BOUNDARY
HUNTER

BOUNDARY HUNTER

A. R. MOORE

MINDBRIDGE PRESS

mindbridge
PRESS

ISBN: 978 0 9822151 2 8
Library of Congress Control Number 2018934992

Book Cover by Sarah Turner

Book Interior Design by Felicia Kahn

Printed in the United States of America.

Published by Mindbridge Press

First Edition

To American Embassy Beirut's Nasty Boys. Simply put, there is no finer embassy bodyguard force on the planet.

Courtesy of Art Balek

BOUNDARY
HUNTER

1

IT WAS SPRINGTIME in Washington, DC, and the cherry blossoms were in full bloom when a tall man with graying hair walked into the Salvation Army and dropped an armload of two-button, single-breasted suits on the counter. All the suits were either blue, black, or gray. As the volunteer clerk sorted through the pile, she noticed that each of the jackets had the inside lining torn just under the left armpit. The puzzled look on her face indicated she had no clue why the suits were torn. After twenty-six years, the man's shoulder holster had left its mark. The burred hammer of the .357 magnum revolver the man carried early in his career had been particularly brutal to his jacket linings; the more recently issued Sig 228 had been less destructive. The man smiled inwardly at the realization that the new recipients of his recycled suits would have no idea where those suits had been or what they had witnessed. Nor would they know anything about the man who had worn them.

His goodwill mission complete, the middle-aged man got in his truck and drove Route 50 East to the Chesapeake Bay. After several days of searching Annapolis and the surrounding areas, he finally found what he was looking for. Near the end of the dock, she rocked rambunctiously at her berthing like a race horse tethered at the starting gate. The broker handed him the keys, and the man climbed aboard. As he eased the boat into the Severn River toward the main channel, the big spoke wheel felt good in his hands. Chest high and solidly built of marine-grade stainless steel, it steered with smooth fluidity the classic thirty-five-foot sloop. Custom crafted of hand-laid fiberglass and gleaming aluminum, with a pilot house, a winged keel, and a single-mast tall racing rig, the sailboat was sleek and beautiful and built for speed. At the mouth of the river, the man hoisted sail and angled the boat against the brisk breeze of the bay. Just as he had anticipated, the boat surged forward like the thoroughbred she was. With a few minor sail adjustments, the skilled sailor settled her down, yet she still strained against her lines like a leashed dog too big for its owner. There amid the wind and the water and the warming sun, a calming sense of place came over him. He had charted his course. The boat had attitude, and she had character, so he bought her, just as his career was coming to an end.

Most men spend their entire lives wondering how they would respond when confronted with extreme hardship or danger. During the course of his career, Cameron "Cam" Coppenger had answered that question more times than he could count. Cam Coppenger had served his country honorably for twenty-six years as a Special Agent with the State Department's Diplomatic Security Service, and he was tired, bone tired. He was tired of the mindless tribal wars and the vindictive violence of terrorism, tired of a world filled with hate, erroneously justified by differences in culture, religion, or politics. There was a reason the Foreign Service allowed full retirement for its officers at age fifty. The mental and physical stress of living and working in some of the most dangerous and unhealthy locations on earth had taken its toll. So when retirement came, Cam embraced it. The timing was critical; he feared he was losing both his humanity and his sanity.

Longing to reconnect with his southern roots, Cam moved his boat to the Alabama Gulf Coast where he could flex the muscle of his sleek sloop in the well-defined breezes of Mobile Bay. He named his boat *Fadeaway* after the codeword used for Secretary of State George Schultz during the Reagan administration. *Fadeaway* was an apt name for Cam's sailboat, which would be his refuge, his sanctuary, an escape from the weariness and cynicism that had accumulated from years of dealing with the troubles of the world. He simply wanted to fade away into retirement, and the boat was his vehicle for doing so.

Fadeaway needed a bit of work, but Cam enjoyed working on boats. He considered it therapeutic. She was certainly big enough to live aboard, with a forward V-berth, an enclosed head with shower, a comfortable salon, and a small galley. The boat's higher pilot house design allowed him to fully extend his 6' 2" frame inside the cabin without bending over, and he liked that. A career in the Foreign Service had taught Cam how few possessions he needed to be happy, and he loved being around water. So choosing to live on his sailboat was an easy decision. He found her a home on a Mobile Bay backwater known to locals as Dog River. Once settled,

Fadeaway was to become his man cave, a place to sort out issues. During the process of refurbishing his boat, Cam hoped she would refurbish him. That was his plan, his first step toward the inner healing he desperately needed.

On a warm Saturday afternoon in April, dressed in cargo shorts, a Hawaiian shirt, flip flops, and an old Auburn ball cap, Cam was sitting at the oyster bar of his favorite dockside restaurant, Judge Bean's, when a TV news flash interrupted the Braves/Padres baseball game.

"*We interrupt this program to bring you breaking news. Unknown gunmen have attacked the ticket counters at San Diego International Airport with automatic weapons, resulting in significant injuries and loss of life. No additional details are known at this time, but all flights in and out of San Diego have been canceled.*"

Jake, the owner/bartender, glanced at his only patron and said, "Cop, did you just hear that?"

"Yeah, I heard it," Cam responded solemnly, so weary of such news its impact was lost. *Poor souls,* he thought, *no rhyme, no reason, no justice.* Cam called out to the shucker, "Can I get another dozen oysters?" Then to Jake, "And another Blue Moon."

Since Cam's relocation to the Gulf Coast, he and Jake had become fast friends, and through that friendship found themselves on similar life missions. Jake was a retired New Orleans police detective. After *Katrina,* he had opened Judge Bean's as his own personal retreat from thirty years of the crime, violence, and mayhem that had come to define inner-city policing. In his sixties, Jake was a bit older than Cam, but he like Cam had burned out, too. Though he had never asked Cam the specifics of what being a Special Agent with the Diplomatic Security Service actually entailed, he understood the frustrations of trying to do good in a world full of evil.

Jake kept his pistol-grip shorty 12-gauge behind the bar. So far, he had only used it once. A sixteen-inch hole in the ceiling above the bar was evidence of the warning shot he deployed early in the restaurant's history to break up a bar fight between rival shrimpers. Firing the blast probably hadn't been necessary, but Jake knew that word would spread, and the hole in the ceiling would become legendary along the Redneck Riviera. The incident had given Judge Bean's a serious reputation, so far making a second deployment of the shotgun unnecessary. Cam appreciated Jake's instinctual application of psychological deterrence and had bonded with him immediately.

Jake plopped the sweaty brown bottle down on the bar and asked, "How do you think it went down?"

Cam didn't answer.

Jake continued his train of thought. "I think it was one of the Mexican drug cartels, a revenge killing. Mexican cartel guys are right here in Mobile, over at the port, expediting shipments smuggled in shipping containers. US Customs only inspects about ten percent of the containers that enter this country, you know. Hell, those cartels ship drugs, guns, cars, even people in those containers, almost with impunity! What do you think?"

"I don't want to think about it, Jake," Cam said. He busied himself with forking a fresh, plump Apalachicola oyster onto a saltine, topping it with a squirt of cocktail sauce and horseradish. Pulling his ball cap over his eyes, he consumed the oyster and took a private moment to clear his sinuses. Then he contemplated the attack on the San Diego airport.

Cam's last assignment with DSS before retirement had been as Chief of the San Diego Resident Office (SDRO). His primary mission in San Diego had been to investigate the huge amount of passport fraud on the Mexican border. Cam knew the lay of the land in San Diego. He was well-versed in the drug smuggling, gunrunning, and human trafficking along the nineteen hundred miles of the US/Mexican border. He was also aware of the false documents, tunnels, official corruption, and violence that facilitated the smuggling. The Mexican border was a leaky sieve, and despite the committed efforts of the men and women of US Customs and Border Protection (CBP), many of whom he knew personally, Cam understood that compliant politics in Washington made their job practically impossible. As he evaluated the San Diego attack with his last swig of Blue Moon, Cam wondered if his ongoing concerns for security breaches along the Mexican border were finally coming to a head.

"Another Blue Moon?" asked Jake.

"No thanks," Cam replied, his concentration broken, "Gotta go, my friend." As much as he tried to hide behind flip flops and flowered shirts, Cam Coppenger was still a Special Agent at heart. He wondered if he would ever be able to flip the switch and move on. And with that thought in mind, he walked down the dock to his boat, went below, put on a Jimmy Buffett CD, and pulled out his laptop.

2

INVESTIGATORS QUICKLY LEARNED the identity of the attackers at the San Diego airport. Later that day, news stations were already reporting claims of responsibility by the radical Palestinian terrorist group, Liwa Tahrir, translated The Liberation Brigade. The group was led by an old foe Cam knew well from his Beirut days. Khalid Khalidi, the leader of Liwa Tahrir, was simply known throughout the Middle East as Ismail.

A product of the Palestinian refugee camps in Lebanon, Khalid Khalidi had known death and destruction as a child. What began as a desperate effort to survive led to Khalid becoming head of a criminal gang enterprise. That criminal gang, when mixed with the politics of an ardent pro-Palestine movement, evolved into the The Liberation Brigade, which was not an expansive terrorist network like Al Qaeda or ISIS, spanning the globe with followers from many different countries. Rather, The Liberation Brigade was a small group of close associates that resembled an organized crime syndicate, a mafia, numbering no more than a couple dozen members.

Because they were a small group and mostly self-funded through criminal enterprises, The Liberation Brigade had been exceedingly difficult for authorities to crack. Due primarily to the group's reputation for extreme ruthlessness and violence, members of the Brigade ruled by extortion and operated with impunity throughout the world. Politicians, police, and citizenry were afraid of them. And Ismail was the boss. Through the years, millions of American dollars, European euros, and Saudi riyals thrown at Palestinian relief causes in the form of aid, or bribery, rarely found their intended mark. Corrupt gang leaders like Ismail were perfectly positioned to benefit from the well-intended but wasted wealth. Ismail became financially wealthy, and then he became politically powerful. His life experiences had taught him that violence was a useful tool. His ruthlessness was legendary.

As a young man, Ismail's experience growing up in the refugee camps imprinted upon him a natural resentment of Israel and its occupation of Palestinian territories. Regaining control of Jerusalem became his cause. For much of his terrorist life, Ismail had directed his anger and vindictiveness toward Israel, but after 9/11, America's involvement in Afghanistan and Iraq had resulted in a decade of killing his fellow Muslim brothers. With America's recent recognition of Jerusalem as the capital of Israel, Ismail concluded that real change to the Palestinians' plight would take place only if the American people felt the kind of pain and loss he had experienced most of his life. The San Diego airport attack was Ismail's opening salvo.

———

Sitting in the salon of his boat, Cam searched his contact list and called Sal Ellis, the FAA rep in San Diego.

"Hey, Sal." Cam Coppenger here." When Sal answered in a harried voice, Cam asked, "What's going on?"

"A mess, Cop. Two men stepped out of a vehicle at the passenger drop-off with AKs, took out the traffic cop and ticket lady, and then went inside and shot the place up! Two thirty-round magazines each, a couple of grenades, and in sixty seconds they were done … thirty dead and another thirty to forty injured, including women and children. The attackers retreated to their vehicle and escaped before anybody could respond. They ditched the stolen car a couple blocks away."

"Did the cameras get a good look at them?"

"No, they wore masks. Don't know anything about the driver. They've shut us down nationwide as completely as 9/11. No flights anywhere until we get a handle on it. Took 'em one minute. Dammit, Cam, it's a mess. I gotta go," Sal hung up.

Having no TV on the boat, Cam wandered back to Judge Bean's to catch the latest news. Jake and a bar full of patrons, some wearing old Vietnam War caps and MIA tee shirts, stared intently at CNN on the flatscreen.

"What did you find out?" Jake asked, anxiously.

"Not much more than what you see on the news," replied Cam. "The Liberation Brigade, led by a guy named Ismail, claimed responsibility. They hit the airport so hard and so fast there was no time to respond."

"Who is this Ismail guy?" Jake inquired.

"An old adversary of mine," advised Cam. "We had some run-ins in Beirut. He's a wealthy, powerful, ruthless, radical Muslim with a cause, and it looks like he has brought his holy war to America."

Every ear in the bar turned toward Cam. Jake took the hand towel off his shoulder, planted both fists firmly on the bar, and asked, "What does he want?"

"He wants your attention to his cause," replied Cam sternly. "He wants you to feel his pain. He wants you to feel that pain until you do something about his cause."

"What cause is that?" asked one of the bar stool patrons.

"He wants Jerusalem to be given back to the Palestinians," explained Cam.

"That'll never happen!" exclaimed another barstool patron.

"I know it, and you know it," Cam responded, "but he doesn't know it ... his god and his imam tell him differently."

"What's an imam?" asked a third from his barstool perch.

"A Muslim preacher," Cam explained, his patience wearing thin. "Only with more fire and brimstone than you've ever heard in a Baptist Sunday sermon."

A gruff voice called from a darkened corner, "Wasn't you one of them *secret* agents in Washington, one time?"

"Something like that," Cam replied, looking at Jake with exasperation. Cam was deeply troubled. The emergence of Ismail as the instigator of the airport attack exacerbated his concerns for what the coming weeks might entail.

Cam suspected that Ismail wouldn't stop with just one operation. What concerned him most was how simple, yet effective, the airport attack had been. Two men with automatic rifles had temporarily shut down the nation's entire air transportation system in less than a minute. *What a rotten way to start retirement*, Cam thought as he walked back to his boat.

Cam's phone rang as he entered *Fadeaway's* cabin. He didn't recognize the number but knew the 202 area code was Washington, DC.

"Cameron Coppenger?" asked the female voice.

"Who's calling?"

"Special Agent Tina Gruder at the FBI's Counterterrorism Center in Washington, DC." Her voice was youthful and ended the sentence with a vocal fry.

"How did you get my number?" Cam asked, suspiciously.

"Your headquarters at State gave it to us," said Agent Gruder. "Mr. Coppenger, I'm sure you've heard of the incident in San Diego and that claims for that incident have been made by one Khalid Khalidi, known also as Ismail. We know you have considerable knowledge of the so-called Ismail, Mr. Coppenger. I have been asked by our Director to inquire if you would come to Washington to meet with us about this individual."

"Well, if it is in fact Ismail, there's no so-called about it. He's the real deal," Cam explained. "But you know I'm retired, right?"

"Yes. We are aware of your retirement, Mr. Coppenger, but you come highly recommended by one of our senior agents."

"What about Sid Lewis? He knows as much about Ismail as I do, and he's just down the hall from you guys."

"Senior Supervisory Special Agent Lewis will be in the meeting. He recommended you to the Director."

"I have absolute confidence Agent Lewis has all the knowledge and background on Ismail that you will need. I'm nine-hundred miles away from Washington, on a sailboat, without a suit or tie to my name. I'm sure Sid can handle it."

"We'll pay your expenses!" Agent Gruder implored.

"No, thanks. Have a spectacular day, Agent Gruder." Cam ended the call, went to the head, put on another Jimmy Buffett CD, and pushed San Diego out of his mind.

———

With the FBI request behind him, Cam looked forward to his first spring of retirement aboard *Fadeaway*. The sound of water gently clapping against the hull, the mainsail halyards clanging rhythmically against aluminum masts, even the seagulls cawing from their pier perches were all soothing sounds to Cam. Those sounds were part of what made marina life so worthwhile. Then there were the relaxing nights: the gentle rocking of the boat, cool fresh air drifting down through the open hatch above his head, and on clear evenings, stars that glistened like tea candles.

Under sail, *Fadeaway* was everything Cam hoped she would be. Her tall racing rig and winged keel harnessed the wind like jet thrust, driving her forcefully in exhilarating beam reaches across the bay. In his skilled hands, she handled the 150 Genoa with ease, tacked crisply, and then quickly accelerated back to maximum hull speed with jackrabbit agility. In the deep water of the Gulf, *Fadeaway* was steady and powerful, slicing her way through heavy swells like a surgeon's scapel. For Cam, boats were time machines. He believed that every day he spent on the water was not deducted from his lifespan. In his home port of Mobile Bay, Cam had found his apex. Sailing was his fountain of youth.

Days rolled into weeks, and Cam settled into a routine. Waking at daybreak, he typically had morning coffee and a bagel with fruit in the cockpit of his boat. Later in the morning, he ran or biked nearby bayside trails. Occasionally, he worked up a sweat on a punching bag yard workers had suspended in the maintenance shop. A wrestler in high school, Cam had always been be able to handle himself should the need arise, and he wanted to keep it that way. Midday, he piddled on his boat, ran errands, or fished off a nearby pier. Late afternoon, he wandered to Jake's place for a solid meal, and then he settled into a waterfront seat with a good book and watched the sun set to the west across the Gulf of Mexico. As the sun set on his quaint piece of paradise, one private game he played was to figure out where the sun was rising on other parts of the planet. His career in the diplomatic corps had given him opportunities to live all over the world. Cam took full advantage of the Foreign Service, having lived and explored every continent but Antarctica. The more exotic an underdeveloped country, the better he liked it. Wherever the sun set on earth, Cam Coppenger had either lived there or visited. Through the course of his career, he had collected stunning photographs of sunsets from all over the world.

As the hot and humid summer months approached, Cam had

one more boat project he had been putting off: *Fadeaway's* pesky Yanmar diesel engine had been acting up and needed overhauling. Cam knew little about marine diesels, which explained his procrastination. What he did know was that he didn't want to be stuck in the hold of a smelly engine compartment in the middle of a hot sticky Alabama summer. So as June approached, he flipped up the deck hatch and went to work.

Covered in grease and oily diesel fuel from stem to stern, Cam had almost completed the Yanmar's disassembly when he heard a woman's heels clopping purposefully down the dock. The clopping stopped at his boat. Peeking through the companionway, Cam looked up to see a set of tanned legs. Familiar, long, lean, and golden brown. "Kate?" Cam bumped his head solidly as he stood for a better look.

"Hello, Cop," the legs replied.

"What are you doing here?"

"Looking for retired Special Agent Cameron Coppenger, obviously." She smiled at the grease monkey who emerged from the bowels of the boat's engine compartment.

Cam rubbed his smarting forehead with a blackened hand, making his dirty face even dirtier. "How'd you find me?"

"Apparently you've forgotten what I do for a living."

She was right. Stupid question. Kate Allison had been a Deputy US Marshal with the US Marshal's Service (USMS) for almost as long as Cam had been a Special Agent. Assigned to the Marshal's Fugitive Warrant Unit, she specialized in finding and apprehending the most dangerous criminals in the country, and she was good at it. Long, tall, and stunningly beautiful, with shoulder-length brown hair, refined features, and a gorgeous smile, Deputy US Marshal Kate Allison could get any man to open any door for any reason. The Fugitive Unit, keenly aware of man's greatest weakness, routinely used her as bait. She could reel them in—hook, line, and sinker.

"But I'm not a fugitive," Cam feigned, knowing full well she was not there on business.

"You're a fugitive from my heart," replied Kate with a wink.

Cam stood in the cockpit and surveyed Kate looking down at him from the dock. Slim, 5'10", and the daughter of a state trooper in Florida, Kate had been a runway model in college before embarking on her career as a Deputy US Marshal. She still knew how to ride the fashion pony. Dressed this day in a culotte short/ top combo with a turned-up collar and espadrille wedges, she looked magnificent. In her mid-forties, she could pass for a decade less. He wondered where in that outfit she kept her Glock 23.

"Gonna invite me aboard, Captain?"

"Yeah … sure!" Cam recognized that she could still knock him off balance with a smile.

He admired her form as she stepped backwards down into the boat. Firmly aboard, Kate turned and smiled at him. "Well, are you gonna stand there, or are you gonna kiss me?" She smiled the charming smile that had opened the front door of every fugitive stash house from New Jersey to New Orleans.

"After I get cleaned up?" All Cam could think about was how filthy he was.

Kate laughed and gave him an elbow bump, knowing she had the upper hand.

"Where are you now?" Cam asked, wiping off grease.

"Still in Miami, but they've moved me to the Witness Protection Program." Kate looked out toward the bay. "Looks like you have a nice life."

"Love it. Why the move?"

"My gig was up. I guess they decided they wanted someone younger and prettier to open fugitives' doors. But with that promotion you got me, it was time to get off the streets and move into management." Still looking out toward the water, Kate fell into a moment of reflection. "I haven't seen you since Belize."

"I'm sorry about that Kate. I was sent to Africa after Belize. Internet was practically non-existent …"

"Of course, important work intervened."

"Something like that. So what brings you to Dog River?"

"I was in Tallahassee on court business. I thought I'd stop by."

"Tallahassee and Mobile are hours apart."

"I know the distance, Cop. I just drove it. Maybe I just wanted to see you." Kate looked out at the water. "Hey … we might have an amazing sunset this evening! Why don't we open a Chardonnay! You do have Chardonnay?"

The truth was, Cam never kept wine onboard. The bottles were too tall for his tiny box fridge, and without air conditioning, reds never stored well.

"Let's go to Bean's and grab a bite to eat, and then come back for a sundowner?"

Kate's eyes brightened, and she held out her hand for Cam's assistance up to the dock.

Cam went below and grabbed a towel, clean clothes, and a bar of

Lava pumice soap. Then he and Kate walked up the dock to Judge Bean's.

Jake saw them coming and was already calculating the back story of the leggy brunette in Cam's company. As they entered the bar, all heads turned in unison.

Cam had seen it happen many times before. He walked Kate over to Jake and introduced them. "Jake, meet Kate Allison, Deputy US Marshal."

A scruffy patron quietly stood up and exited a side door without finishing his beer. Moments later, a second chair scraped the floor, and another shady character slinked away. Kate glanced over at the side door and smiled.

"I need to get cleaned up, Jake. Would you entertain Kate while I shower?"

"Sure thing, Cam!" Jake put down his bar rag, grinned at Kate, and asked, "What can I get you?"

"Do you have oysters?"

"You bet we do, fresh from Apalachicola this morning!" beamed Jake.

"I'll start with a dozen then! We don't have them in Miami; they are all imported from the panhandle. And Jake, a Chardonnay to go with them?"

Jake signaled to the oyster shucker and then started digging around for a bottle of Chardonnay. Finding one tucked behind a special bottle of expensive Krug champagne saved for a special occasion, he pulled the cork on the Chardonnay and poured Kate a glass. "So how do you know my buddy Cam?"

Kate took a sip from her long-stemmed glass, set the glass on the table, placed both elbows on the bar, and folded her hands. "We met in Belize. I was on assignment looking for one of the FBI's *Top Ten Most Wanted*, and Cam was on temporary assignment to the US Embassy. There is no extradition treaty between the US and Belize, so fugitives from justice typically escape to backwaters like Belize, thinking they will be safe from authorities. Cam's job was to coordinate a new initiative between DSS and the USMS to apprehend these guys. He would pick them up and work with local authorities to have them deported to the nearest US Port of Entry where we were waiting, arrest warrant in hand. Cam helped me capture my *Most Wanted* fugitive in Belize, along with a few others, and I got a promotion out of it. It's also where I fell in love with him."

That last bit of information caught Jake off guard, and his eyes widened. "Lucky guy."

The shucker brought the platter of fresh raw oysters over to Kate just as Cam walked in from his shower at the marina's bath house.

"Much better!" he proclaimed, as he took a seat next to Kate. "Oysters?" asked Cam, "I didn't know you liked oysters!"

"Love 'em," she confirmed. She squeezed a slice of lemon around the array, dropped a bit of Tabasco in the center of the first half-shell, tilted the shell into her mouth, paused for a moment as if to savor its delicate flavor, and let the oyster slide down her throat. Then she downed another. Oyster after oyster, Kate's big brown eyes never left Cam. Cam pretended not to notice. Jake let out a low whistle as he turned and began stacking shot glasses.

The sun was settling on the horizon, so Cam and Kate finished their meal, lifted the bottle of Chardonnay from Jake, and strolled back down to his boat. The evening was perfect, and as the sun touched the edge of the bay in the distance, Cam looked at his watch and called out, " Two twenty-eight!"

"Two twenty-eight?"

"That's how long it takes for the sun to completely disappear once it touches the horizon, two minutes and twenty-eight seconds."

"You've been watching way too many sunsets, Cam Coppenger. Alone." She paused to remember their shared sunsets and the evenings that followed on a little island off the coast of Belize. Wonderful memories, among the best of her life. "I've got to be in Tallahassee in the morning," Kate said, wistfully. And exactly two minutes and twenty-eight seconds later, Kate stood up, took Cam by the hand, and led him down into the cabin. The Alabama sky was ablaze in a beautiful mosaic of orange, yellow, and purple.

3

JUNE DRIFTED INTO July, and *Fadeaway's* Yanmar diesel was still disassembled, critical pieces strewn throughout the cramped engine compartment. Cam was waiting on a key part from Japan and delivery was still weeks away. Dauphin Island's traditional 4th of July Regatta was only days away, and Cam had hoped to have *Fadeaway's* engine running in time to join the celebration. Known for massive boat raft-ups and riotous water-borne parties, followed by spectacular fireworks that night, the July Regatta was a huge event. Of course, Cam could sail his boat without a working engine, but with the huge number of participating boats, many operated by amateurs or experienced skippers under the influence of alcohol, attempting to navigate the traffic jam under sail was unwise. So when the 4th came, Cam relegated himself to Judge Bean's outside deck where he could observe the day's festivities from a safe distance.

Jake wandered over to Cam and opened a conversation, "Heard about the storm brewing in the Caribbean?"

"No. Isn't July too early for hurricane season?"

"The season officially starts in June, so a July hurricane is unusual but not unheard of. Not a cause for concern just yet. It's still in tropical storm status. Looks like Miami might catch a bit, though. Hey, I've been smoking pork butts all morning! Can I get you some?"

Barbeque sounded good to Cam. "Yeah, bring me some of your most excellent barbeque, and a big ol' glass of sweet tea!"

Cam's phone vibrated with an incoming call. His son, Caleb. "Hey Dad! Have you heard about the storm?"

"Just heard about it. What are the weather guys in Key Largo saying?"

"It's headed for South Florida for sure, but they don't know if it's gonna turn into a hurricane."

Caleb, Cam's only son from his brief marriage, was made from the same mold as his father, a long lean build, olive skin, blue eyes, and thick black hair. Their shared traces of Choctaw ancestry had been enough to bring dark features to their otherwise Scots/Irish lineage. Raised primarily in Washington, DC, with his mother, the teenage Caleb had chosen to join his father on three of his less dangerous overseas postings: Australia, Morocco, and Sri Lanka. Caleb was most definitely a citizen of the world and had inherited his father's sense of adventure. Following his father's footsteps to Auburn University, Caleb had majored in computer systems management, a smart field choice that gave him unlimited flexibility in jobs and locations. At twenty-four, he had settled in

Key Largo, Florida, the first and northernmost of the Florida Keys.

Beginning just below Miami, the Keys stretched south/southwest in a chain toward the Gulf, eventually ending at Key West, only ninety miles from Cuba. Caleb's youthful motto was, "Location first, job second," and in Key Largo he was fortunate to find a position at the State's Emergency Management Center. Amidst this tropical paradise, Caleb enjoyed an easy-going life of year-round sunshine, scuba diving, saltwater fly fishing, and fabulous sunsets. Cam was proud of his son's spirit and intelligence, and appreciative of his lifestyle.

"Keep me posted on the storm, will you? You can always come up here to ride it out if you need to."

"Dad, I work for Emergency Management—my job is to be down here working during storms, not running away!"

Of course, thought Cam absentmindedly. *Coppengers always seemed to be in the middle of one storm or another.* "Just be safe!"

"The Op Center is built of solid concrete on concrete pillars sunk eight feet in the ground, designed to withstand 200 mph winds and twelve-foot tidal surges. I'll be fine. Hey Dad, my phone's buzzing. Gotta go."

Jake brought Cam a plate heaped with his signature smoked pork (pulled with a claw-hammer), brown sugar baked beans with bacon bits, and a side of southern-style potato salad. "Have you to talked to Kate?"

"No, but I need to call her." Cam sent Kate a quick text and then dug into his barbeque, which was most excellent indeed. Just as he finished, his phone vibrated.

It was Kate's return text, *No worries. In DC on a WP case. Thx!*

Knowing she wouldn't reveal such information, Cam texted back anyway, *Who this time?*

Kate answered, *Let's just say Mexican drug cartels use up a lot of our resources these days. Happy 4th! Watching fireworks down on the Mall tonight!*

———

In the monuments area of Washington, DC, the Federal Park Police were busy securing the perimeter of the National Mall with pedestrian fencing, consisting primarily of wooden slats and orange plastic mesh held up by metal stakes driven into the ground. They established periodic checkpoint gates every hundred yards or so for pedestrian access. In critical areas, chain-link fences and concrete barriers were positioned to defend against crowd surges and vehicle access. Security screeners would be visually checking all purses, coolers, backpacks, and other bulky items at the checkpoints. Even with all that, security professionals knew events like 4th of July celebrations were impossible to secure completely. There was just too much area, too many people, and not enough security personnel to get the job done. Sniffer dogs would be on standby, but at the insistence of the White House, dogs would only be deployed with probable cause, on a case-by-case basis, because it had been determined that indiscriminate use of dogs might offend the sensitivities of DC's growing Muslim community. Such were the politics since 9/11, and the Park Police had learned to work within the boundaries of such restrictions.

Across town, in the basement of an old safehouse in a seedier part of DC, Palestinian brothers Ramzi and Yousef were busy finalizing their checklist list for the 4th of July celebration. Both men were products of Beirut's fifteen-year civil war, and they were well-schooled in the skills of compacting chaos and mayhem into neat, small packages. Ramzi was stuffing his backpack with two pounds of C-4, a military-grade plastic explosive, wrapped in layers of screws, bolts, and nails, secured by black duct tape. Yousef was packing a small cooler with a similar amount of death and destruction. With a lifelong connection to Liwa Tahrir, Ramzi and Yousef had grown up with Khalid Khalidi in the squalor of the Palestinian refugee camps and were participants in many of his early criminal enterprises. The US State Department's diversity visa lottery, however, a program that randomly gives out fifty-thousand immigrant visas each year, offered them an escape from the squalor and had randomly bestowed upon them the potential for American citizenship. As young men in their prime, they had departed for the land of the free with Ismail's blessing. Dearborn, Michigan, became their home, primarily because of the large Lebanese population there. According to FBI intelligence, Dearborn had also become an enclave of North American operations for the Lebanese terrorist group Hezbollah. The brothers had gone in together to open a small electronics shop in one of the more depressed areas of the city, and they had stayed in touch with Ismail through a local imam who made frequent visits back to Lebanon and the occupied territories of Israel. Now twenty years after winning the opportunity to build a better life in America, Ramzi and Yousef found themselves still isolated and still unassimilated. America's involvement in Iraq, Afghanistan, and Syria, and its unfettered support of Israel had become a festering wound for them.

"We need to finish here and get moving. Penny will be waiting on me," declared the older brother Yousef, as he set the timed detonator for 9:15 p.m. and carefully connected it to the explosive inside the cooler. He then used superglue to seal the lid to the small cooler and glued the latch closed.

Ramzi used two phones to check a cell-phone connection and then attached one of the phones to the explosives in his backpack. He zipped the backpack closed and used a fireplace lighter to weld the plastic zipper together. Reaching under his shirt to confirm the location of his pistol, Yousef checked his watch and instructed, "Let's go!" It was three o'clock in the afternoon, and the crowds would be building.

Taking the Red Line Metro from the Adams Morgan neighborhood, the two men rode together to the Metro Center and then split up. Yousef got off at Metro Center and began walking down 12th Street past Pennsylvania Avenue to Constitution Avenue. Ramzi connected to the Blue Line and rode the subway underneath the National Mall, exiting on the other side at Capitol South station, located at the southeast corner of the Capitol Building. Once at their destinations, their moderate walks over to the National Mall would give them a chance to assess the crowds and the security arrangements for the event and identify the most vulnerable areas. Wearing plain clothes and broad-brimmed hats to protect them from the summer sun and from prying security cameras, there would be no more communication between the two until after the operation was completed. Washington, DC, was a city that celebrated the racial and ethnic diversity of its citizens, and the mixture of cultures, values, and skin tones worked to Ramzi and Yousef's advantage. They blended in perfectly.

The National Mall—a two-mile length of single, park-like city blocks running east/west—starts at the steps of the Capitol Building and stretches toward the Potomac, with the Washington Monument in the middle and the Lincoln Memorial anchoring its westernmost end. The Jefferson Memorial and Smithsonian museums, along with other new additions, border the Mall on either side. The Iwo Jima Memorial, situated on a hill across the river in Virginia, overlooks the entire length of the Mall all the way to the Capitol. The view is world famous. Washington, DC, is a planned city, well laid out by French-born architect Pierre L'Enfant in 1791, and the National Mall was the central focus of his plan. Through the years, crowds have gathered on the Mall, often numbering in the hundreds of thousands, for all kinds of reasons. Generations of citizens have viewed the inauguration of every president in history from the Mall. World War I veterans protested their pensions there in the early years of the twentieth century, war-bond drives were held on the steps of the Capitol Building during World War II, and Martin Luther King Jr. gave his famous *I Have a Dream* speech from the steps of the Lincoln Memorial. The Mall had long been firmly entrenched in the heart of American history. As America's most public park, it was a fitting place for America to celebrate its birthday.

Yousef stepped out of the Metro station, cooler in hand, into the bright sunshine of a beautiful summer day in Washington. The sky was clear blue, setting the stage for a fabulous fireworks display later that evening. As he walked among the throngs migrating toward the Mall, he carefully surveyed the Mall's perimeter security. The low fencing would barely keep out stray dogs, but a crowd stampede—like the one he observed several years earlier during his Hajj to Mecca—would overwhelm such barriers with hardly a hesitation. Looking around, Yousef noted the positioning of police inside and outside the perimeter. Some were stationary, some were on foot, others were mounted on big strong horses trained in crowd control. The police were numerous and alert at this time of day, but the area was just too great and the crowds too overwhelming to effectively prevent covert penetration of the perimeter. On a slight rise in the distance, Yousef noted an elevated police command center set on a trailer. The command center was mounted on a hydraulic scissor-lift that raised it high in the air, providing the police a sweeping view of the Mall. Ironically, no police were positioned at its base.

On the other side of the Mall, Ramzi was conducting a similar assessment of perimeter security. On his side, scores of food vendor trucks and souvenir trailers had set up along Independence Avenue, the road that parallels the length of the Mall on its south side. Most of the vendors lined this street, and the area behind their vehicles was stacked with supplies that backed up nearly to the temporary fencing. Already people within the fence, too lazy to walk back outside the security zone, were calling out to the

vendors, and the vendors, all too eager to make a sale, were happy
to bring food, drink, and other treats over to them. A few police
were making a half-hearted effort to discourage the exchanges,
but the crowds were too great and the watchful eyes too few. The
frenetic activity of small-business commerce, combined with the
constant growl of the vendors' power generators, would provide
good cover for his operation, Ramzi surmised.

Yousef's phone rang; it was his fiancé. "Where are you?" she
fussed, "I've found a great spot for us!"

"I am coming, sweetheart," Yousef lied. "Traffic is crazy!"

Penny, Yousef's fiancé of three months, had arrived early to
the Mall to secure a good place for the concert and fireworks. At
Yousef's direction, she had spread a blanket on the grass down near
the front of the stage and secured it in place with a sizable picnic
basket filled with sandwiches, soft drinks, fruit, and paper plates.
She even brought two garbage bags to carry the trash out at the end
of the evening: one for garbage, one for recycling.

The only child of an American University professor and a
human-rights activist, Penny was liberal, cause-oriented, and
emotionally vulnerable. Middle aged, never married, overweight,
lonely, and with low self-esteem, Penny was a prime candidate for
any man to take advantage of her emotions, and Yousef had spotted
it right away. They had met at an anti-Israeli/pro-Palestinian rally
just months earlier, and Penny quickly fell madly in love with
Yousef—or at least with his brooding dark features and compelling
life story as a refugee. Within weeks they were engaged, and
although he had never met her parents, Yousef gave her a small
diamond ring, picked up the day before in a pawn shop, using

money his imam in Dearborn had given him. He didn't love her, didn't even like her really. Her constant blathering about women's rights annoyed him. But she met his physical needs, and she was destined to serve an important purpose for Allah. Besides, he would be rid of her soon enough.

———

From his vantage point at Judge Bean's, Cam's predictions had come true. The boating scene unfolding before him was absolute and utter chaos, with boats of all shapes and sizes weaving in and out of the harbor, churning the water like a swimming pool at a kids' camp. The image reminded him of the scene in the movie *Jaws*: a bounty had been offered for capturing the big shark, and townspeople, most of them drunk, showed up in every manner of boat, spiking the water with bloody chum, running into each other, falling out of boats, and lighting sticks of dynamite with cigars. A complete breakdown of order. Cam saw a small Marine Police skiff among them, its thin blue light flashing. The poor cop was soaked to the bone from a barrage of water balloons. Chaos had engulfed him.

Jake came out to the deck, surveyed the harbor, and exclaimed in a long, slow southern drawl, "Holy moly! Gets worse every year. Do those women on that pontoon boat have their tops off?"

Cam's fixed his 8X50 nautical binoculars to the boat in question. "Looks like it."

Then Jake inquired with hope in his voice, "Is Kate coming?"

"No, she's working a witness protection case in DC, but she'll be at the Capital celebration tonight. I might come in and see if we can spot her on TV."

———

DC was getting dark, and after several failed attempts, Penny's call to her fiancé finally went through. "Honey, where are you?" she implored, with agitation in her voice. "The concert is about to start!"

"I'm outside!" replied Yousef, with false exasperation. "There was a breakdown on the subway, and the crowds are horrible! You were so smart to get there early! Sweetheart, I have an idea. I could probably get through security much faster if I didn't have this cooler with me. Could you meet me over by the fence, and I'll hand it to you?"

"Why did you bring a cooler?" asked Penny, annoyed. "I have everything we need here in the picnic basket!"

"I brought you something special," Yousef said, deceitfully. "Do you see the police tower that overlooks the mall? Can you meet me there?"

"Okay, Yousef … Sure," replied Penny, hesitantly.

Yousef reached the police tower first, and as he suspected, there was no police presence in the immediate vicinity of its base. All eyes inside the tower above were turned outward, scanning the vast expanse of humanity with binoculars. Yousef could see Penny coming a mile away. She was a very large woman with a propensity for wearing loose, drape-like clothing in loud colors. She moved across the lawn like a circus parade coming to town. Yousef, standing directly under the tower, signaled to her to meet him at the fence line. Penny was about to open her mouth when Yousef interrupted her.

"Here, quickly, take this before we get into trouble!" Yousef instructed, handing her the cooler. "And don't open it! I got you something special, and I want it to be a surprise!" Yousef was flooding her with information, and Penny was slow to take it all in. "I'll come find you once I get inside. I suspect the police may give me a hard time," suggested Yousef, appealing to Penny's expressed suspicion of law enforcement. "I am Muslim, so I may have some trouble! Penny, with this crowd, the cell towers may become overloaded, so we may lose phone service, but I'll find you!" he lied. The exchange complete, Yousef walked briskly away.

Penny, in a state of information overload, looked confused as she turned back toward her blanket, cooler in hand.

A police canine, safely secured in the backseat of a nearby cruiser, barked aggressively as Yousef slipped into the crowd.

On the opposite side of the Mall on a park bench near the food vendors, Ramzi sat eating a Lebanese falafel, backpack at his side.

Deputy US Marshal Kate Allison and her partner, Jimmy Lombardo, had just transported and secured their federal witness for the evening. "Wanna go to the concert with me tonight?" Kate asked Jimmy. "Harry Connick, Jr. is singing with the US Navy Band, and I love me some Harry Connick, Jr.!"

"Yeah, sure, why not?" replied Jimmy in his thick Bronx accent. Kate and Jimmy had been friends for a long time. Part mentor, part protector, Jimmy was Kate's first partner in the USMS, having worked together in the fugitive warrant unit and now in the witness protection program. Jimmy was a bit older than Kate, considerably shorter, Italian, old school, and was a natural at working the *wise guys* still in the federal witness protection program. Most kids growing up in the tough, hard boroughs of New York in the sixties and seventies, when mobsters still ruled by violence, will tell you there was a nebulous line that separated the *good guys* and the *bad guys*. As a kid, Jimmy knew both sides, having friends from the neighborhood who started as criminal gang members and ended up as *made* members of the mafia. He also knew the Irish kids whose dads were cops and who themselves aspired to be cops. Firefighters were the same way. It was a family thing. Growing up, Jimmy had learned to function in both worlds. In the witness protection program, the mob guys loved Jimmy Lombardo. He spoke their language. He understood their moral code. They trusted him.

"I've got some beach chairs in the car. Why don't we run by the hotel and change, find a deli, pick up a couple of sandwiches, and then head over?" Kate suggested. Her plan sounded good to Jimmy. Preparations completed, they parked in a government lot, badged their way into the Mall's security perimeter, and found a spot down near the stage. Jimmy set up the chairs, and they settled in for a pleasant evening on a beautiful night in the nation's capital.

Down on Dog River, Cam had had his fill of the lunacy taking place at the regatta. Somebody had launched a massive bottle rocket onto the floating fireworks barge and set the whole thing ablaze. Fireworks began to go off prematurely, and the fireworks technicians, seeing what was about to happen, plunged off the barge and swam for the pier. Then the action really picked up. Huge rockets were firing off in broad daylight, whistling in all directions. Explosions piled on top of one another, growing in frequency and intensity. Once the technicians had abandoned ship, no one was really in danger—not really—but the event had turned into a disaster. For the panicking event coordinators, the evening was a bust. All the while, sunburned drunks were celebrating the momentous catastrophe unfolding before them. Boaters were taking pictures with their cell phones. Facebook postings went through the roof as locals recorded what would eventually become known as *The Night They Burned Ol' Dixie Down*. On a normal day, it would have made national news. Cam retreated back into the bar at Jake's place as spent firework debris rained down on Judge Bean's tin roof.

With a mixture of humor and concern in his voice, Cam asked Jake, "Any chance of this place catching fire?"

"Naw, not really. And if it does, I'm insured. This place needs a rehab anyway."

"Hey, would you mind turning the TV to the National Mall

celebration in DC? Let's see if we can catch Kate on national TV!"

———

Darkness had fallen on the nation's capital, and the Harry Connick, Jr. concert was underway. Penny stood up from her picnic spot and looked for Yousef. She tried his cell phone, but as he had predicted, the call didn't go through. There were just too many people sending messages back and forth. Her mind was spinning with possibilities. Where was he? Was he lost? Had some bigoted police officer detained him? She tried to call Yousef again, and again there was no connection. She sent him a text, *Where are you? I'm down front near the stage on right side. The concert has started!* Her phone replied back, *Unable to send.* Penny's confusion became worry, but as the concert wore on, her worry turned into resentment. *There was a reason I had never married,* she thought to herself as she looked down at the cheap engagement ring Yousef had given her. *Men are simply untrustworthy.* She kicked the cooler with her foot in distain, then reached over and pulled it next to her. "Some special surprise," she mumbled as she tried to unlatch on the cooler. It was stuck fast. *He knew I'd try to sneak a peek,* she thought. *That's why he sealed it. Just as well, it's probably something cheap.* Her resentment turned to hurt. Resigning herself to another evening alone, Penny reached into her picnic basket and grabbed a sandwich, dejectedly taking a bite.

The concert ended with Harry Connick, Jr. singing *America the Beautiful* to a standing ovation, as the US Navy Band accompanyed him with gusto. Yet still no Yousef. As demanded by the television networks, the fireworks began promptly at 9:01. Penny stopped looking for Yousef.

The show began with a flurry of rockets and grew into a stupendous display of light and sound over the nation's capital. All eyes turned upward to absorb the fireworks show. Conversations ceased, replaced by rolling waves of oohs and ahs among the crowd. Each thunderous explosion was more dramatic than the previous one. All the while, the US Navy Band played traditional patriotic songs by the likes of John Phillip Sousa. Then at exactly 9:15 came another boom, a different kind of boom, one at ground level.

Cam was watching the DC fireworks display on television, and he immediately recognized the different type of explosion, one that didn't belong at a fireworks display. High explosives like C-4 have a much quicker burn rate than the black powder of a firework; the boom is fast and quick. It took the crowd a moment to notice the difference, too. There was a bright flash and loud noise down near the stage, followed by a moment of confused quiet. Then came the screams, horrible, desperate screams that sprang from the gut, not emotion. There were screams of sudden surprise, screams of intense pain, combined with the moaning screams of the dying. Then panic set in. It took the Navy Band a moment to comprehend the problem, and their music trailed off awkwardly and disjointedly like a bagpipe losing its air. Television commentators were slow to recognize the explosive event, and as the television cameras began a jerky sweep of the crowd, evidence of mass hysteria emerged. People were running everywhere, tripping over coolers, chairs, and dead bodies, dragging children behind them, pulling wounded people with them. The dead and dying were scattered throughout the blast site, while the injured sat or lay where they were, overcome with shock. A thin cloud of smoke hung in the air around the blast site. The air smelled of cordite. Yet the fireworks continued, adding to the panic and confusion. The fireworks technicians, blocks away from the blast site, were completely oblivious and continued their work dutifully, until finally someone radioed for them to stop.

Ramzi, still sitting on a park bench outside the security perimeter, smiled menacingly at the victory Allah had just delivered to his brother Yousef. It was now his turn. Standing, backpack in his hand, he watched intently at the mass hysteria pouring out of the exits, trampling down the fencing, and running away like ants in a disturbed anthill. He calculated the largest exit point and positioned himself there, then entered the mass of humanity. Working his way into the middle of the crowd, he dropped his backpack on the ground. The crowd surge carried him forward swiftly, like a Class IV rapid, dropping him safely on the other side of Independence Avenue, clear of harm's way. Ramzi, glancing back to the general area of his backpack, took his cell phone out of his pocket and dialed the number. BOOM! The explosion was swift and intense. Screws, nails and ball bearings ripped through the crowd like a scythe, tearing off limbs, shredding skin and muscle, and puncturing bodies like shotgun blasts. Pink matter splattered the hair and faces of survivors. In the hot humid air of the evening, the shock wave of the blast was visible on TV, rippling across the scene of mayhem like a rock thrown into a pond. The panic was now multiplied with crowds moving like swarms of bees from one location to another, false sightings of more bombs causing the crowds to reverse once again, trampling one another in the process. One man wandered aimlessly, clutching his neck, his torn shirt saturated with thick, slick blood, his carotid artery clipped by shrapnel, blood spurting between his fingers. He collapsed to his knees and then slowly fell forward in death, his body drained of life. Television cameras were catching it all, zooming in on the bloody scene, broadcasting to the nation in real time, introducing Ismail's version of shock and awe to America.

"Praise be to Allah," exclaimed Ramzi, as he jogged off into the darkness.

Cam, watching the horrific scene unfold on television nine-hundred miles away, stood up and called out with rare panic in his voice, "Kate!"

4

CAM SPENT THE rest of the night trying to contact Kate but to no avail. Repeated phone calls were not connecting, and voicemail was not even an option. DC was in emergency mode, and phone circuits were jammed. After multiple attempts, one brief text went through around midnight, *Kate, call me. Cam.* Still, no response. Finally, at wit's end and responding to an innate need to find Kate, Cam began to pack a small duffle bag with the intention of driving to DC. Out of sheer habit, he threw in his passport, retirement credentials, some protein bars, and his personal weapon of choice, a compact 9mm Smith and Wesson MP Shield. He was exhausted with worry but lay down in his V-birth around 0200 to try and at least get some rest before he embarked on his eighteen-hour drive in the morning. He slept fitfully, finally arose at 0500, threw his canvas bag into the front seat of his pickup, and headed for DC, the city he had sworn he would never visit again.

The big V-8 in his Ford pickup handled 80 mph with ease, occasionally slipping up to ninety, and by that evening, Cam had crossed the Virginia state line just in time for the Virginia State Trooper to clock him doing ninety-one. Once stopped, Cam was tempted to leap out of his truck and run back to the trooper and explain that he was a retired federal agent on a mission, but then Cam caught himself. He did the smart thing. He turned off his engine, rolled down his window, turned on his interior light, put both hands on the wheel, and waited on the trooper to approach him with further instructions. Then Cam remembered his gun, and he tried to recall if Virginia had a reciprocity agreement with Alabama for Concealed Carry Weapons permits. Virginia had traditionally been a pro-gun state, but since a new liberal governor had been elected, Cam suspected all reciprocity agreements had been made null and void.

The trooper approached Cam's vehicle and asked for his driver's license, registration, and proof of insurance. Cam reached into his wallet and produced his license, but before he reached over to the glove compartment, he advised the trooper he had a firearm in the bag next to him. The trooper paused, looked down at the Alabama driver's license, and asked "Do you have a current concealed carry permit for Virginia?"

"No, I don't, officer," replied Cam. "Is there a reciprocity agreement with the State of Alabama?"

"Reciprocity agreements with other states are no longer honored," stated the trooper, a bit of weariness in his voice.

Then Cam remembered his retirement credentials. "I'm a retired federal agent. Are you familiar with 18 United States

Code 926?" Cam inquired, trying to sound authoritative without being condescending. "It allows retired law enforcement to carry concealed anywhere in the country. They passed it after 9/11. I have a copy of the code in my credentials. They're in the bag with the firearm."

"Please step out of the vehicle, Mr. Coppenger, and move to the front of your truck. Place both hands on the hood of your truck. Do you have a weapon on your person?"

Cam thought for a moment and remembered his tactical knife under his shirt. "Yes, I have a knife clipped to my inside waistband on my right side."

The trooper moved behind Cam and lightly patted him down, found the knife, and removed it. "Do not move under any circumstance," instructed the trooper. The trooper then went to the truck and opened Cam's duffle bag, found the gun and credentials, and opened the black wallet. Inside the credential wallet, he found the reduced copy of 18 USC 926 and used his flashlight to read the fine print. Looking again at his credentials, the trooper read Cam's name out loud. "Special Agent Cameron Coppenger? I think you may have taught a class on inter-agency motorcade operations a few years back."

"If it was around 1998 or so, that was probably me," replied Cam, relieved that he was about to catch a break. "Part of the State Department's Anti-Terrorism Assistance (ATA) program training, as I recall."

"Great course," offered the trooper. "What's your hurry, Agent Coppenger?"

"Retired now." Then he explained the circumstances of Deputy

US Marshal Kate Allison's MIA status.

The trooper returned to Cam his knife and credentials, walked back to his cruiser, and instructed, "Let's put some of that motorcade training to work. Follow me."

Cam got into his truck and followed the trooper, running full lights and sirens up I-95 toward Washington, DC. The speedometer of Cam's truck held a steady 90 mph. After a while he turned on his truck radio and found it jammed with reports of the July 4th attack. Hundreds of casualties were involved, all captured on national television, and The Liberation Brigade had already claimed responsibility. Cam's phone buzzed. It was his FBI buddy, Sid Lewis. *Not now*, Cam thought, as he sent the call to voicemail. Under full police escort, Cam arrived in DC just before midnight. At the Potomac River, where Virginia turns into Washington DC, the Virginia State Trooper turned off his blue lights, moved to the left lane, and reduced speed. With a slight wave, Cam passed him and entered the capital city. *Comradery and professional courtesy still rang true among law enforcement brethren of all walks*, Cam thought. Just as he entered the city, Cam's phone rang for a second time. "Again?" Cam exclaimed under his breath as he glanced down at the number. It wasn't the FBI this time, it was Kate's number.

"Kate!" Cam exclaimed, answering the phone with relief.

"No, Mr. Coppenger," returned the male voice on Kate's phone. "This is Deputy US Marshal Juan Rivera. Kate asked me to call you."

Cam's heart leapt into his throat. "Where's Kate? Is she all right?"

"Kate has been injured," replied the Deputy Marshal. "Several facial lacerations from shrapnel, and she lost a pretty good chunk out of her leg, but she is alive."

Tears came to Cam's eyes as he heard the report. Kate must have reached up from her hospital bed and grabbed her phone from the deputy because her words were muffled and weak. "Oh Cam!" she cried, "They got Jimmy! He's dead, Cam. Jimmy's dead!"

Cam didn't know Jimmy Lombardo—had never met him—but he had heard Kate talk of him many times, so he understood the context. "Where are you, Kate? What hospital?"

"George Washington University Hospital," said Deputy Rivera. "Room 408."

"I'm on my way!" Cam hung up, failing to clarify that he was already in DC.

Cam was very familiar with George Washington (GW), as it was located just a few blocks from the State Department. Its emergency room was top notch. GW was where the US Secret Service (USSS) had taken President Reagan when he was shot outside the Hilton Hotel in 1981, probably saving his life due to their quick action. *How they had allowed the would-be assassin to get that close to their protectee in the first place was a different issue*, thought Cam, shaking his head wearily.

He parked on 21st Street and entered the hospital. As the door to the fourth-floor elevator opened, Cam realized he probably looked like a shipwreck survivor. He had been awake for forty hours and was unshowered, unshaven, and dressed in old khakis and work boots. The night nurse challenged him as he walked by the nurse's station, but he quickly called out, "Shift change, 408," and that seemed to satisfy her. The hospital staff had seen one rough night of triage. He entered and found two Deputy Marshals he did not know sitting and watching The Weather Channel on the monitor high on the wall. Cam assumed the patient between them was Kate, though he couldn't tell for sure with the amount of bandaging on her head and face. Her bandaged leg was suspended in a traction device. The deputies alertly rose to their feet when Cam walked in. Even though Kate's eyes were heavy with medication, they widened with recognition as Cam approached her bed, and the deputies relaxed. Cam nodded at them as he approached her bed.

She whispered thickly, her mouth stuffed with gauze from a wound that had penetrated her cheek. "Cam! How did you get here so quickly?"

"Been driving all day. How ya feeling?"

Kate rolled her eyes at her predicament and glanced over at her deputy buds. "You guys can go now. I'm in good hands." Having been on the clock for twenty-four hours themselves, the deputies were happy to oblige her request. They each lightly fist-bumped Kate's shoulder as they left.

Cam pulled a chair next to Kate's bed, took her one good hand in his, and checked his watch. Well after midnight. Looking up at the television, he noticed that the tropical storm developing in the Caribbean had been downgraded by the time it reached Key Largo. Caleb was safe. Kate was safe. Without another word between them, Cam laid his head back in the chair and fell into a deep, exhausted sleep.

Kate's injuries were painful and would leave scars, but she would recover, at least physically. Emotionally, her partner's death bothered her deeply. Jimmy had been her friend, her mentor, and her protector. In fact, his last act on earth had been to protect her.

His body, positioned by chance between Kate and the improvised explosive device (IED), had absorbed most of the shrapnel from the blast. The hits he had taken were lethal. Wounded but still functional, Kate held Jimmy in her arms as he lay dying. She couldn't free her mind of the look in his eyes as his final breath left him. He couldn't speak, but his eyes communicated clearly: *Get the guys who did this.*

The next morning, Cam's vibrating phone woke him. He looked down and saw the caller was Sid Lewis of the FBI.

"Cop, Sid Lewis, FBI," he stated in a flat business-like tone. "We need to talk."

"Sure, Sid, what's up?"

"You've seen the news, right?" Sid paused and then continued. "Khalid Khalidi is wreaking havoc in this country, Cop, and the White House wants it stopped. Mid-term elections are coming up in November, and the President doesn't want domestic terrorism to be the dominant issue. Our Director has his marching orders, and we need you."

"It's not domestic terrorism, Sid. International terrorism has come to our shores."

"We know that, and that's why we need you. You've dealt with Ismail. You know him better than anyone in the government. You've done a tour in Lebanon. You know the culture, the politics, and the players. We need you to be a part of our Joint Terrorism Task Force. This comes directly from the Director of the FBI."

Cam paused silently for a moment, already knowing his answer as he glanced over at a sleeping Kate. "Okay. I'm in."

"Great! When can you get here?"

"I'm already here."

"In DC?"

"Got in last night."

"Okay, well ... great. The task force has an organizational meeting scheduled for nine o'clock this morning in the Director's office. Can you make it?"

"Sure. Hey, Sid, you remember I'm retired, right?"

"Yes, of course, but we can fix that—contractor, subject matter expert, executive appointment. White House does it all the time. Human Resources will have all the paperwork ready when you get here. Your security clearance should be good for another nine months." Before hanging up, Sid added, "Thanks, pal. We need you!"

Cam looked at his watch: 0710 hours. Time to get moving. He looked over at Kate, still in a medicated sleep, and rushed down to his truck to retrieve his bag. Casual work clothes were all he had. He'd just have to make do. Returning to Kate's private room, he shaved, showered, and changed shirts. A nurse was checking Kate's vitals when Cam emerged from the bathroom, and she peered at him with officious curiosity. "Gotta go," he explained to the nurse, then looking at Kate, "I'll check in on you later, okay?"

Kate batted her eyes in assent.

Before heading to the FBI building, Cam stopped at the Salvation Army to pick up a sport coat and a tie. As he flipped through the racks, he found an old jacket, worn and wrinkled. The tan, cotton-blend journalist jacket, functional but not faddish, with multiple pockets had just enough wear and tear to fit the rest of his wardrobe. Cam smiled to himself at the thought of entering the FBI

Director's office looking like a gumshoe.

At exactly 0855, retired-now-rehired Special Agent Cameron Coppenger—wearing his worn jacket, a wrinkled safari shirt with cable-knit tie, heavy canvas cargo khakis, and well-traveled work boots—entered the waiting area of the FBI Director's office. Youthful eyes in the room turned as if synchronized, assuming some bumbling freelance journalist had entered the wrong office. The Director's secretary, intrigued by Cam's interesting aura of casual masculinity, was about to say something when the Director entered the room, Sid Lewis behind him. FBI Director Reginald Baldwin had never met Cam Coppenger before, had never even seen him actually, but knew him immediately. "Cop!" he exclaimed, as he strode across the room to shake his hand, "Sid has told me so much about you! Welcome aboard!" And with a single handshake, the Director had just given Cam Coppenger instant gravitas within the task force.

Once seated at the Director's conference table, JTTF member introductions were made. In attendance were several FBI analysts and agents from various offices (each one dressed in a five-hundred dollar suit). There was also a major-events coordinator from the USSS, an explosives specialist from Alcohol, Tobacco and Firearms (ATF), a CBP port supervisor from San Diego, an FAA official from DC, a US Navy Commander from the Pentagon, and the obligatory CIA officer, whose name and title were probably false. Cam's longtime friend, Senior Supervisory Special Agent Sid Lewis, was the designated team leader.

Introductions complete, Team Leader Sid Lewis briefed the group on what the FBI knew so far. "Khalid Khalidi, aka Ismail, is a wealthy Palestinian terrorist who has spent most of his career attacking Israel. However, in recent months, he has turned his attention to public targets in the US. His terrorist group, known as Liwa Tahrir or The Liberation Brigade, is a loosely organized band of Palestinian associates who have honed criminal enterprises, politics, and terrorism to a science. Amid the confusing alliances and politics of the Middle East, The Liberation Brigade has emerged from the ashes of first the Beirut civil war and now the Syrian conflict. It was a small but powerful entity with connections to the Palestine Liberation Organization (PLO) when it was under the control of Yasser Arafat, but more recently, The Liberation Brigade has aligned itself with Iran and Hezbollah. Domestically, we have seen evidence linking the Brigade to Hezbollah cells in Dearborn, Michigan, and to the Mexican drug cartels in Mexico. The attacks themselves are impressive in their simplicity, yet their impacts are substantial. In San Diego, they shut down our entire domestic airline operations for a full forty-eight hours. Due to increased security, airline check-in waits are three hours minimum. In DC, millions of Americans watched helplessly on national TV as an attack unfolded just two days ago. In each incident, Ismail immediately claimed responsibility for the attack, using well-known social media sites. We have reason to believe additional attacks are planned, and our mission is to stop Ismail from launching them. Any questions?" Sid asked.

"Cam Coppenger has been contracted to assist us for this mission and is going to tell us more about Ismail. Cam's experience with Ismail in Lebanon goes back years."

Cam leaned forward in his chair and cleared his throat, "The

Liberation Brigade is a small group of criminal thugs turned terrorists. Ismail is their leader. He is brutal, ruthless, and rules by intimidation and violence. Criminal enterprises fund his operations. Most if not all of the Brigade's membership came out of the Palestinian refugee camps of Beirut, which remains their base of operations, though they move in and out of the Occupied Territories in Israel as well. Ismail is primarily a criminal gang leader, but as a young man he found power and wealth in terrorism. His uncle was one of the Black September PLO terrorists who massacred Israeli athletes at the '72 Olympics in Munich. You may remember the Pan Am flight that was hijacked in Rome in 1984 by members of the PLO. Ismail was one of the hijackers. The plane bounced around several European locations until it finally settled in Beirut where the tires were shot out as it sat on the runway. Negotiations for release of hostages went on for two days, until finally Israel agreed to release 127 PLO prisoners in exchange for six Jewish passengers. Unfortunately, two American servicemen were killed aboard the plane before the hijackers were allowed to slip away under the cover of darkness into the neighborhoods of West Beirut. It was rumored they had a large amount of undisclosed cash in their possession at the time of their escape. Iran acted as a go-between during the negotiations, thereby setting the stage for a thirty-year relationship with Ismail's terrorist group."

The young CIA analyst, seeking to establish her credibility within the group, asked knowingly, "But aren't the Iranians Shia Muslims and the Palestinians primarily Sunni? Why are they working together?"

"If you spend enough time in the Middle East, alliances are

often a matter of convenience," Cam replied. "You may have heard the old Arab proverb, *the enemy of my enemy is my friend?* That holds true for much of Middle Eastern politics."

"Where did he get the name, Ismail?" asked the older ATF agent.

"It's a biblical name. If you know the story of Abraham, his wife Sarah was supposedly infertile, so she arranged with her handmaid to bear Abraham a son. That son was named Ismail. Later on, however, Sarah did in fact conceive and bore Abraham another son whose name was Isaac. According to the Bible, Isaac became father of the Jewish people, and Ismail became father of the Arabs."

"So Arabs and Jews came from the same father, Abraham?" asked the ATF agent.

"That's how the story goes," replied Cam. "Khalid Khalidi adapted the moniker Ismail, claiming to be the *father* of the Palestinians, and the name stuck."

"Have you ever had an encounter with Ismail?" asked an FBI analyst.

"We go way back. Not long after the Pan Am hijacking, I was assigned to the US Embassy in Beirut as a Regional Security Officer (RSO) for the State Department. The civil war was winding down, but fighting was still going on. One of my assignments was to monitor the whereabouts of Ismail for future apprehension and prosecution. During one of the ceasefires, I learned that one of our embassy's allied militias had Ismail cornered in an abandoned mosque near the Green Line. I went to the site, assessed the situation, and asked our ambassador for permission to go in and get him. I had an international arrest warrant for his role in the hijacking, but my request was denied. The reason given was that any such action would jeopardize the fragile ceasefire, and I was ordered to stand down. Of course, the ceasefire fell apart anyway the very the next day, and Ismail was long gone."

"You fought in Beirut's civil war?" asked another agent.

Cam glanced at Sid and then at the CIA analyst, "The United States had NO combatants in the Beirut conflict. We were peace-keepers only—and victims, probably victims more than anything." He paused, recalling the American ambassador assassinated in 1976, the 241 US Marine peace-keepers killed in the 1983 barracks bombing, the two US Embassy bombings, and various other embassy officials kidnapped and assassinated during that period.

Cam fell silent as he contemplated the horrors he had experienced as a young agent in war-torn Beirut, climbing over rubble, sorting through burned and mangled bodies, slipping on blood-slickened pavement. He glanced down at his boots, the same boots he had worn in Beirut all those years ago. They were scuffed and scarred, worn out and resoled many times since, but they were still with him, a part of his life. Suddenly, he felt as old and worn out as his boots.

With Cam's bona fides well established among the task force members, Sid called an adjournment. As the team filed out, Cam remained seated, head down, deep in thought. Sid broke Cam's silence, "You okay?"

"Not really. I'm tired of this, Sid, flat out tired. When does it stop? How can we make it stop?"

5

IN THE DAYS that followed his return to DC, Cam developed
a routine. He spent his daylight hours working, analyzing, and
coordinating with the task force, and he spent his nights with Kate
in her hospital room, briefing her on the progress of the task force.
As her physical wounds healed, her bandages became smaller, and
as summer shifted into early fall, she was able to talk more and
move around. The human skull is amazingly strong, and none of the
shrapnel had penetrated bone. Her wounds would certainly leave
superficial scars, but the surgeons assured her that they would be
minimal. The gash in her calf would leave a golf ball-size dent in
her leg, and the hole in her cheek might give her an extra dimple,
but her hair would grow back and cover most of her other scars,
including a partially torn ear. Cam and Kate joked about who was
going to have the best bar-scar stories. In their line of work, there
were always scars, and the better the scars, the better the stories.

But Kate carried mental scars as well. Cam sensed this and was determined to spend as much time with her as he could during her recovery. Evenings after work, he brought her White Castle burgers from Georgetown, or Uno's pizza (her favorite) from Union Station, or a hot fresh Cinnabon from the airport. He tucked away his man card and rented chick-flicks for them to watch at night, like *Sleepless in Seattle* or *Bridges of Madison County*, but not anything by the Nicholas Sparks guy whose male characters always seemed to die. Most importantly, Cam let Kate grieve. Jimmy had been one of her best friends, and it had been her idea to go to the concert, her idea to sit close to the stage. She felt responsible for his death. Nothing Cam could say or do changed her mindset. He listened, held her hand, and tried to offer distractions until time could begin the healing.

The visitation chair in Kate's room had a reclining option and that suited Cam fine. Each night, he slept in the chair, and early each morning he showered and changed in the room's private bath that always had that hospital smell. The arrangement suited both of them, and the night-shift nurses let it happen. They were experienced in the fine art of health care and understood the mental component to healing. Soon Kate was well enough to leave GW. The USMS had assigned Kate to one of its witness protection safe houses during her recovery. Eventually, she reported to Department of Justice headquarters on light duty, surrounded by hundreds of fellow deputies ready to assist, on duty and off.

On the day of Kate's release from the hospital, team leader Sid Lewis called an all-hands meeting of the JTTF and advised the following: "Our computer forensics guys have traced recent

Liberation Brigade communications between locations in Mexico and Lebanon, and we believe Ismail is in Lebanon. We have obtained a federal arrest warrant for Ismail and placed him on the FBI's *Ten Most Wanted List*. A reward of five million dollars has been offered through the State Department's *Rewards for Justice* program. Tomorrow, a reduced JTTF team will be sent to Beirut to continue our investigation. Due to his extensive overseas experience, I am placing Cam Coppenger in charge of that team. Country clearance cables to our embassy have been sent. Go home and pack your bags for an extended stay. Firearms will be transported via diplomatic protocols. Do not forget your passports."

Last-minute international assignments of unknown duration were familiar to Cam, and so were the politics. The junior FBI agent and the ATF agent picked for the team looked at one another with surprise. They had not worked outside of the US before, but the female CIA analyst knew the drill.

As the meeting concluded, Cam briefed his small task force, "Bring a suit if you want for embassy meetings and such, but safari gear is better suited for the environment, and you'll be better received by the locals. Bring sturdy shoes; penny loafers aren't gonna cut it. I recommend shoulder holsters for your firearms, as we will be sitting and traveling in vehicles much of the time. Make sure your qualification cards are current in case you actually have to use your weapon over there. If you don't have a global phone with a transferable SIM card, get one, and an international travel charger to go with it. Bring your JTTF radio and surveillance gear as well. Two bags only. Bring one hard-side lockable suitcase with wheels in case you have to carry your luggage through several terminals. Keep a smaller backpack with you at all times to carry your laptops and other work gear. Do not travel with any classified/sensitive material, electronic or paper. Leave the Americana logos and sports team apparel at home. Make sure your prescriptions are up to date, and if there are any pending birthday/anniversary dates coming up, put the cards in the mail today. Bring both your *official* and *personal* passports, the Lebanese will not allow you entry if you have an Israeli stamp in your passport. Questions? Good, see you tomorrow at Dulles. Don't be late."

After dismissing his team, Cam sent a brief text to Kate advising her of his new assignment.

Her reply was brief and straightforward, *Copy that. Be careful. GET THESE GUYS.*

———

The eighteen-hour United Airlines/Lufthansa flight from Dulles via Frankfurt to Beirut landed without incident. The team was met at the arrival gate by a US Embassy expediter who facilitated their movement through immigration/customs control. *Official passports do have their privileges*, Cam thought to himself as they exited the arrival area of the airport, but Cam also knew that such procedures would alert every disparate political entity throughout Beirut of their presence in the country. Beirut's airport had a well-entrenched intelligence network of eyes and ears that saw and heard everything.

The expediter walked the JTTF members to a waiting embassy

van where they were met by the embassy's Regional Security Officer (RSO).

"Welcome to Beirut, Mr. Coppenger!" offered the RSO, instinctively extending a hand. "I'm Tyrone Bell, RSO." Bell was a stout African-American with a shaved head and a closely trimmed goatee. He carried himself with an athletic, military bearing. He looked vaguely familiar to Cam.

The Lebanese driver got out of the van, came around hurriedly to Cam, and shouted, "Crowbar!"

Cam looked up to see his old friend. "Elie!" Cam exclaimed. They engaged in a deep, lasting embrace between men with a long history of shared experiences. RSO Bell recognized the nature of the greeting, which seemed a bit odd to the others.

"You got fat, Elie."

"You got old and gray, Crowbar. Welcome back. It's good to see you."

The team loaded their luggage into the back of the van and piled into the side door. The RSO entered the front seat with the driver. As the van pulled out, the RSO started his briefing, "We're about forty-five minutes from the embassy. It's really only about ten miles, but traffic is horrible. Always horrible. You'll be staying on the compound rather than one of the hotels downtown. The traffic conditions and security concerns make daily commutes here impossible. You've already met Elie. He'll be your driver and security specialist for the duration of your stay."

Elie glanced into the rearview mirror and raised his hand in acknowledgment.

"They've had a garbage strike here for nine months, and the

garbage is piled in the streets, alleyways, parking lots, right down to the edge of the sea. It's a mess. Smells even worse. The fires you see at night are the locals burning the mountains of garbage in their neighborhoods."

As the embassy van exited the airport and negotiated a large vacant lot piled high with garbage, Cam spoke up. "This looks familiar," he said, already knowing what it was.

The RSO pointed, "That's the site of the Marine barracks bombing in 1983."

"Brings back memories." Cam soberly recalled broken concrete, smashed and burned bodies, and smoking ruins where 241 US Marines and seventy French peacekeepers were massacred by Hezbollah suicide truck bombers early one Sunday morning.

The van moved through the crowded and congested streets of Muslim-dominated West Beirut, dodging double-parked cars and plodding around mounds of putrefying garbage. Cam recognized familiar landmarks. Others, he didn't know. The place had changed. Along the famous Corniche—the scenic park-like route that meandered along the edge of the Mediterranean Sea—he noticed many new and modern shops, restaurants, and hotels. Young couples with baby strollers crowded the sidewalks. The van passed a Starbucks packed with American University of Beirut (AUB) students, each privately worshiping a smartphone. The city center seemed vibrant and alive. Construction cranes dotted the skyline. Industrial sounds of new construction rose above the din of traffic.

Along the Corniche, just past AUB, Cam pointed to his right. "That's the site of the first US Embassy. It was blown up in 1983. Sixty-three people died in that attack. Seventeen were Americans."

A portion of the site now contained a modern high-rise. The rest was a vacant lot. Nothing of the embassy's existence remained, no monument, no plaque, as if the Lebanese people wanted to erase the incident from their memories.

Still on the Corniche, at the center of downtown, the van approached the old but still architecturally beautiful St. Georges Hotel, situated prominently along the waterfront. With its faded yellow paint, cracked concrete and a facade still peppered with marks from bullets and shrapnel, it was obvious no renovation had been attempted.

"What happened to the St. Georges?" Cam asked.

"Lebanese politics! Elie said, "No one can agree on who owns it and what to do with it!"

Just beyond the St. Georges was the Zeitouneh Bay Marina, embellished with sleek, gleaming million-dollar yachts from all over the Mediterranean—yachts owned by royalty and business moguls, legitimate and otherwise, typically docked at the Med's most exotic locations. Cam couldn't help but notice the contrasting symbolism of the vibrant marina compared to that of the forlorn shell of the St. Georges, each within mere steps of one another. To the right, directly across the avenue from the marina, a huge bronze statue of a heavy-set man in a western-style suit gazed out to the sea.

"Who is that?" asked the CIA analyst.

"Lebanese Prime Minister Rafik Hariri. He was assassinated here at this intersection by a suicide car bomb in 2005," the RSO explained.

"Who killed him?" the analyst asked.

"That's still up for debate," replied the RSO. "A full investigation has yet to be completed. Most think Syrians with Hezbollah assistance."

"But he was Muslim, wasn't he?" she asked.

"He was Sunni. Hezbollah is Shia," replied the RSO. "Lebanese politics are complicated."

Recognizing something familiar, Cam quickly asked Elie to pull over at the Hariri Memorial. Rising up behind the giant statute was the Phoenician Hotel, now fully restored. Just behind the Phoenician was another high-rise, windows blown out, concrete walls pocked with chips from bullet and shrapnel impacts, and larger holes from rocket, mortar, and artillery shells.

"That's the old Holiday Inn!" Cam said. "I'm surprised it's still standing!"

Just like the St. Georges Hotel, the Holiday Inn had never been refurbished from the war damage. Located in the heart of downtown Beirut, an area that had seen some of the heaviest fighting of the war, the Phoenician and Holiday Inn buildings stood as contrasting reminders of Lebanon's political history. One was a modern symbol of recovery, the other a painful reminder of its past. Below the hotels stood the statue of Hariri, Lebanon's admired political leader who had rebuilt much of the war-torn city and was then assassinated for his efforts.

"Beirut has changed a lot," Cam observed.

"In some ways," replied the RSO. "In other ways, not so much. Currently, there is no direct fighting taking place, but now they have garbage wars. Prime Minister Hariri, a wealthy Sunni, rebuilt a lot of downtown after the war, but then he was assassinated. The rebuilding continued, then Israel hit Hezbollah targets as well as Beirut's infrastructure pretty hard in 2006 after Hezbollah launched an attack into Israeli territory. Now, with the Syrian conflict, Iranian-backed Hezbollah has sided with the Syrian régime against the ISIS-infused rebels, and Beirut has once again become a staging ground for a full gamut of Middle Eastern stake-holders. This place always seems to have a fuse smoldering somewhere."

"My head already hurts," declared the CIA analyst from the back of the van.

"Welcome to the crossroads of the Middle East," remarked the RSO, cynicism cloaking every word.

The van grew quiet after a while, its occupants absorbing the sights and sounds and smells of a culture much different from that of DC.

Then the ATF agent asked from the back seat, "Crowbar?"

"That was his codename!" interjected Elie, smiling. "In the old days, everybody at the embassy had a codename. Mr. Coppenger's codename was Crowbar! The Nasty Boys named him Crowbar because he was long and lean and tough as nails!"

"Nasty Boys?" inquired the FBI agent, looking at Cam.

"The Nasty Boys was the name given to our embassy bodyguard force by some Special Forces guys during the Lebanese civil war, and it stuck," explained Cam. "People think embassies are protected by US Marines, but they're not. Marines only exist at embassies to protect classified information. If you don't store classified information, you don't get Marines. So US embassies worldwide hire security personnel from the local population, sometimes as contractors, sometimes as full-time employees. Most embassies are comprised almost entirely of locally hired Foreign Service National (FSN) staff, with American Foreign Service officers providing supervision. At the height of the Lebanese civil war, we had seventy-five Lebanese bodyguards providing twenty-four hour protection to American personnel anytime they left the embassy compound. That's in addition to the local guard force that provides perimeter security to the embassy. In the old days, the ambassador traveled in a nine-car motorcade with an armored limo, twenty eight Lebanese bodyguards, and a handful of American RSO's. The Nasty Boys were the best damned embassy bodyguard force on the planet. I trusted them with my life." Cam reached up and patted Elie on the shoulder. "Still do."

As the van pulled up to the embassy gate, the RSO advised, "We'll get you situated in your rooms, but the ambassador has called a Country Team meeting in one hour."

"Who is the ambassador?" asked Cam.

"Ambassador Pruett," replied RSO Bell.

"Wilson Pruett?" Cam sighed slightly.

"You know him?"

"Unfortunately. So Wilson Pruett made ambassador. Is he still a pompous ass?"

The RSO gave Cam a sideways glance, a diplomatic pause that said volumes without saying anything.

Cam muttered to himself, "Great."

The gate guards completed their comprehensive search of the van, and the hydraulic vehicle barriers were lowered, allowing it to proceed into the compound. The guards saluted the RSO smartly as the van passed. Looking at the outward-facing guard towers spaced along the perimeter wall, Cam realized the compound hadn't changed much since the last time he was there. AmEmbassy Beirut was simply a walled compound that surrounded several old estates located on a mountainside in East Beirut. Looking outward, the location was beautiful, a fabulous view of the Mediterranean Sea to the west. Looking inward, not so much. The compound was functional but not pretty by any means. One estate villa became the embassy chancery offices, another became the ambassador's residence, and several others had been modified to house embassy staff. One of the properties did have a swimming pool, which was the focal point of recreation for the small staff of Americans assigned there.

"So this is what an embassy looks like?" asked the ATF agent.

"Not exactly," replied Cam. "After our two previous embassies were blown up by truck bombs in the 1980's, the State Department decided to focus on security rather than aesthetics. I guess Uncle Sam has determined that Beirut hasn't stabilized enough to warrant investment in a decent facility."

Pointing to a blackened concrete shell at the base of the compound, the FBI agent asked, "What was that?"

"That's the Baaklini Building," replied Cam. "After Hezbollah blew up our first embassy downtown with a car bomb in 1983, we moved here to the suburbs of East Beirut, reportedly safer, and started work on the Baaklini Building. Hezbollah blew up that building in 1984 with another car bomb before we could get the security measures installed. Third time's a charm. The US Government simply bought the surrounding properties and put a wall around it."

"Geez, why haven't they done anything with the Baaklini Building in all this time?" asked the CIA analyst.

"Money, priorities, politics … and ghosts. Beirut has a lot of ghosts."

Elie broke the impending silence, "Hey, Crowbar, remember those?" He pointed at two old white Chevy suburbans parked to the side of the drive, sitting askew, flat tires, dented doors, rusted cattle bumpers, and cracked windshields.

"Beirut Battlewagons!" exclaimed Cam.

"Are those bullet holes?" asked the FBI agent.

"A few," shrugged Elie, looking over his shoulder at Cam. "From back in the day."

"What is that on top of the vehicles?" asked the ATF agent.

"Homemade gun turrets," replied Cam. "In the days before armored Humvees, we made our own, so we had the Navy Seabees bulk up the suspensions of the Suburbans, put steel plates in the doors, cut the roofs out with a can opener, and mount turret rings for M60 machine guns. We used two battlewagons in each motorcade, one in the lead and one as tailgunner."

"Sounds like the wild-west," stated the FBI agent, as if it had never occurred to him that embassy duty was potentially that dangerous.

"In the 80's, Beirut was a dangerous place. Still is," Cam replied.

Inside the compound, the van pulled over to a series of shipping containers lined up side by side, each with a heavy hinged door on the front.

"Home sweet home," announced RSO Bell as he got out of the vehicle. The FBI and ATF agents looked at one another as they studied their new accommodations.

"Shipping containers?" asked the CIA analyst. She was accustomed to Hiltons.

"They're not so bad inside," explained the RSO. "I don't think the ambassador anticipates you staying very long. Besides, this is all we've got for temporary personnel."

"What do you mean by *not staying long?*'" asked Cam.

"I'll explain later," advised the RSO, looking directly at Cam. "Anyway, welcome to the Root; the bath house is over there. Country Team meeting is in one hour. I'll come get you ten minutes before."

Cam went over to the van and gave the smiling Elie another hardy embrace, retrieved his bag, and then went to his shipping container. On entering, Cam was surprised to find the containers so comfortably furnished. Years of military application in places like Afghanistan and Iraq had resulted in gradual refinements that included a partitioned sleeping space, a sitting area, a small kitchenette with microwave, and air conditioning. The windowless walls were lined with insulated paneling, the floors a low-maintenance industrial carpet. To Cam, the shipping containers were like living on a sailboat, only with air conditioning, more headroom, and no view.

About the time he finished unpacking, Cam heard a knock at his door and opened it to find RSO Bell.

"Mr. Coppenger, do you have a minute? Thought I'd give you some background before we got into the Country Team meeting," explained the RSO.

"Sure, come in, and the name is Cam."

"Or Crowbar?" asked the RSO, jokingly. "You've got quite a reputation around here. The Nasty Boys that are still around hold a lot of affection for you."

"Those were tough times, but special. My guess is you have military combat experience, so you know how it is."

"Absolutely."

"Where did you serve?"

"Two tours in Iraq. I was with the 1st Marine Expeditionary Force during the Fallujah offensive."

"Fallujah? That was some tough fighting!"

"Yes sir. Urban warfare, clearing houses room by room. Could have been a lot rougher had it not been for solid teamwork."

"Teamwork is an important element to survival. That's for sure!"

"Our paths have crossed before, you know. You taught our new-agent class high-speed driving at BSR in Summit Point, West Virginia."

"Bob Scott School of Racing? I thought you looked familiar! Did I pass you?"

"You passed me, all right ... on the course and on the track!" joked Bell. "So how do you know Ambassador Pruett?"

"Wilson and I were first-tour junior officers together in Khartoum, Sudan. He was a newly hired Political Officer, and I was a newly hired Assistant Regional Security Officer. He was arrogant even then and exceptionally careless in his handling of classified material. I issued him so many security violations in his first year that he was sent back to Washington for retraining. That probably delayed his promotion eligibility by a year or two. He has hated me ever since. Kinda surprised he made ambassador. Didn't think he had the disposition for it. I always knew he was an ambitious prick."

"Oh, he's a superstar, now. Washington's golden boy! Ambassador Pruett was instrumental in the recent nuclear arms deal with Iran, and now the White House has sent him here to facilitate a peace deal in the Syrian conflict. I need to tell you, Mr. Coppenger, he was not too happy to see your team's assignment here. He doesn't want anything to get in the way of his negotiations, so expect a tight rein while you're here."

"I understand. Thanks for the heads up."

RSO Bell looked at his watch, and then began to round up everybody for the Country Team.

Joining with the rest of the task force, Cam proceeded to the secure conference room of the chancery building. As they entered the foyer, Cam instructed his team to leave all electronic devices on the table outside the secure conference room. The RSO led the team inside and found most of the seats at the huge conference table already occupied by embassy personnel. Cam directed his team to the perimeter seats lining the room and took a seat next to the RSO at the end of the table, which was opposite the ambassador's designated seat at the head. Random muffled conversations filled the room for a few minutes until Ambassador Wilson Pruett entered. Then the room went quiet, and everyone stood, as was the custom, until the ambassador, dressed astutely in a custom-tailored suit with vest, raised his hand in polite false modesty. Then everyone sat back down.

Bill Romano, the Deputy Chief of Mission (DCM), opened the meeting by noting the presence of the DOJ task force and advising that, based on the team's clearance cables passed from Washington, the meeting was to be conducted at a SECRET level or lower. No TOP SECRET was to be discussed. The DCM looked to his left and suggested all attendees introduce themselves. In attendance were the embassy's Political Officer (POL), Economic Officer (ECON), the CIA's Chief of Station (COS), the Defense Attaché (DATT), the Consular Officer (CONOFF), the Administrative Officer (ADMIN), the Public Diplomacy Officer (PDO), and the USAID Officer (AID). After introducing himself, RSO Bell introduced Cameron Coppenger as head of the DOJ task force, and Cam in turn introduced his team. The DCM asked for any old business, of which there were a few minor discussions among the various Country Team members that involved embassy operations, and then he asked for new business, giving Cam the opportunity to explain the purpose of his team's visit to Beirut.

The ambassador, ever the diplomat, listened studiously to Cam's briefing on the San Diego airport attack and the National Mall bombing. With a thumb under his chin and a forefinger placed strategically above his lip, the ambassador gave no hint of recognizing Cam whatsoever.

When Cam was finished with his briefing, Ambassador Pruett asked pointedly, "Mr. Coppenger, what is your exact grade and position within the DOJ?"

Cam had not even considered his grade since he wasn't working for status or money. Frankly, he had no idea what his salary was before taxes, but he had enough experience in the Diplomatic Corps to know where the ambassador was going with the question, so he replied, "I am a political appointee designated by the Department of Justice to head an investigation into the Lebanese-based terrorist group Liwa Tahrir, known also as The Liberation Brigade." And as he looked around the room, Cam added, "And it appears I am the senior DOJ official at Embassy Beirut." With that brief response, Cam had covered most of the bases important to those ensconced in the culture of diplomacy. He had White House backing, the full authority of an important Washington agency, and was on a high-profile mission relating to matters of extreme national security. RSO Bell smiled inwardly at Coppenger's response, then thought to himself, *Crowbar 1 – Ambassador 0.*

Next, the ambassador asked, "What exactly do you hope to achieve during your stay in Lebanon, Mr. Coppenger?"

"Sir, our mission is to locate Khalid Khalidi, apprehend him with the help of local authorities if possible, and ultimately bring him to justice within the American judicial system."

Both the ambassador and the DCM leaned back in their chairs simultaneously while the Political Officer shifted uncomfortably in his seat.

"What do you mean by *local authorities if possible*? You do realize you are in a foreign country, Mr. Coppenger?" responded the ambassador.

"Yes sir, I am well aware of that," replied Cam. "I fully understand the concepts of international cooperation toward mutually agreed-upon objectives," he added, inserting all the diplomatic catch-phrases he could remember.

This was getting good, the RSO thought to himself and wondered if he should take notes.

Ambassador Pruett retorted, "Do you know for a fact, Mr. Coppenger, that the Government of Lebanon mutually agrees that apprehending Khalid Khalidi is a good thing?"

"Agreement is what I hope to achieve during our visit, Mr. Ambassador," replied Cam, fighting the urge to call him Wilson.

"You do understand the fragile state of politics here in Lebanon? Any American action appearing to take one side over another could be extremely detrimental to diplomatic relations between our countries," lectured Ambassador Pruett, his voice cloaked in a patronizing tone.

"Yes sir, I have seen the result of diplomatic failures in Beirut," replied Cam sarcastically, thinking of the mutilated CIA officer's body he once had to retrieve from a parking lot on the outskirts of West Beirut. Looking around the room, Cam realized that most of the junior officers in attendance probably had no knowledge of the incident.

"You are also aware, I assume, that AmEmbassy Beirut has been tasked with helping broker a peace deal between the Syrian régime, Sunni rebels, and other regional interests, including the Russians and the United States, as well as major stake-holders in Lebanon, including the Iranian-backed Hezbollah Party? Any distractions from other quarters within Lebanon regarding the Palestinian issue could be disastrous to the overall peace process. You do understand that?" inquired the ambassador, half lecturing, half warning in the kind of diplomatic speak that Cam understood clearly.

"Yes sir, quite aware," replied Cam.

"I'm not sure you are, Mr. Coppenger," retorted the ambassador sharply. "Significant issues with global implications are at stake in Lebanon at present, for which I am responsible, and these issues far outweigh apprehending one bad actor in a region filled with bad actors. Issues of diplomacy are far more important than those of common criminals."

At that point, Cam realized Ambassador Pruett had no idea of the impact Ismail and his Liberation Brigade were having on the American homeland. Pruett had been out of the country too long. He didn't comprehend the shock, the weakened confidence, and the national sense of panic gripping the American public due to one terrorist's actions. Ambassador Pruett was no longer a public servant. He had become a myopic government official who put personal ambition and world politics ahead of the American people.

"Do you understand the relationship between the art of diplomacy and the restrictions of enforcing American law in a foreign country, Mr. Coppenger?"

To break mounting tensions in the room, Cam decided it was time to risk introducing a bit of southern humor into the inquisition. "Yes sir, I've understood the fine art of diplomacy ever since I was a young boy growing up on a sandy dirt road in South Alabama," replied Cam.

The abrupt change in tactics threw Ambassador Pruett off guard. "And how is that, Mr. Coppenger?" he asked.

With a good dose of southern self-deprecation, Cam explained, "When I was a boy, there was a mean old hound dog that lived down at the end of our road. Every day, I had to ride my bike to baseball practice, and every day that old hound dog would come after me. I tried riding fast, I tried riding quietly, I tried walking by with my bike between me and that hound dog. I even tried throwing dog biscuits to the critter. Nothing worked. Then one day my daddy told me to use my baseball bat and clobber that dog right square on the head. The next day, I did just what my daddy told me to do, and you know what? It worked! From that point on, that ol' hound dog continued to bark, but he never came back out into the road. So Mr. Ambassador, in my view, diplomacy is simply the fine art of keeping a barking dog at bay until you can find a big enough stick."

The RSO fought hard to suppress a smile while the rest of the conference room laughed out loud. Even the DCM, recognizing a deft diplomatic maneuver when he saw one, cracked a smile as he looked over to the ambassador.

"It's not always about big sticks, Mr. Coppenger," replied the ambassador stiffly. "It's also about speaking softly and reaching compromise."

"Yes sir," replied Cam, growing tired of the ambassador's words and ready to get on with meaningful action.

"As long as you and your team understand that," repeated the ambassador. Then looking directly at Cam, he reiterated, "Let me make myself crystal clear. I do not want you or your task force to do anything, *anything*, during your visit here in Lebanon that might have even the slightest implications for the Syrian peace process. I expect you to brief the DCM daily on the progress of your investigation and clear all scheduled meetings with Lebanese officials through my office first. Is that clear?"

"Yes sir, crystal clear," responded Cam, giving the ambassador the last word while telling himself that technically the ambassador was not in his chain of command. At the same time, Cam understood that Wilson Pruett was the President's personal representative in Lebanon, confirmed by the Senate, and was the highest-ranking USG official in the country.

Having made his point in front of the entire Country Team, Ambassador Pruett asked if anyone had questions, and when there were none, he concluded the meeting. All attendees stood to attention as the ambassador left the secure conference room.

After the meeting, the DCM pulled Bell aside. "What do you know about this Coppenger guy?" Romero asked.

"I only know him by reputation," responded the RSO.

"What do you mean?" asked the DCM.

The RSO shrugged. "Cam Coppenger is a bit of a DSS legend, sir," he said.

"How so?" asked the DCM.

Bell gave the DCM a sideways glance. "This is still probably classified, but you may recall that before 9/11 the World Trade Center in New York was first attacked in 1993," he explained. "The culprit was a guy named Mohamed Muladi, a Pakistani national operating under the guidance of Osama bin Laden. By the time the car bomb went off in the parking garage beneath the Trade Center, Muladi was already on a plane bound for Pakistan. Once there, he disappeared into the mountains where he went into hiding. Cam Coppenger—the agent you just asked about—was on temporary assignment to Pakistan at the time. Somehow he tracked Muladi down and found him living with clansmen in a remote mountain village outside of Islamabad. Acting completely on his own, without embassy authorization and using only a trusted interpreter as a guide, Special Agent Coppenger single-handedly captured Muladi, threw him in the trunk of his vehicle, and drove to the US embassy.

During the security inspection of the vehicle at the front gate, the embassy guards found the wide-eyed terrorist gagged and hog-tied in the trunk, dazed from his hard journey along rough mountain roads. Agent Coppenger turned Muladi over to the FBI's legal attaché at the embassy, and then went upstairs and told the ambassador what he had done. The ambassador was furious, but there was nothing he could do. Muladi was on the FBI's *Ten Most Wanted* list, and he was in custody. That incident was one of Diplomatic Security's first successes in America's war on terror, and the ambassador got full credit for Muladi's capture. Of course, Agent Coppenger was sent home the very next day."

The DCM, a career bureaucrat, followed with a ton of procedural questions. "Was there an arrest warrant? Were the Pakistanis consulted? Were shots fired? Was anyone killed in the operation?"

"Dunno," the RSO replied with a shrug. "Nobody asked, and Cop never said."

———

Later that evening, Cam's team members bought Lebanese falafel sandwich wraps from the small canteen on the compound and sat at an outside table near the embassy swimming pool. The sun was just beginning to ease itself into the tepid waters of the Mediterranean. To the south was downtown Beirut. The reds, oranges and yellows that filled the western sky were a dramatic conclusion to the team's first day in Lebanon.

"Nice view!" observed the thirty-something CIA analyst.

"Yes, it is," agreed Cam. "Nature's picture show. Get used to it. It's the only decent view you're gonna have here."

RSO Bell, having finished his business for the night yet still carrying his Colt M-4 carbine and radio, was heading to his small apartment on the compound when he saw the team assembled by the pool, so he stopped by. "Everybody settled in?"

"Oh yeah," responded the ATF agent. "Shoe boxes make great hotels … if you're a rat."

"Tell me about it," agreed the RSO. "I lived in a shipping container for eighteen months in Afghanistan."

"That ambassador of yours is a piece of work!" declared the FBI agent.

"I prefer the word, *focused*," replied the RSO, ever mindful of who wrote his yearly evaluation.

"So have you had any encounters with Ismail here in Lebanon?" asked the CIA analyst.

"Not really," replied the RSO. "Given his alliance with Hezbollah and Iran, he has pretty much left us alone during the Iran nuclear weapons negotiations. But now that the deal is done, expect Iran to reactivate The Liberation Brigade as a player in its proxy war against us, *The Great Satan*. We shouldn't discount the possibility of Iran playing a role in the San Diego and DC attacks," offered the RSO, while looking directly at the CIA analyst. "That said, Ismail has always given the Israelis fits. His ties to Hezbollah in southern Lebanon, various PLO factions, and the occupied territories keeps them pretty busy."

"Do you have any contacts within the Israeli Government?"

Cam asked.

"Not formally. Just the Shin Bet guys when we cross paths working protection," advised the RSO. "I pretty much leave the Mossad stuff to the Agency. But you can be assured that if they are Israeli and are here in Lebanon, they are either Shin Bet, the security guys, or the intelligence guys, Mossad. The Lebanese have no love for the Israelis."

The CIA analyst interrupted, "I'll be meeting with the Chief of Station tomorrow. Is there any background I need to be aware of?"

RSO Bell contemplated the question and then responded, "You just need to be aware that Beirut is a complicated place, a theater filled with bad actors, all with blood on their hands in one form or another. For the most part, during the war there were no easily identified good guys or bad guys. Boundaries became blurred as militias deteriorated into mafias. When the war ended in 1990, most of the war lords were exonerated of their atrocities, at least legally. That was the only way to stop the bloodshed. So there currently exists a form of detente in Lebanon where known bad actors are allowed to thrive within their respective communities, protected by complicated alliances and powerful politicians within a very weak and fragile government. But memories run long and deep in this part of the world."

"What role did the Palestinians play in the civil war?" the FBI agent inquired.

"You'd need a week-long seminar by our political officer to fully comprehend Lebanese politics, but I'll give you my take." RSO Bell explained, "Palestinian refugees, which began coming to Lebanon in 1948 after the establishment of Israel as a State, flooded into Lebanon in 1970 after being expelled from Jordan in what became known as *Black September*. Lebanon's civil war started in 1975 when Lebanon's minority Christians clashed with Lebanon's growing majority of Muslims over, primarily, the issue of Palestinian refugees. The refugee camps became festering wounds of unimaginable squalor and hardship. The result was fifteen years of unbelievable savagery and destruction right in the heart of Beirut. To say it was Christians versus Muslims would be a dramatic oversimplification. There were so many sects, militias, alliances, and outside interference that it would have taken a university full of Middle Eastern scholars a lifetime to sort it all out."

The FBI Agent pushed Bell farther. "So give me a crash course."

Bell continued, "The Lebanese Armed Forces (LAF), Christian Maronites, the Palestine Liberation Organization (PLO), the Amal Movement, Druze, Phalange, Shia Muslims, Sunni Muslims, Syrian Ba-athists, Iranian-backed Hezbollah, and Israeli-backed South Lebanon Army (SLA), were all involved, as were others. Beirut was a chaotic, bloody mess. In 1982, a faction of the Phalange Militia—allegedly under the direction of its ally Israel—attacked and killed hundreds if not thousands of Palestinians and Lebanese Shiites in West Beirut's Sabra neighborhood and adjoining Shatila refugee camp. That event became known as the *Sabra and Shatila Massacre.* That massacre, more than any other event, is probably what put your terrorist Ismail on the path he is currently on. Then in 1985, in what became known as the *War of the Camps,* Syria's Assad régime enlisted the Lebanese Amal Shiite militia and others to launch another siege on the pro-Arafat Palestinians in the Shatila

Camp, shelling the camp to piles of rubble and killing hundreds more Palestinians in the process. And that's just a sampling of how complicated the war was."

Having given his best explanation of a situation that defies explanation, the RSO stood and took his leave from the group, retreating to his small apartment within a compound surrounded by high walls, razor wire, and armed guards in towers. To the newly arrived task force, the premises looked and felt more like a prison than an embassy.

As jet lag set in and individual task force members began to yawn, the group disbanded and retired to their assigned quarters for the evening, leaving Cam alone with his thoughts. In the 1980's, from that same mountainside location overlooking the troubled city, Cam had spent countless hours watching the exchange of salvos along Beirut's Green Line, the arbitrary demarcation that separated Muslim West Beirut from the Christian East. After years of civil war, rifle sniping had escalated to rockets and howitzers, and the level of destruction to the heart of the city increased proportionally. Most impressive was the night fighting. With each shell's impact, the ground throbbed and the sky flashed brilliant spectrums of white, red, and orange, illuminating the surrounding buildings with extremes of light and shadow. Steady streams of .50 caliber machine gun rounds laced the night sky with tracers like silent strings of Christmas lights waving slowly to the heavens, followed by the delayed staccato of the heavy gun's report. Sporadically, the muffled stutter of shoulder arms bracketed the quiet intermissions, twinkling like camera flashes from darkened windows. Fifteen years of death and destruction, two-thousand

years of architecture reduced to wasted rubble. Directly below
the pool area were the skeletal remains of the Baaklini Building,
site of the second embassy truck-bombing. Cam was once again
reminded of the personal tragedies that the politics of hate creates.
He thought about the young pretty Lebanese employee widowed at
eighteen and pregnant at the time her young husband was killed in
the second embassy bombing, her son never knowing his father. He
thought about the kindly older embassy telephone operator, shot
by a sniper at her kitchen window as she washed dishes, and the
continued sniper fire as her son struggled to get her into his car for
treatment. Those years had been hard, and Cam's thoughts drifted
to a certain Lebanese girl, a stunning dark-haired beauty who had
entered his life like a guiding angel during those tragic times. He
wondered where she was now, what had become of her.

The next day, the RSO accompanied the JTTF team on its
obligatory briefings from the relevant Country Team members,
each of whom had been present at the Country Team meeting
the day before. The embassy's Political Officer offered nothing
new, repeating much of what the RSO had already told them.
He suggested that the task force would most likely find it
exceedingly difficult to identify a Lebanese government agency
willing to discuss Liwa Tahrir's presence in Lebanon. In fact, the
POLOFF predicted that many Lebanese officials would refuse to
acknowledge that Ismail even existed. The CIA Station Chief pretty
much agreed, adding that Lebanon, long known for its intrigue,
was loaded with conspiracy theories, most being completely
baseless. But according to the COS, conspiracies were important
to Lebanon's political stability since they aided Lebanon's national

tendency for deflection, and deflection created confusion, and confusion in turn helped keep the country's political turmoil at a low simmer rather than a rapid boil. When Cam asked the COS what the CIA was doing with regard to Ismail's presence in Lebanon, he was answered with what Cam recognized as a strategic pause, followed by a diplomatic smile, communicating without saying, "No comment." It was obvious to Cam that the ambassador had already given the COS his marching orders, and those orders did not involve an immediate pursuit of Ismail. The ambassador set USG priorities in Lebanon. Syria, not Ismail, was was Embassy Beirut's priority. However, the COS did offer one helpful piece of advice. The only group within the Lebanese Government who might help would be the police, specifically, its Internal Security Force (ISF). As the briefing drew to a close, the COS made one additional comment. As if an afterthought, he suggested that the Israelis knew Ismail's every movement. Such were the subtleties of embassy diplomacy.

Embassy briefings completed, the team assembled in the RSO's office. Cam asked the RSO an open-ended question. "Given what we just heard, how much cooperation can we realistically expect from the Lebanese in finding Ismail?"

"Not much," replied Bell. "Every faction in Lebanon has an entrenched support network to ensure its survival. Unholy alliances have been forged over the years between groups that may not traditionally have shared interests, except for the shared interest of survival. There is a careful balance of detente that currently exists in Lebanon that reaches all the way to the Parliament, and no one—not politicians, government officials, nor the military—wants

to do anything to disrupt that balance. Ismail and his group Liwa
Tahrir are part of Hezbollah's political base at this point in time,
and no one within the government has the power or inclination to
take on Hezbollah. In Lebanon, Hezbollah, with Iranian backing, is
the five-hundred-pound gorilla."

"What do you recommend we do?" Cam asked.

RSO Bell hesitated, then replied, "If you go the formal
diplomatic route and approach the ISF guys, Ismail will know about
it by sundown. He'll go underground on you. Hell, he probably
already has copies of your passport photographs from when you
came through the airport. And it's not like you can just walk into
these Palestinian enclaves and start asking questions. You wouldn't
last a day. Frankly, without Agency assistance, your team is dead in
the water."

"Okay, you just told me what not to do. I need your advice on
what to do," Cam said.

RSO Bell paused once again—the pause that each team
member was beginning to recognize as embassy-speak—and then
continued, "If you want to be successful, I think the COS had the
best suggestion."

"The Israelis?" asked Cam.

"I didn't say that," refuted Bell, looking at each team member as
he spoke.

"Is there any official Israeli presence in Lebanon?"

"Hardly," replied Bell. "With the exception of the South
Lebanese Army (SLA), which was a proxy militia aligned with
Israel during the war, the Lebanese despise Israel. Most Arab
countries do. In fact, if you attempt to enter Lebanon with so much

as an Israeli entry visa stamp in your passport, you will be denied. The closest official Israeli representation you are going to find will probably be in Cairo."

"Where can I find members of the SLA?" asked Cam.

"They're all in Israel now," replied the RSO. "After Israel's withdrawal from South Lebanon when the war ended, any Lebanese SLA members who tried to remain in Lebanon would have been walking dead men."

"What about unofficial representation?" Cam asked diplomatically.

"I'm sure Mossad is here," replied Bell. "Identifying them is a different question."

The CIA analyst spoke up. "Where do the journalists stay in Beirut?" she asked.

"The Commodore Hotel downtown, generally," replied the RSO, impressed with her thought process.

"That's where we will find Mossad then," she concluded.

"Do you think your chief upstairs can give us some names?" asked Cam, feeling like progress was finally being made.

"I think so," she said. "Let me ask privately"

Cam then looked around the room and stated authoritatively, "This conversation didn't happen. Is that clear?" The team nodded in agreement.

Later that day, CIA analyst Judy—or whatever her real name was—entered the workroom where the team had assembled. She closed the door and announced quietly, "I just met with the COS, and he gave me a name. Do not write this down. Just remember it. Hans Kolb is a reporter for the German language publication, *The*

Arabic Eye. He is based here in Beirut and reporting on the Syrian conflict. He makes routine trips to Damascus, but he should be in town today."

"Good work and thank you!" replied Cam. "I need you to go with me to the Commodore this afternoon. The rest of you stay here." He turned to Judy, "How good is your Arabic?"

"Shway, shway … fair," she replied. "I scored a 4/5 in language training, but that was Egyptian Arabic, not Lebanese."

"Better than mine," replied Cam.

"Do we need to brief the DCM?" asked the FBI agent, remembering the ambassador's instructions from the previous day. The young agent, inexperienced in the subtleties of diplomacy, should have let that sleeping dog lie, but by asking the question he had introduced an elephant into the room.

In response to the agent's question, Cam turned and instructed everyone to take a seat. "We haven't discussed this, but we need to now. In the diplomatic and political arenas there exists the concept of *plausible deniability.* The concept is based on the idea that politicians, diplomats, or agency heads do not always want or need to know everything that takes place under their authority. By insulating them from certain activities, we as subordinates protect them from any repercussions that might take place should certain actions or policies go bad. Usually, the subordinates pay the price. We become the sacrificial lambs for what some perceive as the greater good. In government, plausible deniability allows agency heads to state publicly and somewhat truthfully that they had *no direct knowledge* of an incident in question, thereby preserving his/her position and deflecting responsibility to others. It's a crappy way to do business, but that's how the real world works. Part of my job as team leader is to find Ismail and bring him to justice but in a way that gives our ambassador and the rest of the embassy plausible deniability. But one thing I want to make clear to each of you on this team who have careers to consider within your respective agencies: I will take full responsibility for the actions of this task force. All decisions will be my call, my responsibility. If any of you are uncomfortable with the ethical compromises and blurred boundaries that fulfilling this mission might entail, speak up now. There will be no recriminations. You have my word."

The team members looked at one another, and each shrugged or nodded in unified acceptance. Nobody signed an agreement; nobody swore an oath. It was just understood among professionals that when it came to defeating terrorism some rules were going to be steadfast, some nebulous, and some meant to be broken.

Cam called Elie and scheduled an embassy car for the afternoon.

"Do you want a full security package attached to us?" asked Elie. "The Nasty Boys would love to see you!"

"No, not at this point," Cam replied. High profile was not what he was seeking. "It's a routine meeting."

Later that afternoon, Cam checked the safety on his 9mm and tucked it back inside his concealed holster. He grabbed his canvas briefcase and instructed Judy to bring her laptop bag to serve as props. Then Elie drove them to the Commodore Hotel, located on a hill in the middle of downtown Beirut. About two blocks from the hotel, Cam instructed Elie to let them out, and they walked the rest of the way. The small street in front of the hotel was congested with double-parked cars, cars backed onto sidewalks, and cars parked at odd angles on top of construction rubble or piles of garbage. Others moved slowly in single file, picking their way through the tangled traffic like ants finding their way back home. The sound of shrill horns was a constant. The drivers of the parked cars waited idly outside, chatting amongst themselves, sipping small cups of thick dark espressos, or sleeping in the reclined seats of their cars. In the lobby of the hotel, a slew of journalists from all over the world mingled in groups, chatting with one another in a variety of languages, some bent over laptops, others involved in deep phone conversations, all involving the Syrian conflict. Off to the left, in the bar area, were more journalists, drinking already. The scene reminded Cam of Hemingway's accounts of war correspondents in Paris during both world wars. The international war correspondent culture had always fascinated him. They lived hard and played hard during hard times.

A sign in the lobby stated in five different languages, JOURNALIST WORK AREA, and pointed in the direction of the hotel's conference rooms. Cam directed Judy to sit down next to him on a sofa off to one side of the lobby. She pulled out her phone and pretended to send emails. With an eye on the hotel entrance, Cam waited, watching the door, scanning the lobby, looking for anything that seemed out of place, any indication of someone following them. One young loner, apparently Lebanese, caught Cam's attention. He sat in a chair on the opposite side of the lobby, had no briefcase, no laptop, no reading material, and was obviously not engaged with the buzz of journalistic activity surrounding him. Cam instructed Judy to walk across the lobby at an extreme angle to see if the lone man followed her with his eyes. He did not, but he seemed nervous and checked his watch constantly. An attractive young Lebanese woman came striding over to the lone individual with a smile on her face. As they proceeded to the check-in counter, hand in hand and with no luggage, it quickly became apparent to Cam that a romantic rendezvous was the couple's only clandestine mission that day. After a few more minutes in the lobby, satisfied they were not being watched, Cam walked Judy down the hallway toward the journalists' work room. Entering, they found long rows of tables and chairs arranged into workspaces, each with tangles of cables and electrical wires running from them into a utility closet nearby that connected that room to various news outlets across the world. A smattering of journalists were hard at work over their laptops, their work schedules hinging largely on the time zone with which they were communicating. Other journalists, having met their respective deadlines for the day, sat chatting and smoking cigarettes. A large blue cloth hung on the wall, surrounded by tripods with heavy TV cameras attached and piles of other equipment scattered randomly on the floor. Sitting atop each work desk, a small sign indicated the news service assigned to that space. Cam and Judy roamed among the workspaces until they found *The Arabic Eye* desk.

"May I help you?" came a voice in German-accented English from behind them.

Cam turned and found a fortyish Caucasian wearing rumpled clothes and sporting shaggy hair pulled back in a ponytail. He wore the narrow frameless eyeglasses that Europeans love so well. "Hans Kolb?" asked Cam.

"Who's asking?" replied the man.

"I'm Cam Coppenger from the US Embassy. We'd like to talk with you about events in Syria if you don't mind." Cam lied.

"Do you have a card?" asked the man, still not identifying himself.

Cam realized he was being evaluated. "No, I don't. We just arrived two days ago."

"Who arrived? You said we," quizzed the man. "What section of the embassy are you connected with?"

"The US Interests Section," Cam lied again, pulling a phrase from his days in Cuba, knowing that such a nebulous answer would give pause to anyone not completely familiar with embassy lingo. Then he took the offensive. "Are you Hans Kolb? We were told he could be a knowledgeable source of information."

The man evaluated both of them for a moment. They were obviously American, the worst at hiding their nationality, which in his estimation had something to do with America's extreme sense of national pride. "Yes, I am Hans Kolb," he revealed. Then he pushed further, "How did you get my name?"

"From the Public Diplomacy Office at the embassy," Cam lied again.

"Jeff Slater?" inquired Hans, already knowing there was no one at the US Embassy named Jeff Slater.

"No, one of the secretaries," deflected Cam. Then looking at Judy, he asked, "Do you remember her name?"

"No, no, I don't," stammered Judy, surprised to find herself playing the role of a field agent, not that of an analyst.

"What is it you want?" asked Hans.

Cam decided it was time to make his pitch, so he looked at Hans straightforwardly and stated cryptically, "We need to talk to you about events in Syria … and elsewhere."

Hans deciphered the meaning behind Cam's words and, being initially satisfied Cam was in fact affiliated with the American Embassy, responded, his German accent less notable, "We should meet for coffee sometime … tomorrow perhaps? Khamamah's on Hamras Street? Nine o'clock?"

"Yes, absolutely," replied Cam. The meeting arranged, Cam and Judy walked out of the hotel, turning in the opposite direction of their car and stopping erratically several times as a counter-surveillance tactic. After a moderately circuitous route, they found Elie still parked two blocks away and then headed back to the embassy. It was late in the afternoon by the time they entered the embassy gate.

Cam and Judy walked over to the task force work room where they found the FBI and ATF agents reading threat assessments and political status reports. Cam was about to instruct the team to break it down for the day when the RSO stuck his head in. "Hey, you folks up for some home cooking tonight?" he asked. "My treat!"

"Sure!" responded Cam, speaking for the group. "Your place? What time?"

"How about 7? I want to get in a workout first," suggested the RSO.

"See you there," came Cam's reply.

A little before 7, Cam and his task force assembled at the RSO's flat, located on the bottom floor of the ambassador's residence. Elie came, too.

"Welcome to my humble abode!" declared RSO Bell, calling out from the kitchen. "Hope you like spaghetti with canned Ragu sauce!"

Cam chuckled, remembering his past life of eating canned goods from the stateside shipment allowance. Each officer assigned to a hardship post received that bounty. "This used to be my residence, you know," Cam revealed. "I guess they like having a security officer live close to the ambassador." He looked over at the huge Norfolk pine that reached up two stories from the RSO's indoor garden into the ambassador's living space above.

RSO Bell's residence was indeed a strange living space, but then everything about the embassy compound in Beirut was strange. Once a maid's quarters, Bell's flat had been constructed out of a partial basement and a patio, and it contained a narrow galley kitchen, one small windowless bedroom, a bath, and a sitting area. Adjoining the sitting area was a two-story, glass-enclosed sunroom containing an indoor garden with the huge Norfolk pine. "Does that pine still serve as the embassy Christmas tree every year?" asked Cam.

"You bet!" replied the RSO. "It has become a tradition for the RSO to host an annual tree-decorating party every Christmas. The tree has gotten so big we have to use the ambassador's balcony upstairs to decorate the top! Then on Christmas Eve, everybody brings a bottle of champagne and tries to knock an ornament off with the exploding cork. A Beirut Christmas tradition!"

From his sofa seat, the FBI agent peered over into the garden and saw the ground littered with hundreds of champagne corks and an assortment of colorful broken Christmas ornaments. Remnants of glitter still hung in the tree limbs.

The RSO had no dining room or dining table, there just wasn't space. But he did have a coffee table, and after clearing off stacks of magazines and other clutter, the team gathered around it with plates of pasta, canned sauce, and canned beverages. However, the bread was fresh. Elie, while waiting at the Commodore Hotel earlier that day, had wandered to a bakery and bought an armload of fresh-baked French baguettes. Cam had experienced this kind of meal many times in his career of hardship postings.

Stomachs full and with numerous crushed beer cans littering the floor, the guests leaned back in their seats and shared stories. The stories were one of the things Cam loved most about the Foreign Service. When two or more Foreign Service veterans got together, they told stories, and the stories were always good ones. Exotic locations, cultural eccentricities, hardship, and danger were all essential elements to a good story, and the Foreign Service had them all.

Early October in Lebanon with Halloween approaching, the conversation turned to the supernatural. Judy, the analyst, looked at Cam and asked, "You said last night there are lots of ghosts in Beirut. What did you mean by that?"

Cam glanced over at Elie and replied, "Embassy Beirut has seen a lot of tragedy over the years, constant violence and death. Elie and I have seen our share of it."

The ATF agent pointed over Cam's shoulder at an ancient, heavy steel door located a few steps above the sitting area. "What is that?"

"The embassy's dungeon," replied Elie, smiling to lighten the mood.

Both the FBI agent and CIA analyst looked sharply over at Elie, not knowing what to believe.

Elie continued, "Actually, at one time, that door was the entrance to an emergency escape tunnel from the residence. All these old villas had one. During the war, they used the tunnels as bomb shelters."

Cam added, "The tunnel also provides quick access to the ambassador's residence in an emergency." Then turning to the RSO, he added, "But that's not all."

"What does that mean?" asked Judy.

"During the war, the tunnel and adjoining rooms served as the embassy's morgue," explained Cam. "An American ambassador was assassinated in '76, and two embassy bombings in the 80's resulted in numerous American casualties. Also during that time, a couple of embassy officials were kidnapped, tortured, and killed. One was a military attaché and the other a CIA officer. I had to retrieve the body of the CIA officer from West Beirut after someone found the guy dumped on the side of a road. You have to remember that once the airport shut down, the only way of getting the bodies home was by helicopter, and with constant power outages, ice was always in short supply. So the bodies were kept here in the basement since that was the coolest place on the compound. I bet those rooms still smell like death."

"I didn't know that," replied the RSO solemnly, "but that explains the stains on the floor."

"Institutional amnesia," suggested Cam. "During the war, those basement rooms were stocked with boxes of body bags and temporary wooden caskets built by the embassy's maintenance shop. That's where we kept the bodies until they could be choppered out." He looked over at Elie and saw his friend's mood had darkened. Those had been sad times for Elie and for all of Lebanon. Cam realized that he and Elie were the only people in the room who had known the true horrors of those times. Cam stopped talking, not wanting to cause his friend more discomfort. Yet a haunting question from those days remained. Looking directly at the RSO, Cam asked in a low and serious voice, "Do you ever hear noises coming from that tunnel? Noises like echoing footsteps, heavy doors closing, or squeaking hinges and the like? Even when you know you're alone in the house?"

The RSO turned, a surprised expression on his face. "Yeah, I do, particularly late at night. Even when the ambassador is gone, stuff moves around in there. At first, I tried to check out the noises, even installed motion-activated surveillance cameras, but I never found the source of the noise." The RSO became quiet, then added, "Now I know why."

The next morning, after a breakfast egg falafel and weak Nescafé coffee from the canteen, Cam and Judy connected with Elie and departed for their 0900 appointment at Khamamah's Coffee Shop.

Practicing traditional counter-surveillance techniques, Elie dropped off his riders a couple blocks short of their destination where they again took a casually cautious route to Khamamah's. They arrived early, giving them additional time to observe and individually assess everyone in view, inside and outside the establishment. Apart from the normal commotion of everyday street life in downtown Beirut, no one seemed out of place except one fit European who sat in the corner reading a paper and drinking coffee. His position had been perfectly selected, as it gave him a complete view of the café's kitchen door, the front entrance, and every patron inside, the seat Cam would have chosen had it not already been occupied by the European. Cam always believed that newspapers were much better props than smartphones for surveillance. Papers allows the eyes to be up as opposed to a small computer screen that draws the eyes down. But times were changing and papers were no longer as plentiful as in days past, so they stood out. Cam guessed the fit European was Hans's Mossad backup, and he was okay with that. The Israelis were not the threat for this mission. Cam and Judy sat at a table against the wall in close proximity to the fit European.

Diplomatically late by ten minutes, Hans Kolb entered the café. Cam stood and greeted him. Without taking a seat, Hans turned to Judy and asked in more refined English than Cam spoke, "I don't believe we've been formally introduced."

Judy stood, "I'm Elsa, from the US Interests Section."

Cam smiled inwardly at Judy's new persona. Before they could take seats, Hans suggested they walk to a nearby park.

"Of course," replied Cam. Just as he paid the check, Cam looked up to see Jason Kasich, the embassy's young Public Diplomacy chief, walk in the door. "Dammit," Cam mumbled to Judy.

Jason stopped and looked at Cam and then at Hans, recognizing both but not yet drawing any conclusions. Beirut had grown into a bustling city of two million people but was still a small town in many ways. Without acknowledging one another, Cam and his companions exited Khamamah's.

Stepping into the hectic street activity, the trio found it

impossible to walk side by side. Parked cars, street vendors, construction debris, and garbage cans were constant sidewalk obstructions, so they walked without conversation, moving along the sidewalk erratically as cars next to them weaved through the congested traffic. Cam glanced back over his shoulder several times, but the fit European from the coffee shop was nowhere to be seen. After a few blocks, they came to a weedy vacant lot near a private school. The lot had been haphazardly modified to resemble a park-like setting. Walled on three sides, there were concrete benches and a couple of shade trees in desperate need of water. Before entering, Hans stopped at a sidewalk vendor and ordered three Nescafés. The pause gave each the chance to survey the surroundings. Cam casually glanced around and found another of Han's backups across the street, leaning against an old Volvo and reading a paper. He, too, looked European, youthful, and physically fit. Cam made a mental note that Mossad really needed more old fat guys working surveillance. Hans distributed three small cups filled with weak instant coffee, and they proceeded to one of the dirty concrete benches. Cam made another mental note that the nearby construction noise, the screams of school kids next door on recess, and the constant din of street traffic would make any electronic eavesdropping impossible. Hans had picked his location well.

Hans opened the conversation, "How long have you been in Lebanon?"

"We arrived three days ago," Cam replied.

"Have you been here before?"

"I was here with the embassy during the war, which is part of the reason I wanted to talk with you."

"Oh?" answered Hans. "Go on."

"You were referred to us by some of my embassy contacts as a person who might be able to help us find somebody."

"Who at the embassy?" Hans inquired. The one-day delay in meeting Cam had given Hans time to do background checks on Cam and his team.

"Friends of Israel."

Hans appeared satisfied. "What exactly do you need?"

"Help in locating and apprehending the Palestinian terrorist Khalid Khalidi."

"I see," replied Hans, offering no denial that he knew exactly who Khalid Khalidi was.

"Is this about the two recent terror attacks in America?" Hans asked, dropping all pretense of ignorance to Cam's mission.

"Yes. We have an international arrest warrant for Ismail, but due to the political climate in Lebanon, we can't get to him. And we have very little support from within our embassy. Syria has the ambassador's full attention."

"Do you want him dead?" Hans asked bluntly, trying to establish the boundaries of Cam's request.

At that point, Cam had not seriously considered assassination as a primary option. The FBI was a law enforcement agency, not Mafia. "No. We want to apprehend Ismail and bring him to the US to be criminally prosecuted."

"And if you were to capture Ismail, how would you get him out of the country?" asked Hans, well aware of the logistical complications of such an operation.

Cam shrugged, "That depends on the circumstances. But this

mission has the full backing of the White House."

"But not the full backing of your embassy," Hans observed. "Give me a few days to consider the many different aspects of your request. I'll be in touch."

Their preliminary meeting over, Hans got up and exited the park on foot, turning right. Cam and Elsa, or Judy—whatever her name was—waited a few minutes, finished their coffees and departed, turning left.

Within minutes of their return to the embassy, the RSO entered the task force workroom and advised Cam in a firm voice, "The DCM wants to see you."

This doesn't look good, Cam thought as he proceeded to the second floor of the chancery. Upon entering, the DCM's secretary pointed Cam to the cracked door of the DCM's office. Inside, he found Ambassador Pruett, along with his second-in-command, Bill Romano. The tension in the room was palpable.

"Have a seat, Mr. Coppenger," instructed DCM Romano, directing him to a wooden chair positioned in the center of the office directly in front of the DCM's desk. It was a position of subjugation and a standard interrogation ploy. Cam was familiar with the tactic.

"Where were you this morning around nine o'clock?" queried Romano.

"Judy and I were meeting with one of our contacts."

"Who?" asked the DCM.

"A reporter from *The Arabic Eye*," Cam replied with a half-truth.

"Was that reporter Hans Kolb by any chance?" inquired Romano.

"Yes," replied Cam, matter-of-factly.

"Do you know who Hans Kolb really is?"

"I have my suspicions."

"Did you clear this meeting with anyone at the embassy?" asked Romano.

"I did not. This morning's meeting was simply a fact-finding mission."

Ambassador Pruett, standing off to the side, could no longer hold his tongue. "Maybe you failed to comprehend my specific instructions regarding your investigation while here in Lebanon, Mr. Coppenger."

Cam opted to wait for the follow-up question before replying. He could smell the ambassador's wrath.

"What part of my instructions to *clear all meetings first* did you not understand, Mr. Coppenger?" implored the ambassador. "Do you not realize the implications of an American Embassy officer caught meeting with an Israeli Mossad agent in Lebanon, particularly during this time of crisis? Well, DO YOU?"

"Yes sir, I do," replied Cam, while at the same time wondering if the COS cleared every one of his meetings with the front office first. He already knew the answer. But this confrontation with the ambassador was not about policies and procedures within embassy operations; it was about embassy priorities, conflicting missions, and personal ambitions. Nothing Cam could say or do could fix that dilemma, not at his pay grade. He braced for the storm.

"You deliberately ignored my instructions, did you not?" berated the ambassador.

Cam perceived the interrogation was becoming personal, so he replied calmly, "I didn't ignore your instructions, Wilson. I simply misinterpreted them." Using the ambassador's first name had just slipped out. Given Cam's earlier lecture to his team on *plausible deniability*, his response to the ambassador was a genuine one. Calling him by his first name—not so much.

"You will refer to me as AMBASSADOR PRUETT!" exploded the ambassador, looking first at Cam and then at the DCM. He turned and glared out the window, fists on hips, fuming.

Obviously, the DCM had less of an emotional investment in the issue than did the ambassador, but Bill Romano had his marching orders.

"Cam," the DCM opened, "you and your team have lost the confidence of the Chief of Mission. You are going to have to leave post. We're sending you back."

"Seriously? Just like that?"

"Seriously. Just like that."

This wasn't the first time Cam had been kicked out of a post, and though he had nothing to lose career-wise, being booted was still a strange feeling, one of failure, a blow to the gut. Cam hated losing, particularly to a man he didn't respect.

The DCM continued, "Have your team pack their bags and be on a plane out of here tomorrow. ADMIN will arrange the tickets. We'll send a cable back to Washington tonight, explaining the circumstances."

Cam's instinct was to fight back. He turned and looked directly at the ambassador. "Sir, Ismail has launched direct attacks against the United States. He has killed scores of Americans!"

Ambassador Pruett responded with callous indifference.

"Perhaps if *your* president had not recognized Jerusalem as the capital of Israel, we wouldn't be having this conversation."

Cam was stunned at the implications of what the Ambassador had said. *My president?* Cam thought to himself. *Isn't he our president? How can one man be so out of touch with reality?* Cam had spent a career fighting this kind of politically-biased, bureaucratic mindset and realized the futility of arguing further. He stood and acknowledged solemnly, "Yes, Sir," then exited the office and walked downstairs to brief his team members.

Cam entered the team's work area and closed the door. "Well guys, we're being sent home."

"What?" asked the FBI agent. "Why?"

"Insubordination is the official term," Cam explained. "You know that earlier lecture I gave you on *plausible deniability*? Well, it has a downside. When you're caught disobeying official orders, heads roll. In this case, my head rolls."

"Is this about our meeting with Hans?" asked Judy.

"Apparently so. But you all need to understand this. We were sent on a mission doomed to fail. Local authorities here are not in a position politically to help us apprehend Ismail. We don't have the resources to get him ourselves, and the ambassador has other priorities."

"What now?" asked the ATF agent.

"Go to your quarters, pack your bags, and be ready to fly home tomorrow. Make sure you are paid up at the canteen, and change your money back before the cashier closes. Nobody worry. This is on me. My responsibility." After the task force filed out of the workspace, Cam sent Sid a classified message, *AMB just PNG'd*

our team, heading home tomorrow, will explain later. Then he
sent an unclassified email to Kate, *Mission aborted, headed home
tomorrow.*

6

THE NEXT MORNING, RSO Bell escorted the JTTF team to the airport in the same van that had brought them to the embassy the day they arrived. Elie the driver was noticeably absent, replaced by a man Cam did not know. For the most part, the van was quiet but for idle chit chat about traffic and crowds at the airport.

"Where is Elie?" asked Cam.

"Saturday is his day off," replied the RSO. Cam thought his terse response a bit strange.

The van pulled into the departure area where they were met by the embassy expediter. As the team piled out of the van, the RSO apologized, "I'm sorry about this, Mr. Coppenger. I tried to warn you about the politics."

"It isn't your fault, Tyrone. You're a good agent. I hope our paths cross again. Thanks for the intel. Be safe, keep your head on a swivel, and take care of my Nasty Boys, will you?"

"Yes sir!" RSO Bell smiled as they shook hands. Then the expediter led the team through airport check-in procedures.

Lufthansa Flight #243 climbed into the morning sky on schedule and banked gradually toward Washington, giving Cam the opportunity to view the shimmering blue Mediterranean from his window seat. He recalled that all his previous visits to Beirut had been by US Navy helicopters based in Cyprus. In those days, the helicopters traveled low and fast, landing on the embassy tennis courts—usually at night, without lights, barely touching down, engines at fast idle, off-loading and on-loading supplies and personnel, all within a two minute window. Actually, Cam never really cared much for choppers. He saw them as ungainly machines engaged in a constant struggle to defy the laws of physics. He believed that the average government agent was only allotted a certain number of safe chopper rides in a lifetime, and he suspected he had already used up his allotment in places like Haiti, Pakistan, and Sri Lanka. Truthfully, Cam Coppenger didn't care if he ever got on another one.

The A-300 punched through the cloud cover, reached altitude, and leveled off. As if on cue, the short person in front of Cam whose head he could not see slammed the seat back hard against Cam's already-cramped knees, snapping him abruptly back to reality. The sharp pain only worsened his mood, and Cam shifted his contempt from helicopters to commercial jetliners. The fact was, Cam hated commercial air travel, the way the airlines manipulated passengers, the mindless screening procedures, the cattle-car design of the planes themselves; plus, he was prone to air sickness. Essentially, Cam's disdain for commercial air travel centered around the issue of control, or to be more specific, the complete control one must surrender in order to fly commercially. Cam hated not being in control.

Predictably, flying along at 33,000 feet somewhere over the Atlantic, Cam found himself missing home. He longed for the simplicity and tranquility of an easy-going retirement on the Gulf Coast. He missed the rhythm of the bay tides and the therapeutic routines of life aboard a boat. Then it hit him. Like a bolt of lightning, it hit him. Cam was done. He was finished playing Special Agent for the government. He realized who the enemy was, and the enemy was not necessarily a terrorist like Ismail. Terrorists were always going to be among us in one mutation or another. Cam's real enemy was the two-headed dragon of governmental politics and obstructionism over which he had no control. Throughout his government career, the bureaucratic beast had always played some role in every mission he had undertaken. Like landmines on a battlefield, bureaucratic obstacles had to be anticipated and either neutralized, negotiated, and/or circumvented for any mission to be successful. Now, as he contemplated his dismissal in Beirut, he found that the two-headed dragon had reared its ugly head yet again. As a government agent, Cam had certainly suffered his share of bureaucratic defeats. In each instance, he had learned a lesson from those defeats and gained experience, confident he would return to fight another day. But this battle was different. The difference now was that the white knight of yore no longer had the strength or the fortitude to continue the fight against the black dragons of government bureaucracy. Not in a traditional way at least. Metaphorically, Cam found his diplomatic armor had become rusty, his shield of integrity had cracked, his righteous sword of justice had become bent and dull. Cam knew Ismail could be defeated. What couldn't be broken down, at least in Cam's eyes, were the systemic shackles that bureaucracies placed on good men trying to win against evil. He was not a quitter by nature, but he was enough of a realist to know when the deck was stacked against him. Given the current environment, Cam concluded there was no legal way to get to Ismail. Like any good military strategist, there comes a time when retreat is the best option, and that is what Cam decided to do. In the remaining hours of his flight back to Washington, Cam contemplated how he would break the news to his friends Kate and Sid.

Racing backward against the earth's rotation, the team's Lufthansa flight landed at Dulles in the early evening. It was still Saturday, so the task force disbanded to their respective homes. Cam said nothing to the team members about his decision to quit the task force; he wanted to talk to Sid first. He simply instructed his team to stand by for further instructions. Cam took a taxi to the government lot in DC where his pickup was parked. He checked his messages and saw Kate's response to his earlier text in Beirut, *What happened? I'm back in Miami on a WP assignment. Call me.*

There was also a message from Sid, *Got a cable from the ambassador. Meet me at the office when you get in. We need to talk.*

His truck was parked just a few blocks from FBI headquarters, and Cam knew Sid would be working, even on a Saturday night. He decided to walk the distance. It was a cool fall evening, and he needed the extra time to clear his head and make sure he was making the right decision. Cam used his building pass to enter the

JTTF bullpen where he found his boss immersed in briefing papers and intelligence reports. Cam glanced down at Sid's desk and saw a cable he presumed was from Beirut. Sid looked up from his work, lifted the Beirut cable from his desk, and offered it to Cam, "Here's the ambassador's report from Lebanon if you care to read it."

"Not necessary," replied Cam. "I'm sure it's just diplomatic justifications and bureaucratic ass-covering for why they kicked a JTTF task force on an anti-terrorism mission out of the country."

"Pretty much," replied Sid. "Lotta use of the word insubordination ... so what happened?"

"In a nutshell, Sid, our mission didn't fit the ambassador's agenda. The ambassador never wanted us there. His priority is the Syrian peace negotiations, and he didn't want our pursuit of Ismail to interfere with those negotiations. Typical case of conflicting foreign policy initiatives."

"It happens. It happens a lot, actually, so what do you suggest we do at this point?"

"Sid, I need to level with you."

"I wouldn't expect you to do otherwise."

"The reality is, as long as Ismail stays ensconced within those Palestinian tribal areas of Lebanon, there isn't much we can do. Hezbollah is protecting him, powerful Lebanese politicians are protecting him, and even our own ambassador is resisting USG efforts to apprehend him."

"What about the CIA?"

"I suppose the Agency could send a team inside the camps to snatch him, but we'd have to find him first. Even asking the question would send him underground. In Lebanon, every street corner has eyes, and every house is an armory, and the chances of a successful snatch would be very low. The possibility of another *Black Hawk Down* scenario would be very high, and I don't think the White House has the stomach for that kind of risk, particularly this close to an election. Besides, the ambassador has already given the Chief of Station a cease-and-desist order. I'm sure if it."

"So what do you recommend?"

"Continue to investigate, gather intelligence, disrupt his network … and play whack-a-mole until we can figure out how to cut the head off the snake."

"Innocent Americans are dying," reminded Sid, stating the obvious. "And the White House is on our Director's butt 24/7 to fix the problem."

"Are they on Ambassador Pruett's ass as well?" Cam asked, sarcastically.

"You know the answer to that," retorted Sid. "Conflicting policy initiatives."

"Therein lies the problem."

"All right. Go home and get some rest. We'll start fresh on Monday."

Cam took a deep breath and then followed, "Sid, there's something else I need to tell you." He paused and then continued, "Effective immediately, I am resigning from the task force."

Sid snapped his head back, his mouth agape, "What are you saying, Cam?"

"I'm quitting, Sid."

Sid groped for words. "Cam, if this is about Beirut, rest assured that situation in no way is a reflection on you or your ability to serve on this task force. You still have the full confidence and support of the Director. He told me that just this morning!"

"This is not about Beirut, specifically, but it *is* about what my experience in Beirut has revealed to me. I can no longer work within a government bureaucracy, Sid. I just don't have it in me."

"What do you mean?" asked Sid, trying to comprehend the thought process of a friend and colleague he respected greatly.

"Sid, I respect you too much to patronize you, but you would have to leave the bureaucracy before you could clearly see the bureaucracy for what it is. You don't know it now, but you will one day. Call it whatever you want—Big Brother, the Establishment, the Deep State—but governmental bureaucracy is a monster with many names. It's a beast and something that dedicated agents have to fight every day to be successful. I fought the monster for twenty-six years, and I just don't have the energy to fight it anymore. Time to pass the sword and let somebody younger and with more energy fight the fight."

Sid tried a different tactic, "Cop, there's a mid-term election coming up next month that could result in a significant change in foreign policy! The Bureau is already ramping up for a greater emphasis on law and order!"

Cam just shook his head as he surrendered his radio, building pass, and burgundy-colored official passport to Sid who took them but was too stunned to grasp the permanence of the gesture. "I'm too old for this," Cam reiterated. "I'll be happy to consult with you from time to time as a civilian, but I retired for a reason, and I need to stay retired." Cam nodded goodbye to his friend before he exited the office.

Outside in the cool night air, Cam felt like a burden had been lifted from his shoulders. He walked back to his truck and then looked at his watch. It was 2115 on a Saturday night in the nation's capital, and he didn't have a hotel reservation. He was bone-tired. The camper shell on his pickup would have to be his accommodation. Without moving his truck from the government lot, Cam dropped the tailgate and climbed to the platform bed he had built into the back of his camper. Still fully clothed, Cam removed his worn out boots, got into his three-season sleeping bag, and fell fast asleep.

7

EARLY THE NEXT morning, a DC city street sweeper roared past the government lot where Cam had bedded down, waking him from a deep drug-like sleep. He checked his phone through blurry eyes for the time and set his watch to 0600 hours. Then he set it again for 0500 once he realized he was headed for the Alabama Gulf Coast and Central Standard Time. Cam climbed stiffly out of the camper onto legs still sore from the cramped flight, stretched, and entered the cab of his truck. As he headed west on Constitution Avenue early that Sunday morning, the streets of DC were deserted. The homeless people who occupied just about every park bench along that part of Constitution were beginning to stir from underneath their piles of donated blankets. Breakfast would be waiting on them at any one of the several soup kitchens in the city. Cam felt hunger pains in his own stomach, reminding him he had forgotten to eat dinner the night before. To his left was the National Mall, site of the July 4th terrorist attack. A few joggers were shuffling slowly along the gravel paths that bordered it. No remnant remained of the mayhem that had taken place only a few months prior. Life in DC had moved on. As he drove down Constitution, stopping every block for red lights that controlled empty streets, Cam had time to think. The tranquility he had found from yesterday's decision had been replaced with a foreboding sense of mission failure and unfinished business. He needed to call Kate. As he crossed the Potomac on the Roosevelt Bridge and headed west on I-66, he dialed her number.

Kate answered on the second ring, breathing heavily amidst a background of wind noise. She was already up and exercising along some part of Miami Beach. "Hey! You back?"

"Yep. Got in late last night."

"Where are you now?"

"On I-66, heading over to I-81. That'll take me to Alabama."

"Alabama, huh? Sooo, what happened?"

"Well, the unclassified version … I got fired."

"The FBI?"

Cam clarified. "No, the ambassador. I quit the FBI."

"You *quit?*"

"I can't do it anymore, Kate, not under government rules."

"What rules?"

"The catch-22 rules the government insists you play by. Damned if you do and damned if you don't."

Mindful of their open phone line, Kate asked cryptically, "What about our Subject?"

"I don't know, Kate. I just don't know. I feel like I've let you down."

Kate remained silent, quietly processing the information.

Cam broke the silence. "Look, Kate, I gotta go. I need to think about some things. Let me call you later."

"Sure, Cam." She hung up. The exchange was uncomfortable.

Interstate 66 ended at Winchester, Virginia, and Cam exited South onto I-81. It was October, and the autumn leaves were at their peak in the Shenandoah Valley. Cam dialed his son's number. With his customary enthusiasm somewhat subdued by the early Sunday morning hour, Caleb answered. "Hey, Dad. What's up?"

"I'm back from Lebanon and thought I'd check in with you." informed Cam.

Beirut was one of the few places in the world Caleb had not explored with his father. "How was it?" he asked.

"A troubled place. I'm on my way back to Mobile now."

"Have you heard about the hurricane in the Caribbean?" asked Caleb.

"No. I haven't," replied Cam, realizing he had not listened to news in a week. "Is this another false alarm?"

"Not this time, Dad. They've named this hurricane *Larry*. Computer models have it growing to a Category 4 and hitting the Gulf Coast sometime later this week."

"*Larry?* Kind of a stupid name for a hurricane. So is Mobile the target?"

"Mobile … Pensacola … New Orleans. We don't know for sure, yet. And I don't name the hurricanes. I just work 'em. In fact, I'll be heading up to Pensacola tomorrow to work out of the emergency center there."

"Great! Maybe we can get together? It'd be good to see you!"

"Maybe, but I might be working a lot of long hours. This thing has the makings to be a real monster. Get ready!"

"I will, and thanks for the heads up. Let me know when you get into town."

"Will do, Dad … talk soon!" Caleb disconnected.

With his home port under threat, Cam drove at a faster pace. By mid-afternoon, he was passing through Tennessee, and late that evening he pulled his truck into the parking lot of the Dog River Marina on Mobile Bay. Even at the late-night hour, the boatyard was alive with activity. Cranes pulled boats out of the water while workers busied themselves with putting some of them on jack stands in the boatyard. Others were being placed on trailers to be hauled to higher ground. The night air was filled with beeping tractors, idling diesel engines, men shouting, and tires grinding on gravel.

Cam walked to Judge Bean's and found Jake outside on a ladder, screwing plywood over the windows of his oyster bar. "Think that'll do any good?" asked Cam, sarcastically.

Jake looked down and saw his old friend. "Didn't help with *Katrina*. It was the water that got us."

"Need any help?"

"Yeah, sure … hold that corner. This is the last one."

"What do they say about the storm?"

"Cat 3 right now, though they expect *Larry* to be a Cat 4 by landfall."

"Dumb name for a hurricane. Where do they expect it to hit?"

"Weather channel says Mobile most likely."

"When?"

"Tuesday night/Wednesday morning."

"So what is your plan?" Cam knew he was close to getting on Jake's nerves, but asking questions helped him form his own plan of action.

"I'm gonna finish up here and find a way to haul my camper trailer to a safer location. My Miata won't tow much." They laughed at Jake's joke.

Cam reassured his friend, "Don't worry about the tow, we can use my truck."

"Thanks, buddy, but aren't you going to be towing your boat out of here?"

Cam admitted his shortsightedness. "Can't. I sold my trailer to some guy from Texas this summer. Didn't think I'd be moving my boat again except for haul-out maintenance."

"So what will you do?"

"Don't know. But I'm beat right now. I'm turning in. Good night, Jake."

Cam stopped back by his truck, retrieved his bag, and headed to the dock. He found *Fadeaway* rocking quietly at her berthing, her engine still disassembled, missing one key part. Most of the other slips were empty, and many boats were queued in line to be hauled out by one of the two lifts at the marina. Throughout the night, the sounds of a busy boatyard echoed the impending crisis, and Cam's angst over the approaching hurricane and his awkward conversation with Kate resulted in a fitful rest with little sleep.

The next morning, forecasters concluded that Mobile would be directly in *Larry's* path. The charming coastal city had absorbed the blows from many hurricanes through the years: *Frederic* in '79, *Erin* and *Opal* in '95, *Danny* in '97, *Georges* in '98, and most recently, *Ivan* in '04 and *Katrina* in '05; Now *Larry* headed straight for the mouth of Mobile Bay. Cam was bothered that hurricanes were sometimes given a masculine name. Naming any hurricane after a man showed just how little the government knew about storms. For him and for most other knowledgeable men of the sea, a hurricane was unquestionably female, reflecting all the moods, the mysteries, the unpredictabilities, and the inevitable wrath of the fairer gender. Cam's conclusion was drawn, not from prejudice or chauvinism, but from fifty years of experience with Mother Nature and human nature. To Cam, giving a hurricane a man's name was just plain wrong.

Weather forecasts warned of eight-to-twelve-foot tidal surges in many parts of the bay. Cam had grown up around hurricanes, and like Jake, he too understood that the water, not the wind, often caused the most damage to fixed objects. During his tour in Sri Lanka, Cam had experienced the Asian tsunami of 2004, which took the lives of over thirty-thousand people on that tiny island nation. He had first-hand knowledge of the destructive power of water.

Cam found Eddie, the marina's harbormaster, standing in the middle of the boatyard, surrounded by six anxious boat owners. In one hand, he held a cell phone to his ear. In the other hand, he held the marina's haul-out priority list, which he was using to direct boatyard traffic. Cam was late to the game, and he knew it. After waiting his turn, he asked the harried harbormaster in the calmest voice possible, "What are owners without trailers doing?"

"Ya got four options," replied Eddie. Then he stopped to answer a call. Apparently, the caller had the same question Cam had asked, probably the hundredth time Eddie had answered the same question in the past couple of days. "Ya got four options," Eddie repeated to the caller. "You can move her up the bay to a more protected cove, but those coves are already congested. You can dry dock her here and hope for the best. You can leave her moored in her berthing, but you'll be liable for any damage she does to my dock. Or you can take her to deep water, but I can't say I'd recommend that unless she's a battleship or a submarine. Text me back with your boat name and decision. I need to know soonest. Make sure your insurance is paid up." Eddie hung up and looked at Cam with exasperation, "Now *what* was your question?"

Cam had already assessed his situation and concluded that dry-docking was his best option. He was betting with a losing hand, and he knew it. Cam hated operating from a position of weakness. But simply folding and walking away just wasn't an option in the hurricane game. He asked Eddie, "What's the waiting list like for hauling and storage in the boatyard?"

Eddie looked at his clipboard and estimated, "Certainly not today, I can put you down for tomorrow, but it'll be late afternoon at best. Yours is the thirty-five-foot sloop, isn't it?"

"Yeah, named *Fadeaway*. Put me down for a haul out, and thanks, Eddie!"

Cam walked behind Jake's place, found a sturdy cardboard box, and headed down to his boat. He retrieved the few removable items worth salvaging, including his laptop, phone charger, a few of the boat's electronics, toolbox, a mason jar filled with foreign coins, a family photo album, important papers, and his rare signed copy of Harper Lee's *To Kill a Mockingbird*. Then he took the jib off the forestay and the mainsail off the mast, rolled them up the best he could, and tossed them below deck. Leaving the cabin hatch unlocked, Cam placed his box of possessions behind the seat of his truck and returned to Judge Bean's for some breakfast. He ordered a fried egg sandwich and coffee. "When do you plan to shut down, Jake?"

"Sometime tomorrow before the storm hits. The guys working the yard are gonna need to eat. What did you decide to do with your boat?"

"Eddie will haul it and put it on blocks tomorrow."

"You know the yard is gonna be under water, don't you?"

"Yeah, but I don't have a lot of options with the engine still inoperable. I guess *Fadeaway* and Judge Bean's are going share the same fate, huh?"

Both shrugged at each other, then grinned with knowing eyes the look of men who have dealt with crises.

"When do you want to move your camper, Jake?"

"We'll get your boat on blocks, move my car, then head out sometime tomorrow ahead of the storm."

"Where to?"

"Dunno. Drive until the storm quits and then turn around."

"I-65 northbound will be a mess."

"We're not going north. That'd be like trying to outrun a falling tree. Let's go due east or west and get out of the storm's path."

Cam liked the way Jake thought. "Sounds like a plan," he said. He was finishing his sandwich when Caleb called.

"Hey Dad!" Caleb said. "Just thought I'd let you know I'm in Pensacola now."

"Great! Where will you be during the storm?"

"At the Emergency Management Center. Built to the same standards as the one in Key Largo. The Feds gave Florida a bunch of money after *Andrew*, and they built storm forts all over the State."

"Will you have any time to get together before the storm hits?"

"Honestly, no. We've been in full prep mode ever since they named her *Larry*."

"Ok then. Just stay safe."

"Will do, Dad. You, too. Talk later!"

———

Tuesday was D-Day. The boatyard workers were up early scrambling to get their work done before *Larry* made landfall. Eddie the harbormaster was eventually able to get *Fadeaway* hauled and blocked in the already-congested storage yard. Cam sensed the effort was futile, but given the circumstances, the storage yard was the best option available. Under overcast skies with a light sprinkle dampening their shoulders, Cam and Jake disconnected the power and water to Jake's camper, cleared the foundation blocks from underneath, inflated the tires, and hooked it up to Cam's truck. Jake checked the locks on his boarded-up business one last time, then stopped and went back inside to retrieve his shorty 12-gauge from behind the bar. As he climbed into the truck, Cam quipped,

"Riding shotgun?"

Jake smiled. "Looks like it."

"Where to, partner?"

"I'm betting *Larry* makes a gradual swing to the northeast once she makes landfall. Let's head west," calculated Jake.

"New Orleans?"

"Right," said Jake, patting the pistol-grip shotgun in his lap. "We could park the camper somewhere in the middle of the Ninth Ward, have some gumbo, and wait the storm out."

"On second thought, let's head to California. Everybody goes to California in hard times."

Cam put the truck in tow gear and headed for Highway 98, westbound toward Mississippi. As he pulled away from the boatyard, Cam slowed to avoid a large bay-side alligator attempting to cross the road, apparently moving to a safer location in the bayou. "Never seen that before," Jake commented.

"Animals seem to know … they always know," replied Cam. While waiting at the gator crossing, Cam's phone buzzed, a text from Kate.

Be safe, the text read.

Cam texted back, *Always*. Kate's message caused Cam to think about his son Caleb, running to the storm while he was running from it, an uncomfortable feeling for him. Cam looked back toward the bay. The skies had darkened to an ominous blue/gray, and the wind was picking up. The sea grass alongside the two-lane blacktop had already begun to bow to Mother Nature's will.

Within twenty-four hours, *Larry's* assault on Mobile was over. Cam and Jake had gotten no farther than Natchez when they bedded down for the night at a rundown truck stop. Throughout the evening, the trailer had been buffeted by gusty winds, and it had rained sideways for a while. Other than that, they had dodged *Larry's* haymaker. Watching the news in the truck stop's café, Cam saw that *Larry's* fist had caught Mobile Bay flush on the chin, and then, as Jake had predicted, the hurricane had veered off to the east after making landfall. By mid-morning, *Larry* was heading toward Atlanta with significantly reduced winds and rain. The televised pictures of Mobile were not pretty. As a Category 4 storm with sustained winds of 150 mph, Hurricane *Larry* had left his legacy. Trees and power lines were down everywhere. Several of the beautiful old live oaks along Mobile's famous Government Street, some five feet in diameter, had toppled over into the roadway. Clumps of Spanish moss from the ancient trees lay everywhere, like old gray wigs left over from a Mardi Gras bender. Macho TV weathermen in severe storm gear were standing knee-deep in water as they reported from downtown Mobile, giving testimony to the storm surge that had encroached over a mile inland. Beach houses along Fort Morgan Road, the spit of land that extended westward across the mouth of Mobile Bay from Gulf Shores, had been twisted, torn apart, or forced to lean northward on stilted legs, as if a tsunami had hit them. Dauphin Island, a barrier island on the southwest side of the bay, had been completely submerged and then washed in two by the storm surge. The Dauphin Island houses were nowhere to be seen. Bayside shrimpers would be dredging up rusted cars, refrigerators, and washing machines from those houses for years to come.

Jake looked at Cam. "Well, what do ya think? Is there anything to go back to?"

"Do we have a choice? Do you have another idea?"

"I've been through this before with *Katrina*, Cam. Sometimes it's better not even to look back but just move on to the next dream."

"We should at least go back and help Eddie clean up. We're like turtles. We carry our homes on our backs. We are retired, after all."

"Good point. Eddie could probably use our help, and Mobile certainly can. We have a new mission."

"They'll need a few days to get the roads cleared, and then we can head back," estimated Cam. "We'll need to pick up a couple of chainsaws while we're here. As I recall from my experience with *Frederic*, it's pretty much guaranteed there won't be an axe or chainsaw available within a hundred miles of Mobile by the time we get there. Power will be out for at least a week if not longer."

After a maddening couple of days waiting around Natchez, watching bad movies on Jake's DVD player in the camper and eating bad truck stop food, Cam and Jake stocked up on supplies, reconnected the trailer, and headed back toward Mobile.

As they crossed the Alabama line, evidence of the destruction began to reveal itself. For mile after mile, acres of tall southern pines were bent to the ground like giant snare traps. In other areas, spin-off tornados had snapped the pines like matchsticks, leaving entire forests of jagged stumps protruding to the sky like deadly punji sticks. Scattered rural farm houses looked as if they had been victims of domestic abuse, disheveled and battered. Mobile homes, those that weren't strapped down, had been rolled across the ground while those that had been strapped down were torn apart. Sheets of corrugated tin roofing hung loosely in the tops of broken trees. Others had wrapped themselves around tilted telephone poles, like shredded battle flags of a defeated army. A dead cow lying bloated in a pasture, had a broken 2x4 sticking from its abdomen. Human victims, punch-drunk and still in shock, roamed their soggy properties, zombies after a hurricane apocalypse.

As Cam and Jake approached Mobile, evidence of American resiliency and hope was already taking root with teams of neighbors assembling, chainsaws shrieking, power generators running, and privately owned front-end loaders and bulldozers already in action. Yet FEMA was nowhere to be seen. The government had gotten pretty good at reacting to disasters, but expecting bureaucracies to be proactive and have people and materials prepositioned is not what the government does. The sounds of gradual recovery were promising, particularly the chainsaws, but to Cam's ears, these sounds also stirred a different emotion. He had first heard the chainsaws with *Frederic* in '79 but also heard them later in his career. Truck bombs in Beirut, earthquakes in Haiti, tsunamis in Sri Lanka … all carried the same trademark sound. To Cam, the shrill whining of those two-stroke engines were grim reminders, sorrowful moans of death and destruction.

An interesting fact about most hurricanes is that after they pass they leave behind beautiful clear blue skies, as if the angry vortex had sucked all the negative energy into its gut to be hauled off and regurgitated elsewhere. Such was the irony Cam and Jake encountered as they negotiated their way into the Dog River boatyard. Beneath the beautiful blue October sky lay absolute and complete destruction. Judge Bean's was gone. Except for twisted pier pilings where it once stood, only heaps of broken debris remained. Disassembled chunks of weathered lumber had been shoved into piles among the muddy sea grass. Jake kicked at a few shattered boards, but the muck was so deep he couldn't investigate further. He glanced at his feet and saw a unopened bottle of champagne sitting heads up in the muck. He pulled it up and wiped the mud from its label: his prize bottle of Krug champagne, vintage 1988, purchased to commemorate his retirement and the grand opening of Judge Bean's. Disasters sometimes leave irony in their wake, offering smattering glimpses of meaning for those so inclined.

Cam laced up his old worn boots and began his search for *Fadeaway*. As he expected, the storm surge had lifted every boat in the yard and dashed them violently about the marina, piling them in broken heaps on top of one another, stacking them haphazardly like split firewood. Rotting seaweed intertwined at the tops of eight-foot fencing meant the flood surge had been at least that high. He stumbled among all matter of debris, dead smelly fish strewn everywhere across the mud. A fat water moccasin, disoriented and pissed, hissed at him from broken boards under his feet. The small limp carcass of a drowned deer tangled in broken tree limbs gazed down at him from above. A child's doll lay on the ground, face and hair smeared with brown matter, one eye stuck closed in a cruel wink. In Cam's experience, lost dolls always seemed to be part of a disaster's landscape.

After a considerable search, Cam finally found his boat, hardly recognizable, sitting askew amid a jumble of ruined fantasies. Her mast had been ripped off, taking a hunk of decking with it, yet some of the mast stays still held, forcing her to drag the broken mast through the storm like a severed limb hanging by tendons. Suspended awkwardly above the ground, *Fadeaway*'s hull was impaled upon pier pilings. Pierced through, hull to deck, the image suggested her shapely female form had been savagely raped by the destructive forces of a storm with a man's name. Though Cam had anticipated as much, he was still stunned by the visual. He had left her alone, a statue on a pedestal, open and vulnerable to attack like some diplomatic post on Main Street, and she had suffered due to his negligence.

Fadeaway was ruined, and Cam felt gut-punched. The image of his lost fantasy would change his perspective forever. He told himself that never again would he attach himself emotionally to an inanimate object. Boats were simply pieces of equipment that had to be maintained and cared for to provide useful service. Boats would no longer be a *her*, they would be an *it*, and *its* were not named but were described by make and model. Furthermore, Cam vowed he would never again play a defensive role with a boat, sitting back, hoping to absorb the blows of an oncoming storm. He had learned that lesson during his professional career and should have applied it to his personal life. Someone called out "Coppenger!" Cam looked over to see the UPS man standing in the muck with a package, the missing part for his boat engine.

Jake brought the missing engine part and the bottle of champagne over to Cam, and they sat down together amidst the debris. Then Jake popped the bottle with an explosion of warm fizz, and the cork flew in a high arc, landing somewhere in the bow of Cam's broken boat.

Looking at the label, Cam declared, "Expensive stuff!" He took a long chug and with the back of his hand wiped the foamy bubbles from his four-day beard.

Taking the bottle from Cam, Jake offered a toast. "Here's to broken dreams, resilience, and fortitude." Then he downed the remainder, finishing with a deep, grumbling burp that blended poetically with the chainsaws revving in the background.

8

CAM ALWAYS BELIEVED that a troubled man should be left alone and given a physical challenge—a mountain to climb or a body of water to cross—and he would solve his problem. That was how men figured things out. Cam had concluded years ago that a man's sense of value and worth were best realized through a lifelong succession of pushing boundaries, and for that reason, challenges had always been a part of his life. Hurricane *Larry* presented a new kind of challenge for Cam, the kind of challenge he needed to lift his mood. The dirty, heavy, physical labor of storm cleanup would give his hands something to do and give his mind time enough to clear his thoughts.

With his storied boots laced high and a truckload of tools at hand, Cam set about post-storm recovery. But before joining the chorus of chainsaws already at work in the yard, he decided to make a call. Many cell towers were down, but after several tries,

Cam got through to Caleb.

"Hey, Dad! That was some storm, wasn't it? You okay?"

"The boat is in shambles, but we're good here. Just wanted to check on you. What's your plan?"

"I'll be in Pensacola for another few days to finish up, but I'm beat. I've been on the clock for forty-eight straight hours. Hey, I was thinking of taking some time off and heading over to San Diego to do a little surfing. Maybe hitch a ride on Amtrak's *Sunset Limited*."

Caleb shared his father's love of trains, as well as his disdain for flying. They had taken train trips together in exotic locations all over the world. As part of their trek to Machu Pichu, father and son had taken a Peruvian train trip along the Urubamba River Valley from Cusco to Aguas Calientes. In Morocco, they had taken trains from Tangiers to Marrakech, then on to the beautiful blue and white coastal city of Essaouira. And then there was the memorable trip through the mountainous Sri Lankan tea country aboard an ancient British railcar that wound its way through scores of tunnels cut into solid rock. Some of their less remarkable trips had been aboard America's Amtrak, not known for its reliability, continuity, or ease of access, but they were memorable just the same.

"Wanna come with me?" Caleb asked.

"Very tempting, but I need to help Eddie clean up the boatyard a bit, and I need to address insurance issues with the boat. But it sounds like a fun trip! When do you plan to leave?"

"In a few days. Do you know if the trains are still running out of Mobile?"

"*The Sunset Limited* discontinued service from New Orleans to Jacksonville after *Katrina*, but we could drive over to New Orleans and leave from there."

"Sounds like a plan! I'll let you know."

Call completed, Cam turned around and saw Eddie walking by. "Hey Eddie, how's it going?" Cam already knew the answer.

Eddie, a Vietnam-era combat veteran, was a serious man with little time for foolishness. "You see it," replied Eddie. "Been through it before. It'll take a while, but we'll recover. Appreciate your help."

Cam shrugged, "Glad to. Gotta stick together." Then Cam saw Jake cross the yard with a disheveled stranger walking in front of him. As they came closer, Cam noticed that Jake had his shorty shotgun pointed at the stranger's neck.

"Found this guy in the yard plundering stuff out of wrecked boats. Do either of you know him?" Jake asked.

"Never seen him before," replied Eddie.

Cam shook his head as well. "Looks like a trespasser."

"More like a looter," corrected Jake. "What should we do with him?"

"Shoot him and throw him in the bayou for gator meat." There was no humor in Eddie's response. The looter's eyes widened.

"That's what happened after *Katrina*. All those bodies they found … most of them were looters shot on sight," Jake said.

The man shifted uncomfortably. He was dealing with three tired, angry men with little or no patience. He glanced at Cam, hoping for some hint of mercy. Cam looked up at one of the few remaining trees. "Hanging would be better than a shotgun blast, or we could make it look like an accident. Eddie, do you have any high-strength boat line left over from the storm?"

At that point, the looter stammered, "Mister, please … I was just helping clean up a bit. I-I--."

"Shut up," snapped Eddie. "I'm in no mood for your bullshit."

The looter stumbled backward into the muck, got up, and broke in a panic for the road. Whether the brown stain on his pants was mud or if he had soiled himself was unclear. He ran with the jerky, disoriented run of terror that Cam had seen many times before when a man was about to lose his life. The sticky black muck reduced his sloppy steps to an agonizing slow motion. Jake raised his shorty and fired off to one side of the man, flinging mud into the air closer to the crook than he had intended. The looter shrieked, flailed his arms and ducked his head, and then he slipped and fell into the muck again. He landed hard on a broken board, and a large rusty nail punched clean through his right hand. He raised his impaled hand in horror, the heavy board still nailed firmly to his palm, tearing flesh with its weight. On his knees, the crippled man tore the board from his hand and fell over in agony. Still panicked, he rolled and began crawling in the mud like a three-legged dog. From somewhere within the debris, a thick dark cottonmouth sprang from a hole and popped the looter dead center of the coiled cobra tattoo on his shoulder. Adrenaline somehow got the looter back to his feet, and he stumbled toward the road.

None of the men said a word. Jake walked back to his camper as he loaded a replacement round of buckshot into his pistol-grip pump-action. Eddie headed toward his makeshift office, coiling a length of stout dock line as he went. Cam picked up his chainsaw, primed it three times, and yanked it into a mournful whine.

After several days of tough, physical work, the boatyard had become recognizable. Eddie posted a notice that several insurance reps had set up shop at the marina office. With that bit of good news, Cam turned his attention to his own recovery efforts. He retrieved *Fadeaway*'s paperwork from his truck and found his agent working out of a rental car, a computer in his lap, his trunk filled with boxes of file folders.

"Hello, Mr. Coppenger!" said the insurance agent in a surprisingly upbeat mood. "Filing a claim today?"

"Guess so," replied Cam. "Looks like the boat will be a complete loss."

"Let's go take a look," suggested the agent.

Cam escorted the agent over to where *Fadeaway* hung suspended, untouched since the storm. The agent moved forward to take some photos, then announced, "Yeah, she's totaled, no need to investigate any further." He climbed some debris to record the serial number from the transom and then opened Cam's file and confirmed, "Looks like you had a full replacement cost policy. I can write you a check today."

"How much?" asked Cam.

The agent looked down at the file, then consulted a fat reference index. "One hundred and five thousand dollars, less a disposal/environmental fee of around $5K, so how about an even $100K?" That figure was good enough for Cam, especially since he had only paid eighty thousand for the boat. They shook hands and walked back to the agent's car. The agent wrote the check, made some entries into his laptop, had Cam sign some papers, and replaced the file.

As Cam drove to the bank to deposit the check, Caleb called. "Hey, Dad! What's up?"

"Running errands. When are you headed to New Orleans?"

"Tomorrow, if you're still available for a cross-country adventure?"

Cam was ready for a break. "Absolutely! Pick you up in Pensacola?"

"That'd be cool, Dad … 0600?"

"Works for me."

———

The drive to New Orleans went smoothly. Jake had arranged for Cam to park his truck on a police lot near the Amtrak station. As they shouldered their packs for the walk to the station, Caleb asked, "You packing?"

"My pistol? Yeah, I've got it. Always pays to be prepared."

"Does Amtrak allow guns onboard?"

"Since I'm retired law enforcement, federal law permits me to carry in most circumstances. Besides, Amtrak doesn't have full-time security screening at every station. They just don't have the money. Some stations practice random screening, others don't. It depends on the station."

"That sounds like a disaster waiting to happen."

"Probably. But the government is not going to do anything until there is actually an incident. That's just the way government works."

Cam and Caleb checked in with the conductor at trackside for their seat assignment.

"Where to?" asked the conductor, a hint of bureaucratic

weariness in his voice.

Cam was never quite sure if the attitude came from overwork or if the bureaucratic monster had simply overrun Amtrak.

"LA, then on to San Diego," advised Caleb. Attempting to establish rapport, Caleb asked, "How many cars are in this train?"

"Nine cars," he replied. "Two coaches, one lounge, one diner, two sleepers, one baggage, and then two engines." Punching their tickets without making eye contact, the conductor attempted to terminate the chit chat, "You are assigned to the last car on the end."

"Only two coaches?" asked Caleb, still trying to break through the conductor's attitude.

The conductor looked up at the tandem with tired eyes and replied, "We pick up a third coach in San Antonio from *The Texas Eagle*. People don't ride trains much anymore."

They walked toward the end of the train, packs shouldered, and once they climbed aboard, Caleb raced ahead to claim the window seat.

As Cam took the aisle seat, he mumbled under his breath to Caleb, "Twenty-four and going on eight!" Actually, Cam didn't mind aisle seats; they allowed him to react more quickly should trouble arise. He carried that same mentality into restaurants, airplanes, and movie theaters, always picking seats with a clear view of entries, exits, and fields of fire. Twenty-six years of thinking tactically in code yellow was rooted in his psyche.

Caleb grinned at his dad sheepishly. "Two full days and two full nights sitting shoulder-to-shoulder. How many father/son teams can pull that off these days?"

Caleb was right. They had a good relationship. There were differences, certainly, but Cam had learned to view them as generational. They usually got along surprisingly well. One thing was certain; he was glad Caleb came from the techie generation. As he had done so many times before, Cam pulled out his phone and asked, "Can you show me how this App works?"

Right on time, Amtrak's *Sunset Limited #1* pulled out of the New Orleans terminal and eased over one of Union Pacific's rusting Mississippi River bridges. Within minutes of departure and before gathering speed, Amtrak #1 pulled onto a side track and stopped. After several minutes, a Union Pacific freight train rumbled by from the opposite direction, claiming priority status over all passenger service. Twenty minutes into their two-day adventure, Amtrak was already fifteen minutes late. Such were the conditions of twenty-first century train travel in America.

Caleb spoke up, "Do you realize we just got on this train without a hint of security screening? I mean, we could have anything in our bags, and no one would know! What's up with that?"

"You're right. Budgets, priorities, timing – take your pick. Government only reacts. It doesn't pro-act."

Cam looked over at his son's phone just as Caleb was scrolling down and noticed the subject line, *Hack Attack*. Caleb had tried to scroll past it quickly but wasn't fast enough.

Cam asked inquisitively, "What is Hack Attack?"

Caleb responded casually. "Just a program."

"Really, what is it?"

Caleb hesitated and then opted for a half-truth, "It's an amateur hacking group I'm a member of in Key Largo."

"Amateur ... *hacking*?"

"More or less."

"What does that mean exactly?"

"We get together and mess with rule breakers."

"Like who?"

"Self-serving corporate interests, environmental polluters, corrupt politicians, and the like."

"And how do you mess with them?"

"We stir the pot—educate the population, counter their propaganda, reveal the truth—expose their lies."

"How did you learn to do that?"

"Here and there. Learned some at college, group sessions and the like. A lotta stuff is online these days. Don't worry. We use technology for the greater good. Guns are not the only weapons against evil."

As much as Cam bristled at the thought of his son potentially being among punk hackers who seemed to cause so much trouble in the world, Caleb had a point. Surveillance, counter-surveillance, human intelligence, electronic intelligence, data mining, public policy, financial analysis, forensics, and international cooperation were all important tools in the war against terror. Cam decided to let the hacking issue go for now, but it bothered him.

Amtrak's *Sunset Limited* rolled quietly through the day, moving first across the wetlands of Louisiana, then on to the oil and gas industry sectors of south Texas. Those areas would be the least attractive parts of the route. Cam and Caleb used the time to reminisce about past adventures, talk about future travel plans, and laugh at the challenges of living overseas. They were in Houston by sundown.

Their train arrived in San Antonio by midnight and added a coach car from the *Texas Eagle*. A large extended Amish family entered Cam's car, wearing traditional homemade attire. The men sported chin beards, braced trousers, and wide-brimmed hats. The women wore prairie dresses, aprons, and bonnets. The children were dressed in miniature versions of the same. They carried their own food in large wicker handmade picnic baskets. Cam had seen Amish groups on trains before. He suspected it had something to do with their acceptance of trains as transportation but not automobiles or planes. He had never asked. Yet there was something about the Amish that Cam had always respected. Their quiet dignity, adherence to tradition, sense of community, fierce independence, and solid work ethic were all admirable qualities in his mind. The conductor seated them as a group toward the front of the car, and they settled into their seats quietly before the train pulled away from the station. The big coach seats were comfortable, and the gentle rocking motion of the speeding train soon enticed its passengers to sleep soundly through the night.

By daybreak they were in Del Rio, a dusty Texas border town located within mere steps of Mexico. As the train rolled through the rough, hilly country, crisscrossed by dirt tracks, dry river beds, and littered with low gray scrub, an occasional white-and-green US Border Patrol truck could be seen atop the highest point of the surrounding area. In the immediate foreground, a modest chain link fence ran parallel to the tracks.

Caleb asked, "Is that the border?"

"Yes, it is."

Caleb asked incredulously, "That's it?"

Cam was content to let the visual sink in. "That's it."

"Nothing really to keep anybody from walking across."

The train rolled on at full speed, and as the desert landscape zipped by, Caleb observed in the distance an occasional green flag on a tall flag pole. "What are those flags for?"

"Designated water stations."

"For cattle?"

"For illegal border crossers."

"Who puts them there?"

"Humanitarian groups. By the time the illegals reach this point, they have probably been in the desert for two to three days and are most likely out of water. In this environment, each person needs a minimum of one gallon of water a day. A gallon of water weighs a little over eight pounds. One plastic milk jug in each hand, with a small backpack containing a few clothes, cheese, and homemade tamales. That's how they travel."

Caleb contemplated the image and then followed, "Why doesn't the Border Patrol camp out at the watering holes and catch them?"

Cam smiled at his son and responded, "The Border Patrol has an agreement with the humanitarian groups to only patrol the flagged locations during certain times of the day."

Stunned at the contradiction, Caleb replied, "You're kidding me."

"It's how your government works. The government is full of conflicting policy initiatives. The agreement was probably hashed out in Washington between sympathetic politicians, the humanitarian groups, and the USBP, and then sent downrange to the border."

Caleb looked at his dad with narrowing eyes that suddenly widened as the train flashed over a ravine filled with piles of discarded clothing, worn-out sport shoes, and hundreds of empty milk jugs. All around the area, shredded plastic shopping bags hung from fence lines and sagebrush, rattling in the wind like Tibetan prayer flags over a municipal garbage dump.

"What was that?" asked Caleb, already suspecting the answer would have something to do with illegal immigration.

"A pickup point," replied Cam, "where Mexican smugglers bring their goods for onward transportation into the US."

"Do you mean people?"

"Not just people, but drugs, cash, guns, stolen passports—just about anything an illegal immigrant can carry. The cartels give the illegals a smuggling discount if they agree to carry contraband in their backpacks in lieu of water or food. The illegals prefer it because they believe the smugglers will be less likely to abandon them in the desert if they are transporting goods for one of the cartels. All along the two-thousand mile border are networks of these pickup points, and the cartels recruit Amcits to come down with vans to drive them to safe houses."

"Why American citizens?"

"I don't know current practice. But during my time time in Southern California, for political reasons, it was standing policy that American citizens caught smuggling illegal aliens would not be prosecuted by the Feds. Their vehicles were confiscated and their names put on a watch list, but if you had a US Passport, you were let go. Of course, most of the vehicles driven by the American recruits were often stolen by the cartels specifically for smuggling operations. During my San Diego assignment, finding a decent used passenger van in the entire county was practically impossible. The cartels bought them all up. Mexican smugglers, called Coyotes, charge three-thousand to five-thousand dollars for each illegal smuggled successfully. The cartels get the largest cut, usually around two-thirds, and the coyotes get a third. The Amcit drivers typically get a flat one hundred per head. Multiply that by ten to fifteen illegals per trip, and you've got quite a business plan."

"Unbelievable."

Cam added, "That's just the tip of the iceberg. We finally busted one particular Mexican smuggler who had lived for a decade in an expensive San Diego neighborhood using a stolen American passport. Three to five nights a week, he would drive a van down to the border and bring back a dozen or so illegal Mexican immigrants. Whenever he got caught, he simply flashed his stolen US passport and was released. He did that for ten years, a thousand dollars per night, five thousand per week, twenty thousand per month, all tax free. He had a nicer house in San Diego than most American citizens. We finally got him on passport fraud charges, and he was given a ten-year sentence, but because his kids were born on American soil, which makes them citizens, he will probably never be deported because the government doesn't want to break up families."

Caleb became quiet. Cam couldn't decide if it was shock, anger, or a combination of the two that caused his silence.

On the second day of their trip, the train slowed to enter El Paso. Mexico's sister city, Ciudad de Juarez, was clearly visible across the Rio Grande. Squalor easily distinguished Juarez from El Paso.

As *The Limited* exited the center of the city, a low thin wire fence appeared just below the windows of the train. Well-worn footpaths crisscrossed along both sides of the fence line.

"Is that what I think it is?" asked Caleb.

"The border fence?" clarified Cam. "Absolutely!"

By mid-afternoon the train had crossed into New Mexico, and Cam was looking for a snack. He glanced over at Caleb's pack and noticed a small package of Oreo cookies sticking from a side pocket. *Perfect!* Cam thought, grinning, as he reached down to liberate his favorite childhood indulgence.

Down the aisle was a young Amish boy dressed in gray pants with suspenders, a blue homespun shirt, and wide-brimmed hat. He looked to be about six or so and was laughing as he stood in the aisle, rocking with the movement of the train. Probably his first train trip, he was enjoying himself immensely as he jostled from one side of the aisle to the other. The automatic doors that connected the passenger cars were particularly intriguing to him. Each door had a punch button at his eye level and a kick button at toe level, which automatically slid the doors open for a brief period before they glided back into place. Between the cars were two metal plates on the floor that moved loosely between the cars, allowing passengers to step from one car to the next. When the doors slid open, the outside noise of the speeding train was loud and chaotic. To the small boy, crossing between cars was like moving through a clown's fun house with buttons to punch, doors opening and slamming, and floors moving underfoot. Cautious by nature and perhaps a little irritated at the noise from the constant opening of the doors, Cam was tempted to warn the boy's parents of the dangers on a moving train, but then he realized that this kid had probably been handling pitchforks, jumping from haylofts, and riding horses bareback since he was four. The boy was obviously having a grand time, so Cam let the kid play. As he opened the package of Oreos, Cam looked up to find the Amish boy standing next to him in the aisle, staring intently at the cookies.

"What's your name?" asked Cam.

"Joshua," replied the boy with a slight German accent.

"Where do you live, Joshua?"

"On a farm."

Ask a literal question, get a literal answer, thought Cam, smiling to himself. He restructured his question. "What state do you live in?"

The boy gave him a blank stare.

"Do you like Oreo cookies?"

"I don't know. I think so," replied the boy.

"You've never had an Oreo before?" asked Cam, raising his eyebrows.

Joshua shook his head shyly.

Now there was no doubt the quiet little boy standing next to him had grown up with an abundance of homemade apple pies, peach turnovers, fresh picked strawberries, and hand whipped sweet cream, but Cam was surprised that Joshua had never had a store-bought Oreo. "Would you like to try one?" The boy nodded his head enthusiastically. Cam looked up the aisle and saw an older, bearded Amish man, probably the boy's grandfather, astutely observing the conversation. Cam held the package of cookies up for permission, and the Amish man gave an authoritative nod of approval. Secure in the knowledge that Oreos were not the path to hellfire and damnation for the Amish, Cam gave the boy his first store-bought cookie. Joshua's eyes lit up with delight. Finishing the first one, the boy looked down at the remaining Oreos, and Cam realized the battle was lost. Cam took one cookie, twisted the top off as a demonstration, licked the center clean, and winked as he surrendered the rest of the cookies. Joshua sprinted down the asile to share his new discovery with his cousins, who had been watching the scene unfold from their seats in the front of the train. Cam watched the older Amish man bend down and whisper something into the boy's ear. A moment later, Joshua walked purposefully back down the aisle to Cam's seat, reached into his pocket, and pulled out a miniature hand-carved wooden baseball bat. He handed it to Cam. About four inches long, the tiny bat was perfectly proportioned and sanded as smooth as a Louisville Slugger. Hand rubbed with saddle oil to a golden brown, the bat was a work of art.

"Did you make this?" asked Cam.

Joshua nodded proudly and then sprinted back up the aisle to his family. Caleb, just waking from his nap, observed the exchange. "What was that about?"

"Oreo diplomacy," Cam responded, as he pocketed the keepsake. "Breaking down cultural barriers, one cookie at a time."

———

Farther west in the Mexican border town of San Luis Colorado, Palestinian brothers Yousef and Ramzi were busy loading their improvised explosive devices (IEDs) into a moderate-sized backpack. They had built two separate devices for redundancy, each containing one kilo (2.2 lbs.) of the high-explosive C-4. Each device also contained a separate cell phone detonator. A second backpack was loaded with other essential items, including food, water, a compass, flashlights, wire cutters, duct tape, and a small trench shovel.

"We need to finish up here," advised Yousef, tucking his pistol into the front of his pants. "Our guide wants us to meet him at the bar in an hour."

"When is the train expected?" asked Ramzi.

"The train will be passing through Yuma at midnight. We will position ourselves well past Yuma, though. We want the train to be at full speed when we detonate the explosives."

"Do we know where the guide is taking us?"

"Deep into the desert. Away from prying eyes."

"Can we trust him?" asked Ramzi.

"He has been smuggling in this area for twenty years, and he knows the backcountry better than anyone. He comes highly recommended by the cartel."

"Has he been paid?"

"Abdullah is handling that. Abdullah will drive us to the designated location and wait for us until our mission is complete. Only after the guide returns with us safely will he be paid. But we are wasting time. Come, we must go."

The brothers locked their packs in the trunk of a beat-up Nissan and drove to a rundown old bar called Chiquita's, located in a bad part of town. They entered the swinging door in dim smoke-filled light, brushed past several resident drunks, and spotted their guide sitting alone in the back. He was easily identified by the turquoise bandana he had been instructed to wear on his balding head. Emilio was a rough-looking character with pocked sun-damaged skin, bad teeth, and bloodshot eyes. They greeted each other in Spanish but transitioned to English in low, hushed voices.

"You want Tequila?" asked Emilio in a raspy whiskey voice, motioning over to the short fat saloon chica who was aged well beyond her years.

"No, no … gracias," replied Yousef, clinging to at least one honorable aspect of his religion. "Solamente agua, por favor – in a bottle, please," he added, having expended his knowledge of Spanish.

"You are ready to travel?" asked Emilio.

"Yes, tonight," replied Yousef, "Where should we meet?"

"Señor Khalidi will meet us out back at eight o'clock." Emilio paused to hack a wad of thick yellow phlegm from his chest. "This Abdullah Khalidi … he is an important young man, no?"

Hoping to instill an element of fear into Emilio, Yousef leaned in close and whispered seriously, "He is the son of a very powerful man. Hijo de Ismail … El Jefe," emphasized Yousef. He repeated his message in English, and declared, "Son of Ismail … The Boss!" That information was enough for Emilio, but actually what he understood most was that his mission was sanctioned by the cartel. His real fear resided there.

Darkness fell on the Mexican border town, and a few minutes before 8:00, Yousef and Ramzi pulled their dirty and dented Nissan down a back alley behind the bar. Waiting for them was Abdullah

Khalidi, leaning against an older model Ford Explorer that had been repainted with black primer. Its windows had been darkened with adhesive film; its big knobby tires were worn but functional. The fuse that connected the truck's brake lights had been removed.

"Fen kunt?" asked Abdullah in his native Arabic, "Where have you been?"

"We were told eight o'clock," replied Yousef. Abdullah, in his twenties, was considerably younger than Yousef, but Yousef still responded with deference.

"The Will of Allah waits for no one! Have you learned nothing since San Diego? Where is the guide?"

Ramzi looked around the slummy area. "He said he would be here!" Ramzi replied authoritatively, trying to establish his position within the terrorist cell's hierarchy.

After a moment, the back door of the rundown bar creaked open, and Emilio lumbered out with a small backpack slung over his shoulder, a big shiny .45 protruding awkwardly from underneath his big belly. He peered around in the darkened alley with unfocused eyes.

"Emilio, come here, you are late!" shouted Ramzi.

Emilio drifted his gaze over to the blacked-out truck and began an unsteady shuffle toward the group.

"Are you drunk?" asked Ramzi.

"Solo un poco caliente para el viaje – only a little warm for the trip," asserted Emilio. "Ahora … vamonos … we leave," he ordered, as he climbed into the shotgun seat of the Explorer.

Yousef and Ramzi retrieved their packs from the trunk of their Nissan and placed them in the truck. Abdullah looked first at the drunken Mexican next to him, then at the brothers as they climbed into the back seat. Speaking in Arabic, Abdullah instructed, "Kill him with a knife once he takes you to the location, and leave him on the tracks for the train to devour."

Fully loaded, the blacked-out SUV headed out of town. At the edge of town, two armed men in Mexican police uniforms stepped out of the shadows into the road, blocking the Explorer. The sudden braking of the vehicle woke Emilio from his drunken stupor. In rapid Spanish, he ordered the men over to his open window. He mumbled several lines to them in low commanding tones. The only word Yousef understood was, "Sinaloa," but that one word was enough for the two men to take a step back. The vehicle was allowed to proceed west without further interference. After twenty miles, Emilio instructed Abdullah to slow down. Soon, they came to a rusted old Toyota Hi-lux van that had been abandoned on the side of the road. The van was missing its windows and all four wheels and had been there a while. Emilio glanced back over his shoulder, then told Abdullah to turn off his lights and take the next right onto a rough dirt track. The full moon was bright enough for the desert brush to cast shadows against the rough terrain. After driving a few hundred meters off the main road, Emilio signaled for Abdullah to stop the vehicle behind a small hill.

"We will wait here for our eyes to adjust to the darkness," advised Emilio. Twenty minutes went by without much conversation. Emilio appeared to have sobered up somewhat. As they exited the vehicle, Emilio turned to Abdullah and explained, "Señor Khalidi, we are about three-hundred meters from the

border. Just beyond that is the train track. Stay here. I will take your
men to the border. Then I will come back here and wait with you. I
am a guide, not a terrorist."

Abdullah exploded at the guide's inference. "We are not
terrorists!" he asserted through clenched teeth. "We are soldiers of
Allah, you worthless swine!" Pulling his pistol, Abdullah aimed it
at Emilio through the open window of the vehicle. He was about to
pull the trigger when headlights from an approaching car appeared
out on the main road. After a few tense moments, the car passed
in the distance with the soft hiss of rubber on warm pavement, its
lights fading into the desert darkness.

Emilio never flinched, he simply showed his gold dental work,
then turned and spat on the ground. "Just have my money when
I get back," stated Emilio. "Five-hundred dollars," he reminded
the soldier of Allah. Then motioning to the two brothers, Emilio
instructed, "Come, follow me."

Ramzi and Yousef shouldered their packs and fell in line behind
Emilio, Yousef carrying the supplies and Ramzi the explosives.

Before entering the trail, Yousef turned back to Abdullah and
exclaimed in a low but excited voice, "God be with you!"

Abdullah returned the salute, "And God be with you!"

As they slowly worked their way in the darkness through low
scrub and cactus, the desert dished out its punishment. Through
experience, Emilio avoided most of the pitfalls. Still, long thin
arms of cholla cactus grabbed at their shoulders and hands. One
branch caught on Yousef's face, clawing his cheek in jagged tears,
causing him to stop in his tracks and step backward to disengage
himself. Then Ramzi, following in the rear, stumbled into a deep

armadillo hole, twisting his knee badly. Limping now, Ramzi began to fall behind. In a careless rush to catch up, he tumbled headlong into a well-established growth of prickly pear cactus paddles. As he fell, he reached out with both hands to break his fall and landed squarely on the cactus. Long needle-like spines penetrated deep into the pads of his soft hands. Ramzi screamed in agony. He tried to rise to his knees, but they too were imbedded with needles. He tried rolling over, but then his forearms, butt, and thighs became impaled. He screamed again in torment.

"Mérida!" exclaimed Emilio, as he turned back to examine the commotion. "What have you done, you idiot?"

Enveloped in nature's concertina wire, Ramzi was trapped. He had lifted himself off the ground like a crab, the soles of his shoes and the pack on his back offering the only relief from his torment. Emilio reached down and grabbed Ramzi by his pack straps and pulled him to his feet. Paddles of broken cactus still stuck to his clothing. The fight had been taken out of Ramzi. He couldn't speak, all he could think about was his pain and the horror of being punctured with thick, heavy cactus spines. Even the slightest movement caused the spines to either break off under his skin or press deeper into his flesh. Yousef switched on his flashlight and attempted to shine it onto Ramzi's wounds. Emilio immediately slapped the light from Yousef's hands.

"Esta loco?" hissed Emilio, "Are you crazy?" Emilio looked closely at the whimpering Ramzi and concluded he would be useless for the remainder of the night. "What do you want to do, Señor Yousef?" he asked. "This man can no longer help you."

Yousef evaluated the situation, then turned to his brother. "Give

me one explosive from your pack," he ordered. "Take the other
one back to the vehicle. We can use it later." Ramzi didn't even
argue. His spirit was broken, all he could think about was his pain.
He turned and headed slowly back toward the truck. He moved
like a kitten on broken glass, every step in tearful torment. Yousef
removed several non-essential items from his pack, tossed them in
the brush, and placed one package of C-4 inside. He felt around on
the ground for the flashlight Emilio had knocked from his hands,
and when he found it, he placed it in his jacket pocket.

"Come," said Emilio, "not much farther."

Moonlight led them to the border fence, which was not much
of a fence. Made of wire squares designed for livestock, the wire
sagged from a history of human weight. Emilio pointed to a break
that had already been cut and trampled down. "Here is the border,"
he said. "Go over that rise to the north. You will find the track in
another three hundred feet."

"How will I find our truck when I am finished?" asked Yousef.

Emilio pointed back toward the main road to a mountain in
the distance. "Do you see the flashing red light on the mountain to
the south? That is your beacon tower. Your vehicle will be directly
in line with this path and that light. If you reach the main road,
you have gone too far. Find the old van and turn back. Do not,
under any circumstances, use your flashlight to find us. If you
want to whistle, try that, but do not shout. We will be waiting."
Emilio turned around and faded into the darkness at a quickened
pace with his shoulders hunched, moving like a lone coyote on the
prowl.

Yousef crossed the broken fence and headed north. The land

was more open here with less undergrowth, and he moved more easily. He came to a dry shallow wash and stepped down the rocky embankment. In the darkness, he kicked what he thought was a large piece of cardboard. It skidded roughly across the rocks. Wondering what cardboard was doing so far in the desert, Yousef looked more closely and noticed that the cardboard contained shredded clothing. Upon even closer inspection, Yousef realized that it was not cardboard at all but the collapsed and dried corpse of a man. Dismembered by animals, the skull missing, the body had bloated, exploded in the desert sun, and dried hard and sinewy like a flat piece of beef jerky. Mummified skin and clothing had held the bones together somewhat, leaving nothing more than a large piece of weathered shoe leather. Yousef, himself a child of the camp wars, was more curious than horrified and quickly continued north. As he crested the small rise that Emilio had shown him, he saw the railroad tracks below. Straight and true for as far as the eye could see, a portion of them gleamed in the moonlight.

Yousef approached the tracks and unshouldered his pack. For some reason, he felt compelled to kneel and put his ear to the cold rail. He heard nothing. Putting the shoebox-sized explosive aside, Yousef pulled the trenching tool out of his pack and began scraping away at the loose gravel ballast that held the ties in place. He felt like the operation should have been more complicated, but it wasn't. He simply attached the cell phone to the detonator imbedded in the plastic and then slid the explosive between the wooden ties under a joint in the rail. The extra ballast he used to cover the hole he had dug. He didn't need Ramzi, but he would have liked to have the second device. Doubts began to enter his mind. Would the single kilo of C-4 be enough? And now there was no backup. Too late, the clock was ticking. Yousef pressed the light on his cheap digital watch. Almost midnight, he noted. The train would be pulling out of Yuma about now. It would gather momentum in the desert night and should be at top speed by the time it got to this location. Yousef loaded his pack and retreated back to the small hill overlooking the tracks where he sat and waited. A distant pack of coyotes yammered in the cold desert night, celebrating their kill.

———

Aboard Amtrak's *Limited*, Cam and Caleb were sound asleep in their roomy coach seats in Car #9, now the next-to-last car in the train. Cam stirred slightly as two passengers departed noisily from the train at the Yuma station, rudely yapping to one another as if it were lunch hour. The Amish family occupied the front section of the car. A dead-head truck driver three rows back was snoring loudly. Across from Cam, a young Goth girl dressed in black was watching Netflix on her notepad, its glow illuminating the tackle box of piercings on her dark but angelic face. In the train's cab, the engineer shoved the throttle forward, and the train pulled smoothly away from the platform. After a precursory run through the passenger cars, the conductor and car attendants retreated to their downstairs lounge compartment for a few hours of shut-eye before the next station stop. On good, straight tracks with modern cars, there is little noticeable difference between a train traveling

35 mph and one traveling at its top regulated speed of 79 mph. In non-congested areas, the big diesel/electric motors are able to quickly accelerate the train to top speed. Within minutes of leaving Yuma, *The Sunset Limited* was racing across Arizona's desert southwest toward California.

————

From his position overlooking the railroad track, Yousef heard a portion of the rail ping with a slight metallic pop, like a cooking pan does when it cools. He looked to the east and saw the faint white light of the diesel locomotive approaching, two, maybe three miles away. Yousef sat up and pulled the phone from his pocket. He turned it on, and there was an unusual delay on the phone's screen. Yousef was puzzled by the delay, and then a shocking thought entered his mind. They didn't think to test the cell phone reception in this part of the desert! "Ibn haram!" Yousef cursed.

He looked back at the red beacon light flashing on the distant mountain range and thought, *Is that the cell phone tower?* The moments seemed like eternity. He heard the train's whistle. Fear, rage, and confusion set in. "Turn ON!" He shouted to himself. Still, the small round arrow continued to rotate like a dog chasing its tail. Yousef cursed again and shook the phone as if the motion would wake it up. Then the screen went blank. Eventually, it blinked twice and finally turned on. Yousef exhaled in relief, but the surging adrenaline had jumbled his mind. The train was approaching. He fumbled with the contact list to find the coded number. He missed it the first time and had to scroll back through the list a second time with trembling hands. "Hnak!" he exclaimed as he found it. Yousef looked up to gauge the distance of the speeding train. In the darkness with only the locomotive's massive light as a measure, time and distance were distorted. He couldn't dial too soon, or the train might begin emergency braking procedures. If he dialed too late, only a portion of the train might be derailed. He couldn't gauge the train's speed; all he could see was one bright light heading in his direction, so he simply guessed and tapped the phone's SEND button. One ring, two rings as a safety mechanism, then BOOM! The C-4 exploded into the night, lighting the surrounding area in a bright camera flash that staggered in the night sky for just a split second and showered Yousef with rock ballast. The rapid detonation pushed quickly and powerfully up against the rail joint with enough explosive force to twist the steel at an awkward angle, shearing the connecting bolts and breaking it in two. That was enough. Yousef had guessed right.

The train's engineer, having just read a freight status message on his onboard computer, looked up just in time to see the explosion immediately in his path. Confused but decisive, he moved quickly to engage the train's emergency braking system, but it wasn't soon enough. Passenger trains need at least a half mile to stop under such conditions; this train had less than two-hundred yards. As every wheel on every truck of the cars locked down, everything slammed forward with the severe braking. Passengers in the forward sleepers were flung out of their beds. Anyone standing was thrown to the floor. Loose luggage rained down from the overhead racks like bricks from a collapsing wall. Farther to the rear, as the dynamic braking action took effect, Cam and Caleb were slammed forward against the seat backs in front of them. The distinctive shrill screech of steel wheels grinding against steel rails filled the railcars like the ear-piercing shriek of a baby's scream.

As the locomotive's headlight penetrated the smoke and illuminated the damaged track, the engineer realized he could do nothing more but brace himself. He glanced at his speed indicator and read fifty-two. *Oh boy, this is gonna be ugly,* was his last thought in life. Hitting the broken rail, the locomotive jolted hard upward and bounced violently off to the left. As the lead 135-ton locomotive dug deep into the desert sand, the surging weight of the second locomotive following behind pushed it askew and turned it backwards, crushing the cab. Car after car followed the path of its lead, folding themselves like accordions against each other, snapping their knuckled joints and rolling sideways. Others lifted up and slammed down on top of cars beneath them.

In the rear of the train, the scene for a dazed Cam began to unfold in slow motion. First came the sound. After the screeching of the wheels, there followed a series of pronounced, rhythmic claps that sounded like heavy doors slamming down a long empty hallway—*slam, slap, bam, bang, whump, wham.* Then came the moaning of heavy metal under stress. Car #9 lifted up, slid off to the left, snapped free, and rolled to its side where it slid for several feet before coming to a rest. The ride was rough and jolting, enough to shatter glass but not catastrophic. Dust and dirt filled the compartments. Snapped airbrake hoses hissed in the background. Liquid was dripping somewhere. Then came the darkness and momentary silence, followed by moans. Sparking wires ignited the four-thousand gallons of diesel fuel spilled from the ruptured locomotive tanks, making lakes of greasy fire on the desert floor. Disoriented, Cam and Caleb had been shoved together in a heap. Ultimately, the wreck deposited them against shattered window glass as it rolled to its side. Caleb was moaning, and even in the darkness Cam could feel blood on his face. Cam's ribs hurt like hell. He felt a throbbing pain in his dislocated little finger. Grabbing it with his good hand, Cam snapped the finger back into its socket. Slowly emerging from his mental fog, Cam moved across the aisle and climbed up the side of a seat. Reaching over his head, he pulled the red metal emergency handle that loosened the rubber gasket around the car's window. He yanked hard, and the heavy safety glass fell partially inward against his head. He pulled again, and the glass fell completely down.

Reaching back to Caleb, he pulled at the hand of his waking son, but Caleb, his arm broken with a spiral fracture, cried out in pain, and Cam let go. He performed a quick triage of his son's other injuries and found a busted nose, a slight concussion possibly, and cuts and bruises, but none of the injuries were life threatening. Stepping on the seat arm, Cam lifted himself out of the tilted car and helped other less-injured passengers climb out to safety. One of the Amish women was looking frantically for her child. As he stood on the side of the car, Cam observed the wreckage through the smoky, dusty darkness. The jumbled cars looked like a junk yard. Moonlight reflected off the dented silver siding of the cars like crushed soda cans. He saw the burning locomotives ahead in the distance.

Cam re-entered his wrecked car and climbed over piles of fallen luggage to look for other survivors. In the aisle under the seats was the trucker, dead, his neck broken. Off to the side was the young Goth girl just coming to her senses. From the glow of her notepad still running nearby, he could see her mouth was bloody and swollen. One foot was trapped awkwardly under a mangled seat, her right femur bone had snapped and protruded jaggedly through the skin toward her pelvis. As she came to, the searing pain in her thigh brought her suddenly to full consciousness, and she began to scream hysterically. When she looked down and saw her injured leg, her screams became even more desperate. Cam covered her leg with a jacket and tried to calm her. Caleb, dazed and bloodied and with only one useful arm, crawled over to the girl to help his dad.

"Here, support her leg like this, and keep her calm," Cam instructed his son. "Her foot is trapped, and we won't be able to move her without some mechanical help. Can you handle this?"

Caleb nodded and took his position next to the girl. He began to offer soothing words to her as she slipped in and out of consciousness.

His medical triage complete in that car, Cam moved to other parts of the wreck to assist survivors. Dead broken bodies thrown from the wreckage by the force of the collisions littered the surrounding desert like road kill. Some of the injured were calling eerily from the desert's darkness. Cam searched like a blind man, listening for sounds of life. He had no idea the cause of this calamity was just steps away.

From the shadows of his hilltop position, Yousef watched with morbid fascination the disaster he had created. "God is good," he declared under his breath as he gathered his pack and descended the path back to his waiting vehicle.

As he approached the truck, Yousef whistled softly a few times to alert the occupants to his presence. Abdullah stepped out of the vehicle and greeted Yousef with a smile. "You did it!" he exclaimed. "Was it a complete success?"

"Complete," responded Yousef, making no mention that he almost botched the operation. "The train has been destroyed – God is great!"

"Yes, God is great!" rejoiced Abdullah. "We will send a message to the world celebrating Liwa Tahrir's great victory tonight!"

Yousef looked over to his brother, a bent shadow leaning painfully against the truck. Ramzi was in torment. He could not sit or lay down, only the soles of his feet were free from discomfort. Emilio was asleep in the front seat, drunk from a fresh bottle of tequila he had stashed in his pack.

Abdullah motioned in the direction of the sleeping guide. "We must now finish our business," he instructed in Arabic.

Yousef nodded and reached for his pistol.

"Not a gun, the silence of a knife," Abdullah directed.

Yousef nodded again and moved his hand from his pistol to a back pocket, retrieving his tactical blade. He approached the passenger door and quickly flung it open, causing the sleeping Emilio to fall sideways into the dirt. The movement was enough to partially wake him just in time to see Yousef thrusting down toward him with the knife. Emilio was able to raise his left arm just enough to deflect the jab of the knife, forcing the blade to drag viciously across the underside of his forearm. Bleeding profusely but not lethally with his feet still entangled in the open door of the truck, the heavyset Emilio rolled aggressively into the legs of Yousef, knocking him off balance. Drawing his own pistol from his waistband, Emilio fired once at Yousef's dark outline, striking him in the upper thigh. Yousef fell backward, writhing in shock and pain.

Abdullah moved in and stomped on Emilio's gun hand, knocking the pistol free. He then landed a knee squarely across Emilio's chest, pinned the Mexican's injured arm, and jabbed a knife deep into his neck, simultaneously severing Emilio's jugular vein and carotid artery. As he withdrew the serrated knife in a ragged jerking motion, black blood spurted in long snakelike streams, landing on the cringing Yousef several feet away, splattering the truck door, and soaking Abdullah's shirtsleeve. Abdullah held the struggling guide down for a few spurts longer. It didn't take long for Emilio's lifeblood to flow out of him.

"Come, we must move quickly now that a shot has been fired!" exclaimed Abdullah, as he reached into Emilio's pack and retrieved the five-hundred dollars he had just paid him. He helped Yousef to his feet and ordered Ramzi to climb in the passenger side of the vehicle. Moving slowly like a woman in labor, Ramzi did as he was told. Abdullah laid the grimacing Yousef in the back seat of the SUV. His leg was bleeding but not spurting; the bullet had torn flesh but not an artery. He would live. Abdullah spun the black Explorer in a swirl of dust up onto the empty main road and headed southwest, deeper into Mexico. As he looked back toward the border, Abdullah could see the glow of flames in the night sky and the faint flashing lights of emergency vehicles racing to the scene from Yuma.

Several hundred yards away in the dark cold desert on hard ground still warm from the day's sun, Cam Coppenger was working feverishly on the broken dying body of a young Amish boy.

"Joshua! Joshua!" he was pleading. "Don't die on me! Open your eyes! *Please!*"

But the boy did die, and something primordial snapped deep within Cam's core.

9

THE SMALL HOSPITAL in Yuma was quickly overwhelmed with surviving victims of the train wreck. Choppers took the most critically injured; others were taken by ambulance. The next closest trauma hospitals, located in Phoenix, Tucson, and San Diego, were all about three hours away by vehicle. Compared to most of the victims, Cam was not seriously injured, but his shirt was covered with the blood of strangers. He looked worse off than he was. Cam checked his wallet and found he still had three months remaining on his government-issued Air Evac membership, good for anywhere in the world. Even though he hated helicopters, he called for one anyway. When the San Diego-based chopper arrived, Cam used his badge as leverage to get Caleb and the now-sedated Goth girl on his flight. As their evacuation helicopter rose into the night sky amid a swirl of flashing emergency lights, desert dust, and tumble-weeds, Cam was provided an expansive view of the disaster scene. It was littered with bright yellow sheets covering the dead. There were many yellow sheets; more than he could count.

With the adrenaline rush gone, the pain in Cam's ribs became pronounced. The thumping vibration of the helicopter didn't help. It hurt to breathe. He was sure some ribs were broken. Cam was thankful their destination was San Diego. The hospitals were first rate, and he knew people there.

Upon their arrival, the hospital's trauma center took immediate action. Caleb had his nose patched and a cast put on his arm. The Goth girl finally had her compound fracture screwed back together and sewn up. They wrapped Cam's broken ribs with a compression bandage, gave him pain pills, and discharged him. There was nothing they could do about fractured ribs, they said, except to prescribe ibuprofen and rest.

The hospital did seize Cam's gun, however, and turned it over to security. Security, in turn, turned the pistol over to SDPD. Cam spent an hour sorting through that bureaucracy, but he eventually recovered his gun after explaining the federal provisions of 18 USC 926c that allowed retired agents to carry firearms. Cam had spent four years working in San Diego; he knew the drill.

With discharge papers in hand and wearing a freshly pressed green hospital shirt that replaced his bloody one, Cam hurried to the third floor of the hospital to check on his son.

"They want to hold me overnight for observation," slurred Caleb, peering through two blackened and swollen eyes and a massive nose bandage. His pain meds were clearly taking effect. "They're concerned about the bump on my head."

"You're looking pretty rough there," teased Cam, dryly. "But I'm glad you're gonna be okay. Great call on the train trip, by the way," he joked, as he lightly touched his own sore ribs.

"Do you think we can get a refund from Amtrak?" Caleb smiled through his busted lip.

"I'm going to head over to Pacific Highway and pick up a rental car. I also need to buy a change of clothes and get a hotel for us. What time do you want me to pick you up tomorrow?"

"That's already been taken care of, Dad. Some of my surfer buds offered me a place to stay in Pacific Beach, and Elizabeth is gonna hang with us until she gets back on her feet."

"Elizabeth?" Cam's eyebrows lifted.

"You know, Dad, the girl with the broken leg. She's down the hall and doesn't have anybody here to help her."

"Oh, that Elizabeth!" Cam winked and then checked his watch. It was still early morning. He calculated that Kate was three time zones ahead, so he stepped into the hallway and called her.

"Hello Cop, what's up?" Kate answered from her desk at work.

"Guess you haven't heard."

"Heard what?" she asked, wondering what sort of news Cam had for her.

"About the train wreck last night."

"Oh my God, Cop. *Your* train? Where?"

"Somewhere in the desert past Yuma," he estimated, calmly. "We're in San Diego now."

"Was it serious? Are you hurt?"

"Banged up a bit, but I'll live. Caleb was hurt a bit more seriously—broken arm, busted nose, concussion maybe—but he'll be okay."

"Were there casualties?" she asked, as she stood and peered over her cubicle to see any late-breaking news coverage on the office television. Fellow deputies had begun to gather around the wall-mounted flat screen.

Cam paused before answering. He suddenly realized how heavy his heart felt, like a brick in his chest. The chaos of the evening had suppressed the feeling for a while, but Kate's question brought it sharply back into focus. He was carrying a burden and needed to share it with someone. "A little boy died, Kate; he died in my arms last night." Cam's throat froze up; he couldn't finish. "Gotta go. I need to sign some papers for Caleb."

"I'm so sorry, Cop," Kate responded, immediately thinking of Jimmy's death. "Thank God you're safe! Let me know what you need. Do you want me to come out there?" By then, Cam had already hung up.

Alerted by Cam's call, Kate moved closer to the television where her colleagues had gathered. Reporters were already at the crash site, and their stunning video images showed in shocking detail the sobering extent of the carnage. According to news reports, The Liberation Brigade had already claimed responsibility for the disaster. The information unnerved her.

———

Leaving the hospital by taxi, Cam picked up a rental car, some toiletries, and a fresh change of clothes. He checked into the Motel 6 in the Little Italy section of San Diego. A step above fleabag-level accommodations, it was the cheapest place to stay that was still close to things. He needed to make the $100,000 boat insurance money last as long as possible. Little Italy was where he had lived when he worked in San Diego, so he was familiar with the area. It was also where his old DSS office was located. Once inside his motel room, Cam found himself restless in spite of his exhaustion. He needed to do something. Maybe a walk would help clear his head. He decided to pay his old office a visit.

Once at the SDRO, Cam tested the door combination and discovered it hadn't been changed. He walked right in. The office appeared deserted until he found a small team of agents in the conference room gathered around a television, watching news reports on the train disaster in Arizona. Special Agent Mike Dunbar turned to find his old boss standing in the doorway. "Cop!" he called out, causing the other agents to turn around as well. "Where'd you come from?"

"Technically, Alabama, via a train wreck in Arizona," Cam replied casually.

Another agent, the only one Cam did not recognize, responded, "Huh?" Turning back to the TV, he pointed, seeking clarification, "You were on *that* train?"

"Car #9 to be exact," replied Cam, enjoying the shock value his partial clues were providing the room full of trained criminal investigators. His former colleagues, looking at the bandage on his forehead and the splint on his little finger, were both perplexed and intrigued.

"How'd you get *here*?" asked Dunbar.

"If you mean San Diego ... by helicopter," Cam said with a

smart-ass smile. "And you need to change the combination to your front door," he added, never missing an opportunity to teach junior agents a thing or two. "Otherwise, just anybody can walk in!"

Slowly recovering from the surprise of finding his ex-boss standing in the office, Agent Dunbar remembered his manners. "Cop, it's good to see you!" He walked over and shook Cam's hand. "Have a seat! Are you okay? Can I get you some coffee?"

"Coffee would be nice," acknowledged Cam. "I'm fine, but I haven't slept since the accident."

Dunbar poured a cup from the office pot and set it down in front of Cam. With television coverage of the train wreck still running in the background, the team of agents gathered loosely around the conference table. Cam recognized all of them except for the one new guy. It was just like the old days.

"Who's running the office now?"

"Eddie Sanchez," replied Dunbar. "He came here from Bogota as RSO. He's in DC this week for a conference on border security."

"I know Eddie; he's top notch. How's the work going?"

"Busy as always. Two agents are in DC working protection for the SecState, two more are up in LA working the arrival of the Korean Foreign Minister, and another is on TDY to Baghdad. It's always busy down on the border. We keep an agent posted at San Ysidro Port of Entry full time now."

"Is the US Attorney's office still supportive?"

"For the most part," explained Agent Dunbar. "It's a numbers game, as you know. There just aren't enough jail cells to handle the amount of passport fraud we detect on the border. Tourists have them stolen in TJ, college kids sell them for party money, and fraudulent applications are an ongoing problem. Earlier this year, we discovered that the San Diego county clerk was issuing birth certificates to anyone who showed up with a name and date of birth. As long as they had the name of two parents who had citizenship—along with their DOB's—no photo ID was required. Of course, illegals who have assumed the identity of a friend or dead relative have that information, so then they take the birth certificate and get a driver's license, are automatically registered to vote, and apply for a passport. Instant citizenship! We arrest them, they get out on a thousand dollars bail, and then they simply slip back across the border to try again under a new identity. And it's not just Mexicans. We've had a significant increase in Haitians down at the border this year. We're not sure why, other than it must be easier to cross a leaky land border than it is to float over in a leaky boat."

"Interesting," commented Cam. Then turning to the television, he asked, "What are they saying about the train accident?"

"Well, first, it wasn't an accident. Liwa Tahrir has already claimed responsibility. You know about the Palestinian terrorist Ismail and The Liberation Brigade, right?"

The information caught Cam by surprise. This was the first time he had heard Ismail's name connected to the train disaster. "Yeah … I have some background on them."

Agent Dunbar, unaware of Cam's recent involvement with the JTTF, continued, "They've already hit San Diego's airport. I'm guessing there is a border link. FBI is handling it as a case of international terrorism."

Contemplating Ismail's involvement in the train crash, Cam

decided not to go into detail with his former colleagues about his brief return to government service. No reason to mention it. They didn't need to know, and there was no way for them to know. They simply saw him as a retired has-been.

But the information Dunbar had just provided was a game changer for Cam. The death and destruction he had experienced only hours before hadn't been an accident. Ismail was behind the attack! That changed things. Ismail's third attack on American soil had now hit close to home. The train derailment had injured Caleb and ruthlessly taken the life of that innocent Amish boy, among many others! As Cam's agent instincts began to kick in, it occurred to him that Ismail wouldn't stop until *somebody stopped him*. He reached in his pocket and retrieved the small wooden baseball bat Joshua had given him. For Cam, Ismail's war had just become personal.

Cam downed his coffee, abruptly stood up, and announced, "Hey guys, this has been great, good seeing everybody, and thanks for the coffee!" As he worked his way to the door, he turned and said, "Let's do this again!"

"Absolutely!" replied Dunbar. "Come back anytime!" With Cam's sudden departure, Dunbar suspected that something must have triggered his former boss, and he turned back to the news reports on the train wreck. He had seen Cop pull a small wooden object from his pocket and wondered if it had anything to do with Ismail and The Liberation Brigade.

From his motel room, Cam put in a call to his buddy Sid Lewis at the FBI.

"Hello Cop, where's my retired homeless task force leader these days?"

"San Diego via an Arizona train wreck."

"You were on *that* train?"

"Yep. Caleb and I both."

"Good grief, Cop, what's with you and disasters these days? Were either of you hurt?"

"Not seriously."

"You know Ismail was behind the derailment, don't you?"

"Yeah, and that's why I called you. What have you learned so far?"

Sid paused. "Well, the *unclassified* version is The Liberation Brigade has teamed up with the Sinaloa Cartel and has a base of operations in Mexico. Their original objective was to establish a drug pipeline to Europe, but the relationship has apparently expanded into other operations. Our intel guys are looking into the connection, but the cartel has everyone down there either on their payroll or living in fear. Human intelligence is hard to come by south of the border. Why are you asking? I thought you were out of the counterterrorism business."

"Sid, Ismail came close to killing me and my son. I'm trying to make sense of it all."

"You're not thinking about pulling a Muladi snatch ... are you?" the FBI agent inquired discreetly, acutely aware of Cam's resume.

"A snatch? Not planning on it."

"Be careful," Sid advised. "You seem to have a target on your back these days. Are you sure you don't want to come back to the task force?" Without waiting for an answer, Sid followed, "Hey, I've got to brief the Director on this Amtrak attack in five. Can we talk later?"

"Sure thing," said Cam. "Later."

"Can I tell the Director you are back on the team?"

"No, Sid, you can't," Cam replied sharply before hanging up.

Leaning back on the cheap motel pillows, Cam was suddenly overcome with deep fatigue. He hadn't slept since before the train wreck. He was exhausted, and his ribs felt like a sledge hammer had hit him. Cam popped four Tylenol and quickly went comatose on a stained bedspread that smelled of wet dogs and cigarettes.

10

A FEW HOURS later, a blue, orange, and tan 737 came roaring directly over Cam's motel and landed on the airport runway just a couple blocks away, waking him from his deep sleep. It was dark. Cam looked at the flashing red numbers on the motel's alarm clock and realized he couldn't trust it. He looked at his watch: 2145. He couldn't remember if that meant 9:45 Central, Mountain, or Pacific Standard Time. He rolled over on the lumpy mattress, and his injured ribs sent an electric jolt through his torso.

"Arrrrrrgh!" he screamed out.

His shout was loud enough to cause a couple walking past his door to stop, pause, and wonder if a crime was being committed in his room. Hearing nothing more, they moved on.

Fully awake, Cam realized he was starved. He got up, showered, rewrapped his ribs, and walked down to Mona Lisa's restaurant for a satisfying meal of the best baked ziti on India Street. By the time he got back to the motel it was late, well after midnight on the east coast. He called Kate anyway. Her phone rang a long time.

"You asleep?" Cam asked when Kate finally answered.

"Of course, Cam. It's three o'clock in the morning," she responded, sleepily. "Are you okay?"

Cam thought he heard a man breathe heavily in the background. "Yeah, but not really," he replied. He wanted to talk about a lot of things, but he stayed with his business at hand. "I have a favor to ask you. It's pretty big, but it sounds like you're busy. We'll talk later."

"Cam, wait, what are you talkin …" Kate stopped in mid-sentence. She was talking to an empty phone line. She slammed the phone down, angry, confused, and unable to go back to sleep.

The next morning, Kate took her personal phone to an empty interview room at the office, closed the door, and aggressively punched in Cam's number.

"Hello?" Cam answered, too asleep to check the caller ID.

"What was that call about last night, Special Agent Coppenger?"

"*Retired* Special Agent," Cam corrected. Cam wanted to reveal the lingering heaviness in his heart and tell her about the Amish boy, but he wasn't mentally prepared so early in the day. He moved on to business. "I have a favor to ask."

"What is it?" Her tone softened.

"Do you remember that Tijuana police chief who had his family threatened and his house shot up by one of the cartels for being an honest cop? Roberto Menendez was his name."

"Yes, I remember. He came to you in fear for his life, and you got him and his family an entry visa into the US. We put him in the

Witness Protection program, and the DEA got some pretty solid convictions out of his information, as I recall."

"Yeah, that's him. I need you to put me in touch with him."

Kate went quiet for some time. "You know I can't do that, Cop. Menendez is under deep cover. It would break every rule we have to reveal his whereabouts. Only his handler has that information."

"I told you it was a big favor."

"Why do you need to talk to him?"

"I need to get some background on the cartels." Cam told a half-truth.

"Google it," Kate said sharply. "Wiki will have the same information Menendez could give you. And his name is no longer Menendez, in case you didn't already know." Kate paused and then asked point blank, "Are you going operational, Cam?"

"Define operational."

"Don't play word games with me, Cam Coppenger. Answer my question."

Cam paused and then played his ace card. "Do you want Jimmy's killers brought to justice or not?"

His question struck her emotional bullseye like a laser beam. Kate went stone cold silent.

"Answer me, Kate ... do you?"

After a long silence, Kate responded, "Let me think about it." Then she pushed the CANCEL CALL button.

———

For three full days, Kate refused to answer Cam's phone calls or respond to his texts. Finally, on his fourth day in San Diego, Cam's phone vibrated from an unknown caller and a brief text appeared, *Hola amigo! Meet me at 2:00 today at Mama's Best Pies in Julian. Oscar.*

Menendez … had to be, Cam concluded.

Cam was familiar with Julian, an old mining town with a wild-west vibe, located in the mountains above San Diego. Famous for fresh baked apple pies, Julian was a popular weekend destination for tourists. The winding mountain road to Julian was particularly popular with motorcyclists, and Cam had ridden his Suzuki V-Strom up there many times. Julian made for a great day trip, and the pies were fabulous.

Ever mindful of prudent security precautions, Cam positioned his 9mm comfortably next to his bandaged ribs and headed to Julian early, taking a circuitous route in his rental car through Escondido. He was not followed. Arriving at lunchtime, he easily found his rendezvous location directly on Main Street. Across the street from Mama's Best Pies was a barbeque place, and Cam was hungry. He set up counter-surveillance at a window seat there and ordered lunch.

Lining both sides of Main Street were rows of motorcycles of all makes and models backed neatly against the curbs, kickstands down, and front wheels turned left in the locked position. Most were Harleys, and the majority of the riders mingling on the sidewalks were dressed in traditional biker attire: jeans, sleeveless shirts or black leather vests, heavy boots, and bandanas tied tightly around their heads. As far as he knew, none were actually outlaw motorcycle gang (OMG) members, but many looked the part. In reality, a good number of them were probably off-duty cops. Cam thought about his own bike rides to Julian and began to miss his V-Strom. He had left his sport tourer with Caleb in Key Largo after what he thought would be a last ride to Key West down US-1, but now he wasn't so sure. Second only to sailing a beam reach on a well-heeled boat, accelerating a well-tuned bike on long sweeping curves was Cam's favorite avenue of escape.

From his vantage point, Cam could observe most of the activity on Julian's Main Street. None of the tourists that entered Mama's were noteworthy. Almost all were Anglos. It was a typical sunny California day in a tourist town. The red-headed waitress brought Cam his plate of chopped smoked pork butt and set a rack of bottled sauces on the table. One bottle was a vinegar/mustard-based yellow, another a thin brown concoction that Cam was sure carried heat. A third bottle was a thick and robust red, probably of the sweet variety. "Good," Cam thought, "These folks know their BBQ." He dug in.

It was almost two o'clock when the waitress asked Cam if he wanted a piece of apple pie for dessert. "I'm scheduled to meet a friend for pie over at Mama's in a few minutes. How is their pie?"

"Next to ours, Oscar makes the best!" admitted the waitress with a grin.

"Good to know," replied Cam as he paid the check. "Oscar is the owner?"

"Yeah, he and his family moved here about two years ago. They are from Mexico, I think. Kinda quiet. Cute kids."

At two minutes before two o'clock, Cam walked across the street and entered Mama's. Once inside, he paused at the door. Lunchtime was almost over, and the crowd was sparse. A few customers were finishing up huge slices of apple pie, each topped with a large scoop of vanilla ice cream. The brown-skinned lady behind the counter looked familiar; she was Menendez's wife. She was busy at the register.

Mrs. Menendez would not have remembered Cam. It had been midnight and dark three years before when Cam had picked up the Menendez family at the border. With three young children in her arms, the terrified mother had been hysterical when Cam tried to introduce himself to her. Earlier that evening, cartel thugs had driven by their house in Tijuana and sprayed it with automatic weapons fire, shattering window glass, splintering doors, chipping plaster walls with bullet holes, shredding curtains, and exploding table lamps inside. Luckily, the family had escaped unharmed, but they were traumatized. Roberto Menendez was one of the few honest police chiefs in Mexico, and Cam recognized early in their relationship that Roberto was a good man trying to do the right thing in a world full of evil. They had worked closely together on several major passport cases, and Cam trusted him.

Menendez, now known as Oscar, was a short, heavyset Mexican with black hair and a thick mustache. He walked in from the kitchen and looked up at a clock on the wall. Wiping greasy hands on a white apron, he looked around and spotted Cam in the doorway. Oscar lifted his chin and eyebrows in recognition and, with a twitch of his head, directed Cam to the back door of the restaurant before retreating back into the kitchen. Mrs. Oscar never looked up from her work.

Following Oscar's directive, Cam went through the rear door marked EMPLOYEES ONLY and entered an enclosed outdoor patio. Colorful pink bougainvillea climbed high wooden fencing. A wooden picnic table sat under a lone shade tree. The ground was littered with cigarette butts. Closed to public access, the area apparently was used by restaurant employees for smoke breaks and informal private parties. An industrial kitchen vent fan was blowing loudly into the courtyard. An excellent location for a private conversation, Cam took a seat in the shade and waited.

In a moment, Oscar emerged from a separate kitchen door and strode across the patio. "Cameron, mi amigo!" he exclaimed softly as he embraced his friend. It was the same kind of deep prolonged embrace that Elie had given Cam in Beirut. Finishing with a hearty pat on the shoulders, Oscar asked, "Como esta?"

"Bien, y tu?" Cam responded.

"Not bad, not bad," replied Oscar. "Thanks to you!"

"You are a good man, Rober … *Oscar!*" Cam corrected himself. "You deserve good things," he added. "Y su familia … como estan?"

"Good, good," replied Oscar with a broad smile. Just then a young brown skinned boy about six came bounding out of the restaurant's back door and launched himself into the arms of his father. Dressed in dusty jeans and sport shoes, he had on a blue t-shirt with the name Blue Jays written in cursive across the chest. His blue ballcap had a white J embrodered on its crest. Oscar introduced them with a broad smile, saying, "Eduardo, meet my friend Mr. C!"

"Hello Mister Sea," said the boy with perfect English. "Do you live near the ocean?"

"Hello Eduardo, nice to meet you," Cam replied. "Actually, I do live on the water!" Then hoping to move the conversation away from himself, Cam asked, "Who are the Blue Jays?"

"My baseball team!" replied Eduardo, enthusiastically.

"The Julian Blue Jays?"

The boy nodded.

"What position do you play?"

"Second base and outfield!"

Oscar proudly interjected, "Eduardo is a good fielder, but he is a much better hitter. He is batting over .300 this year!"

"That's great!" congratulated Cam. "Which is your favorite major league team?"

"San Diego Padres!" shouted Eduardo.

"I like the Atlanta Braves best, but I also like the Padres," Cam said, checking out the boy's uniform. "And in the American League, I like the Baltimore Orioles!"

Eduardo grinned in acknowledgement.

Oscar interrupted the conversation. "Eduardo, I need to talk to Mr. C for a while. Be a good boy, and go inside to help your mother."

Eduardo gave Cam a high-five and raced back into the restaurant as if stealing home plate.

Oscar turned to Cam, "Everything I have here I owe to you."

"You earned everything you have, Oscar. I simply helped you get out of a bad situation."

Oscar shook his head. "You saved my life and that of my family," he declared, his eyes becoming damp with tears. Regaining his composure, he continued. "I heard you wanted to talk to me. What can I do for you, my friend?"

"I need some information on the Mexican cartels."

"Which ones? There are many!"

Cam elaborated, "The Sinaloa Cartel or the Tijuana Cartel, I'm guessing. Maybe the Juarez Cartel over by El Paso. We have reason to believe one or more of them are working with a Palestinian terrorist group called The Liberation Brigade. We believe The Liberation Brigade is behind the three recent terrorist attacks in the US."

"Who is we?" asked Oscar. "The State Department?"

Cam paused for a moment, contemplating how much background information he needed to provide his contact. "Oscar, do you remember when I met your family at the border the night of the attack?"

Oscar nodded.

"Actually, that was a personal decision I made that went outside the scope of my normal duties. I never asked for permission to escort your family across the border. I never sought governmental authorization to take that action, I just did what I thought was right. Do you understand?"

Oscar reached across the table and gripped Cam's arm in comaraderie. "Yo comprendo. I understand."

"What I am about to do is similar to that night at the border. I am retired now, so I have no official capacity. I'm just trying to do what's right."

"Congratulations on your retirement, Cameron. I am retired, too! Now how can I help my honorable friend?"

"I need information, names, and locations."

"And a wingman?" probed Oscar, smiling.

"I would never ask you to do that. You are a family man."

"You didn't ask. I offered!" Oscar's earnest smile hardened. "Those men attacked my family, and they were never brought to justice!"

"You know the identities of the men who attacked you that night?" asked Cam, reminding himself that Mexicans sometimes lived by a different code of honor than that of their northern neighbors.

"I have names," replied Oscar, confidently. "What is your plan?"

"I don't know yet. I'm just getting started. But I need information first."

The back door to the restaurant partially opened, and Oscar's wife stuck her head out, looking for him.

Turning toward the door, Oscar barked sharply to his wife, "Leave us!"

She glanced at Cam for a moment of vague recognition, then did as she was told.

Oscar turned back to Cam. "Now, continue," he instructed in a low voice, transitioning their friendship to a partnership.

"I need to know which cartel is working with the terrorists, where their base of operations is, and who some of the players are. It would be helpful to know their methods of operating, their ports of entry, transportation routes, and such."

"Let me see what I can find out. What is the name of the terrorist group again?"

"Liwa Tahrir ... The Liberation Brigade ... led by a guy they call Ismail. Khalid Khalidi is his true name ... a Palestinian based in Lebanon."

Oscar pulled a stubby pencil from his behind his ear and wrote the information on a ticket receipt, then stuck it in his apron pocket. "I will find out. Give me a week." Nodding in agreement, the men stood and gave each other another shouldered embrace. Oscar unlocked the tall wooden gate at the rear of the patio and let Cam out the back way. Cam paused to observe his surroundings. Sitting in a dirt lot behind the courtyard among a scattering of other vehicles was a beat-up old pickup truck with Tijuana plates. It had been there a while. Dust covered the windshield, and one tire was almost flat.

On his drive back to San Diego, Cam contemplated his mission. Certainly, he believed in the rule of law. He also understood that strict adherence to the rule of law sometimes allowed justice to slip through the cracks. But to use the words he had written hundreds of times in his criminal complaints for prosecution, he was about *to knowingly and with willful intent* break laws, many laws in fact. That was his moral dilemma, balancing justice with adherence to law. Deep, serious questions raced through his head. What does a moral man do when rules obstruct justice? How and when should rules be bent or broken to ensure that justice prevails? Must justice always prevail, or is it the adherence to law that holds a civil society together? Are true patriots justified when they break laws to protect their country? Do the ends justify the means?

A jackrabbit darted across the road and snapped Cam back into reality. He swerved and barely missed it. The jackrabbit had survived life's roulette wheel to live another day. Now refocused on the task before him, Cam mentally slapped himself, *Get a grip, Coppenger, you're not Plato. Keep it simple, and just do the right thing.*

Descending from the mountains into San Diego, Cam took the Pacific Beach exit and called Caleb. "How's it going?" Cam asked when his son answered.

"Hey Dad! Where are you?"

"Just coming into PB and thought I might stop by."

"Yeah, sure, come on! Elizabeth and I are just hanging out!"

Cam liked Pacific Beach. A quintessential California beach town, PB had a vibrant downtown strip located right on the Pacific Ocean. The area was loaded with surf shops, bars, coffee bistros, and burger joints. A medical marijuana dispensary sat prominently on one corner. Kids in board shorts and adults on skateboards roamed the town at all hours. Classic convertibles and Volkswagon vans lined the streets. As he cruised along Mission Boulevard in a rented four-door sedan that was seriously out of place, Cam briefly wondered why he hadn't retired in PB instead of Alabama. Then he passed a series of FOR RENT signs on one of the blocks and was quickly reminded of the cost of living in California: they call it *Sunshine Tax.*

Cam turned up Garnet Street and found the rented beach house where Caleb had been invited to stay. In serious need of lawncare and repair, the house was located just a block down from a house Cam had raided as a federal agent just a few years prior. That house had been used by the Russian mafia for human trafficking of Ukranian prostitutes. For years, the Russian mob had lured scores of leggy young girls into the US, using H1B visas under the guise of recruiting them for a growing pedi-cab industry. But once the girls arrived, their passports were seized by the mobsters, and they were threatened with deportation and often violence if they didn't cooperate with the mafia's true business plan. Sure, the girls could be found throughout the day pedalling tourists along the PB beachfront, but at night the nature of their delivery services changed significantly. Under his direction, SDRO had launched a massive visa fraud investigation into the operation and made several significant arrests of area Russian mob leaders, taking them off the streets for at least a decade.

From the sidewalk in front of the surfer house, Cam could hear the music of the group *Beach Boys* emanating from the open front door. Caleb met his dad at the door and smiled. His nose bandage was much smaller now, and the brusing beneath his eyes had diminished. The electric-blue cast on his arm, covered in surf shop stickers, extended well above his elbow. Barefoot, shirtless, deeply tanned, and in board shorts, Caleb greeted his father with an embrace.

"How are you coming along?" asked Cam.

"Good. No surfing with this cast, but I am loving PB!"

Cam looked over Caleb's shoulder to see Elizabeth reclined on the sofa, her full-leg cast propped up on pillows, laptop in hand. Without her facial piercings installed, she was quite pretty. Her jet-black hair was pulled back in a short pony tail. "Hi Elizabeth, I'm Cam, Caleb's dad."

"I know who you are, Mr. Coppenger," she said, tucking her laptop away. Looking down at her cast, she added, "I never thanked you for rescuing me!"

Pretty and good manners, Cam thought to himself. "You are quite welcome! How are you feeling?"

"Aside from obvious mobility issues, things couldn't be better," she said, looking over to Caleb with affection. "Please, have a seat! What can I have my butler get you?" she asked, making eyes at her new boyfriend standing next to his father.

Smiling at Caleb, Cam asked, "Got any Bama-sweet iced tea?"

"No, but I can make some," replied Caleb, as he plodded off into the kitchen. "You two get to know one another."

Cam shooed a fat calico cat off a well-worn upholstered chair and sat down facing Elizabeth. He opened the conversation as any old guy would do when talking to a twenty-something. "So Elizabeth, where are you from?"

"Imperial Beach," she replied. "My parents are divorced. My mom took off years ago. My father still lives there, and I sometimes live with him."

"Down near the border, huh? Are you a surfer?"

"Not at IB! The sewage from TJ flows directly into the ocean there! A friend of mine almost died from a sinus infection he contracted while surfing that polluted water!"

"Good Grief! Is he okay?"

"He survived, but they had to remove part of his skull due to the infection. He has a metal plate this big in his head!" She held up her hand as a demonstration. "He has a hell of a time getting through airports."

He wasn't sure if she was trying to be funny or not, and attempting to move the conversation to more pleasant topics, Cam smiled. "So what does your father do?"

Elizabeth paused and looked toward the kitchen. "He runs a motorcycle repair shop."

"Really? I've got a bike! Is he a Harley guy?"

"Custom choppers, mostly."

Caleb came into the room with the iced tea loaded with enough sugar to cause diabetic shock. "Hey Dad, did Elizabeth tell you her dad is a biker?" he asked, using the term with deferential reverence in the same way one might use astronaut or secret agent.

Elizabeth shrank back a bit at the revelation.

The information caught Cam off guard, and he was sure his reaction showed it. With a brief delay, he responded with genuine curiousity, "Really? As in biker gang ... uh, club?"

"Yeah," Elizabeth admitted dryly. "The Vagos ... he's getting too old for it though. He's really just a big 'ol teddy bear," she clarified, trying to soften the image. "He has a metal plate in his head, too."

Cam smirked in wonderment. This girl was hilarious, whether she intended to be or not. "Was he a surfer, too?" he asked.

"No ... gunshot, actually," she replied flatly. "A Hell's Angel shot him in the forehead with a .32 a few years ago."

The conversation was becoming awkward. "Is he okay now?" Cam asked, trying to regain a decent level of rapport with his son's new girlfriend.

"Yeah. He's fine. He has a hard head in more ways than one. But his left eye does droop a little bit now." Then exercising diplomatic skills well beyond her age, Elizabeth handed Cam a lifeline. "Caleb told me what you did for a living. Maybe you two could meet one day."

Lifestyles much different from his own had always interested Cam, and the opportunity to gain insight into the outlaw motorcycle gang culture intrigued him. "Yes, I'd like that," Cam answered sincerely. Cam looked down at Elizabeth's pretty, delicate hands and noticed for the first time a capital H tattooed in Gothic script on the back of one hand, and a Gothic A tattooed on the other. Risking yet another awkward moment, Cam pointed to her hands and asked with a bit of fatherly trepidation, "Hell's Angels?"

Elizabeth retracted her hands and glanced over at Caleb.

"Actually Dad, it stands for *Hack Attack*," Caleb replied, smiling sheepishly. "She's one of us."

———

The week went by quickly, and it was soon time for Cam to reconnect with Oscar. He sent Oscar a text, "*Is this afternoon a good time to meet?*"

"*Yes, 3:00 today, back gate,*" came Oscar's reply.

For his return trip, Cam took a different route to Julian. Arriving early, he sat in his car behind Oscar's restaurant and observed his surroundings for several minutes before getting out. There were a few old cars and a battered dumpster but no people. The beat-up old pickup with TJ plates was in a different position. The dust on the windshield had been wiped off and the bad tire inflated. It had apparently been driven. Cam wondered if Oscar had taken it to Mexico recently.

At exactly 3:00, Cam heard the back door of the restaurant squeak open and then detected activity at the back gate to the patio. Cam lifted the gate latch and entered. He greeted Oscar quietly. Oscar relocked the gate and directed Cam to sit across from him in the shade.

"It's good to see you, my friend," Cam said. "What were you able to find out?"

"I have learned much," Oscar said. "As I suspected, the Sinaloa Cartel has formed an alliance with your Arab friends. The cartel is looking to expand its marijuana, cocaine, and methamphetamine markets to Europe, and your Arabs are looking for a good source of heroin. The Arabs have set up a small base of operations in the Baja California town of San Felipe. There are reportedly three Arab strangers living in a beach house near that town."

"Where is San Felipe?"

"San Felipe is on the Baja peninsula on the west coast of the Sea of Cortez about two hours south of the border below Mexicali. It was a sleepy fishing village until it became a tourist resort in recent years. College kids go there for Spring Break now. Its unrestricted access to the Pacific Ocean has also made it an important trafficking route for contraband entering the US."

"Since when did the Sinaloa Cartel become a sponsor of international terrorism?" asked Cam, sarcastically.

"The Sinaloa Cartel has always been a terrorist organization," retorted Oscar sharply, his blood pressure rising. "They do not call themselves the *Blood Alliance* for no reason. What do you call the attack on my house that night? Or the practice of decapitating their rivals? Or the vats of acid that disolve informants to yellow mush?"

Cam nodded in embarrassed agreement.

Oscar continued, "Just because they have not done these things to the norteamericanos does not mean they are not terrorists!"

Cam had obviously hit a sore spot with Oscar, and he immediately regretted making light of the cartel's activities. "You are right, Oscar; I should have spoken differently. I apologize."

The men nodded in mutual understanding.

"Now that their leader El Chapo has been recaptured and extradicted to the US, where he will most certainly be put away for life, extreme elements within the Sinaloa Cartel have declared war on America. Their alliance with The Liberation Brigade is part of their strategy. The cartel believes that a wave of terror within the US might pressure American authorities to reconsider prosecution of their leader," Oscar explained.

"Very interesting. And insightful," Cam said.

Oscar leaned back, slapped both hands on his thighs, and asked, "Now, amigo … what is our plan?"

"Do you know where this house is?" Cam asked.

"There are no addresses in San Felipe. I will have to show you," Oscar said, positioning himself as an essential partner in Cam's cross-border counterterrorism operation.

"Give me a few days. I will be in touch," Cam said, and then he asked, "How did you get this information, my friend?"

Placing one hand on Cam's shoulder, Oscar smirked and stated knowingly, "No hay secretos en Mexico, solo temor a los carteles." Cam's weak Spanish failed him for a moment, so Oscar repeated his response in English, "There are no secrets in Mexico, only fear of the cartels."

11

ON THE DRIVE back from Julian, Cam decided to check on
Caleb in Pacific Beach. As he pulled up to the beach house on
Garnet Avenue, he could hear the music of *The Red Hot Chili
Peppers* playing inside. A blacked-out panhead chopper was
parked on the street out front. Guessing the bike belonged to either
Elizabeth's dad or one of their surfer friends, Cam knocked on the
door with some degree of hesitancy and thought to himself, *Maybe
I should have called first.*

After several loud knocks, a barefoot kid in board shorts
answered the door. Caleb, sitting inside on the sofa next to
Elizabeth, looked up from his laptop just in time to save Cam
from having to introduce himself. "Dad!" he yelled over the music,
"Come on in!"

Cam stepped inside and looked around. Sitting across from
Elizabeth in a side chair was a big, rough-looking dude with a

calico cat in his lap. He tossed the cat casually aside with one enormous hand as he stood up. The guy was huge, at least 6' 5" and a solid 250. His heavily tattooed arms hung from his sleeveless denim vest like a couple of lamp posts. As he stepped into the light from the open door, Cam could see that beneath a shock of dirty hair his left eye drooped. The two men sized each other up a bit as Caleb turned down the music. Then the big man extended his thick grease-stained hand and said, "I'm Angus, Elizabeth's dad. You must be Agent Coppenger."

Cam met Angus' firm grip with one of equal force and, comfortable with the encounter, replied, "The name is Cam, actually. I'm retired now and glad to meet you."

Still holding his grip, the big man continued in a deep voice that had been shredded by years of whiskey and cigarettes, "Elizabeth tells me you saved her life."

Cam glanced down at Elizabeth in surprise. "Well, actually, you can credit Caleb with that. I just showed him what to do," Cam said. "Besides, her injuries weren't really life threatening. She was just in a lot of pain."

"But you put her on your helicopter and got her help," said the big man, still holding a firm grip to Cam's right hand.

Cam's defensive instincts began to creep in. The grip was lasting too long. It's always hard to maintain eye contact with someone with a bad eye, and the big man still had hold of Cam's shooting hand with no apparent intention of letting go. The physical vulnerability was beginning to make Cam uncomfortable. He knew he was being assessed at some primal level, so he tried to relax. To break the grip at that point would have been bad manners.

He shifted his feet for better defensive balance. "I tried to help a lot of people that night," he deflected. Angus never actually said the words *thank you*, but a slight upward twist of his hand before letting go sent a tribal signal of appreciation. At least that's the way Cam read it. A truce had been established. The big man resumed his seat and retrieved a long neck beer bottle sitting on the floor.

Still standing, Cam looked down at Elizabeth. "How are you doing?"

Elizabeth had been working on her laptop and replied with casual deflection, "I'm okay. Doc says at least six weeks in this cast, and then he'll take out the pins."

"What are y'all working on?" Cam asked.

Caleb looked over at Elizabeth, seeking permission before he spoke.

Elizabeth shrugged.

"We're looking into the group that blew up our train," Caleb said.

"What are you talking about?" asked Cam, eyes narrowing.

"Liwa Tahrir," said Caleb. "We umm, *hacked into their system* and are just looking around."

Glancing over at Angus, Cam was not sure how far to take his line of questioning. Cam looked back at Caleb. "What do you mean, hacked into their system?"

"You know, their website and stuff," Caleb explained. "The Liberation Brigade is what they go by. The website is mostly in Arabic unless they are broadcasting to westerners, but Google translator tells us most of what they are talking about."

"Seriously? You are in their secured system now?"

"Yeah, sure," replied Caleb, turning his laptop around with his one good hand so Cam could see the screen. "Elizabeth showed me how. She is top shelf with this stuff."

Cam spoke Arabic better than he could read it, but he recognized The Liberation Brigade's red-and-black logo and saw a collage of graphic photographs depicting the terror attacks in San Diego, DC, and Yuma.

"Do you wanna send them a message?" asked Caleb, a mischievous grin on his face.

Cam looked over at Elizabeth in amazement, then at her father. Angus shrugged and took a swig of beer. "Maybe later, Caleb," said Cam. "You can hack into their system anytime you want … and they can't find you?"

"Pretty much. It takes a little while, but they are not using the newest encryption, so Elizabeth figured out their setup."

"Okay, well, hold that thought, but don't either of you get any smart ideas of contacting them. Understand?"

They nodded in the way kids do when not really listening. Cam recognized that no one in the room had any knowledge of his dealings with the terrorist group. He needed to give the kids a reason for holding off on further action, but not with Angus around.

Angus growled, "If I ever find the guys who did this to my baby girl, they are dead meat!" He finished his beer with a deep belch, then stood up and headed to the kitchen for another long neck. As the huge biker walked away, Cam recognized the green Vagos patch on the back of his vest. He considered Angus' declaration for a moment, quite certain that bikers rarely bluffed. However twisted their motivations sometimes seemed to be, Cam knew that outlaw bikers tended to follow an ancient tribal code of honor that was separate and removed from statutory law. In many ways, Cam felt the same.

———

Over the next several days, an operational plan began to evolve in Cam's head. He called Oscar to explore his options.

"Hola, amigo!" said Oscar when he answered the phone. "Que tal?"

"Bien, bien, amigo," said Cam, neither using his name nor Oscar's over the phone. Then cryptically, "I want to explore some property south of here, tomorrow if possible. Are you available?"

"Absolutely. Tomorrow is good. I will be your guide. We will take my truck. Bring hiking boots, binoculars, your passport, and a pistol if you have one. Pack a bag. We may be there several days."

Early the next morning, Cam and Oscar left San Diego and headed east on I-8 toward El Centro, California. Once there, they turned south toward the Mexican border to Mexicali. With Oscar's truck bearing Tijuana plates and a Mexican driver's license in his new identity, crossing into Mexico was easy going. The authorities hardly noticed, gave a casual glance at Cam's passport, and waved them through. Getting back into the US would be harder. Guns always complicated matters.

"They didn't even check our vehicle," commented Cam.

"Most of the time, they don't care," replied Oscar. "Only the norteamericanos care about smuggling."

From Mexicali, the two retired cops took Highway 5 south for about an hour toward the Sea of Cortez. The landscape was hot and barren. To their right were the mountains of San Pedro Martir, which ran down the center of the Baja California peninsula. On the other side of the mountain range was the coastal town of Ensenada, situated just below Tijuana on the Pacific Ocean. Along the way, random billboards advertised the famous Baja 500 cross-country race.

"Is a Baja race coming up?" Cam asked Oscar.

"Several Baja races," replied Oscar. "They are very popular here. The biggest one is the 500 that starts in Ensenada and loops around here, passes San Felipe, then crosses the mountains back over to Ensenada."

"Have you ever attended a race?"

"I have seen the dust clouds they stir up as the vehicles speed across the desert. And as a young police officer, I searched for the bodies of drivers stranded when their vehicles broke down. The desert is very unforgiving."

As they approached the uppermost tip of the Sea of Cortez, Oscar motioned to an unidentified dirt road on the left, marked by a lone telephone pole sprayed with a band of red paint at eye level. "That road leads to your house of Arabs. We will not stop here, but you will see the house down by the water in a mile or so."

After a few minutes, Oscar pulled to the side of the road. To their left in the distance below them, the Sea of Cortez glimmered in the sun like a vein of turquoise streaked through desert rock.

Against the bleak desolation of the desert, the water shimmered like a gemstone. A lone dirt track ran along the length of the water from the north and ended at a modest two-story stucco house with a red tile roof. A veranda at the back of the house overlooked the water. Beyond the veranda, a long pier stretched well out into the shallow water where an expensive speedboat was moored. Off to one side of the house a thatched-roof shed sheltered some sort of hopped-up dune buggy, the kind that might be used in a Baja race. Parked in front of the house was a dusty blacked-out Ford Explorer.

"This is the house," said Oscar. "My sources say the three Arabs stay here."

Cam looked around at the desolate environment. "How will we establish surveillance and not be detected?"

Oscar glanced to the mountains above them. "When the time is right, we will set up in the mountains there. The caves and abandoned mines will provde good shelter from the sun. You have good binoculars, no? But we must not linger here now."

The men got back in the truck and headed on to San Felipe, located ten miles further south. With the Sierras San Pedro Matir serving as a backdrop, the town of San Felipe was quaint but not impressive. Most of the town was clustered along Highway 5 that ran along the water's edge. A wide sidewalk served as a promenade, and a low concrete seawall separated the beach from the road. Pulled up on the sand below the seawall were rows of wooden fishing boats painted bright colors. The sand was brown and dirt-like, but the water was spectacular. A few high-rise hotels bracketed the town in the distance, but for the most part the town was comprised of low one-and-two story stucco structures with flat roofs. At one time, the diminutive buildings had been painted in bright primary colors, but layers of dirt and grime subdued their formerly brilliant hues.

In the town's center was the popular Hotel Dolphin, San Felipe's oldest and most reputable establishment on the beach, known among tourists for its lively night life. Oscar pulled his old truck up to a space in front of the hotel.

"Shouldn't we pick a place that's less conspicuous?" Cam asked.

"We can gather the most information here," said Oscar, as he reached behind the seat and grabbed his bag. "There will be many loose tongues in the Dolphin bar tonight." Oscar took note of Cam's hesitation at staying in such a public location. "Relax, amigo. I am hiding you in plain sight. You are simply a tourist in a tourist town. Or maybe you are a fisherman … or a Baja racer. Trust me, I know about hiding in the open."

Against his training and instincts, Cam yielded to his partner's strategy. This was Oscar's territory and his people. Still, it didn't feel right.

The lobby of the old three-story hotel was dated but clean. Decorated in the traditional Spanish style with heavy dark wood, thick velveteen curtains, wrought iron fixtures, and Tuscan red tile, the lobby provided a cool respite from the blazing sun outside. A few Hispanic men sat idly in ornate chairs positioned around the perimeter. One fit young man was reading a paper. Others in the lobby seemed to be avoiding the mid-day sun. The registration desk was on the right. A bar already filled with patrons was to the left. At the corner of the bar was a prostitute in heels and tight clothes. She had lost her figure years ago, but her heavily painted face indicated she had refused to acknowledge the realities of aging. In the center of the lobby an indoor fountain bubbled recirculated water over colorful blue and yellow tiles. Straight ahead, stairs ascended to the upper floors. There was no elevator. Checking in at the front desk, Oscar asked for a room with two beds on the top floor. He gave the clerk a bogus name, and no additional questions were asked. Cam paid for the room in US Dollars.

Once in the room, Cam pulled the covers back on one of the well-used beds, lifted the mattress, and checked for bed bugs. Reasonably satisfied, he tossed his canvas bag in a chair, removed his pistol from its concealed holster, and collapsed on the squeaky bed without removing his boots. He wasn't accustomed to the intense mid-day heat, and the drive had been rough on his still-sore ribs.

Oscar, taking the other bed, shook his head and chuckled. "Gringos," he mumbled, as he changed into a fresher shirt. "Take your siesta, my friend. I will let you rest while I go out for a few hours. Meet me in the lobby around four o'clock, and we will have an early dinner."

"Where are you going?" asked Cam.

Oscar stopped at the door, turned, and replied, "Someplace you cannot go, my friend. I think you gringos call it *plausible deniability*."

Cam's siesta passed quickly. He awoke with a foggy recollection of where he was and checked the time. Almost 1600. He showered quickly, rewrapped his ribcage, and returned his 9mm to its holster, which he then covered with a clean untucked shirt. Still groggy from his sleep, Cam descended the stairs and entered the hotel lobby. As he approached the fountain, Cam glanced to his left and noticed a gaggle of men gathered at the registration desk. His grogginess evaporated as he sensed something was out of place. The men were not tourists, nor were they police, yet they were intensely questioning the desk clerk. Cam's agent instincts kicked in. He stopped to evaluate the scene for a moment. Even with their backs turned, he could tell that three of the men were dark but not Hispanic. They all had bulges in various locations around their waists, indicating they were armed. The clerk they were talking to looked up from their discussion, then jutted his chin pointedly in Cam's direction. Two of the group turned and looked at Cam, and when they did, their casual posture shifted to a more alert status. Then the others turned. Cam recognized their reaction, and it was not a friendly one. They had been specifically asking the clerk about *him*, and Cam sensed danger. In a crisis, Cam knew from experience that time always seemed to slow down for the participants, and that is exactly what happened in the lobby. Normally, his first reflex would have been to seek cover, but in this instance, his instinct was to discern the intent of the potential adversaries in front of him. Cam went into hyper-agent mode. Like a scene in a wild-west saloon, he counted them as five and mentally noted the nine rounds in his 9mm Shield. He estimated their distance to be thirty feet. Cam had encountered multiple adversaries at close range before—two rounds to each of three targets' center body mass in less than five seconds—but he had never encountered five targets before. Not in the open without cover. Five would be a challenge. He assessed that all nine rounds would have to count, as he didn't carry an extra magazine. Cam's government-issued Sig had carried fourteen rounds, and for a split second, he regretted not sticking with a 228 in retirement. Amazing what stupid thoughts enter one's mind at such times, and Cam mentally dope-slapped himself at his lapse. Then with computer-like precision, he adjusted his calculation, deciding he would sweep each of the targets with single hits first, then come back and hit three of the most dangerous targets a second time, saving a final round for Murphy's Law. He would move laterally to his right, toward the fountain, making himself a more difficult target while seeking cover. His missing partner never entered his mind. As far as he was concerned, it was just himself and five bad guys.

For a few seconds that seemed like an eternity, the lobby stood still. The hotel clerk had witnessed deadly shootouts in hotel lobbies before, and he ducked behind the counter. Somebody in the bar behind Cam knocked over a glass that shattered as it hit the floor, but Cam never flinched. Three of the five bad guys did. Knowing he had to first prioritize the adversaries who posed the greatest threat—either in attitude or firepower—Cam scanned the group, identifying the two men who hadn't flinched, Mexican cartel gunslingers probably. They looked like killers. The other three must be the Palestinians. One of the cartel guys had a pistol tucked sloppily in his belt. Cam thought, *Good, they were poorly trained.* He suspected they were also one-handed shooters, maybe even Hollywood sideways shooters if he was lucky, giving him yet another advantage. Then he looked for the leader. He noticed two of the Palestinians with wild, scared eyes glance over to the younger man in the middle, which didn't make sense. He was not much older than Caleb, but he was definitely their leader. In a reaction that was not planned but purely instinctual, Cam stared directly at the young terrorist and communicated non-verbally but quite clearly that he would be Cam's first target. The young man shifted his weight insecurely. His eyes and body language indicated that he was not mentally prepared for a gunfight. The tension permeated the lobby like a bad odor. *So this is what a Mexican standoff is like*, Cam thought, bracing himself for combat.

Then, as if on cue, Oscar entered the hotel. His position was to the side and a bit behind Cam's adversaries. *Excellent timing!* thought Cam, not even knowing for sure that Oscar was armed. *Now we now have a tactical advantage.*

Stopping at the lobby entrance, Oscar spotted Cam immediately, but it took him a second to recognize the threat. Oscar's smile quickly became a sobering glare. Realizing Cam's situation, Oscar smartly introduced a second timely distraction. Placing his shooting hand under his shirt, he called out to Cam, "Yo, amigo, do we have a problem? Our vehicle is outside, and we are late!"

Violating the first rule of close quarter combat, all five adversaries turned in unison and looked at Oscar. They had taken their eyes off their target. For a split second, Cam was tempted to draw his pistol and open fire. He was confident he could hit all five at least once before any of them had a chance to reacquire an effective sight picture. But he now realized he had a less dangerous option, so he hesitated. Even though Oscar's entrance had put them at a tactical disadvantage, the five men looked relieved that the tension had been broken. With one well-thought question, Oscar had insightfully given them a way out of their predicament.

As the men disjointedly turned their eyes back to Cam, he

looked at the young leader of the group again, and with a lift of his eyebrows and pivot of his chin, he nonverbally repeated Oscar's question, *Well, do we have a problem*? Cam was ready to rumble, and the bad guys knew it. The young terrorist glanced sideways and away, breaking eye contact. The two cartel guys shifted their weight as well, sending an unintended signal of detente. And just like that, the crisis was averted.

With another timely command, Oscar called out, "Vamonos, let's go!"

Cam used the opportunity to move cautiously across the lobby toward the door, never taking his eyes off *his* targets. Cam and Oscar exited quietly, and the entire lobby breathed a barely perceptible but unified sigh of relief.

As Cam and Oscar pulled calmly away from the hotel in their truck, the retired police chief asked his partner, "What was that all about?"

"Somebody must have been watching us at the hotel and alerted our terrorists."

"Mexico has many eyes and many ears. Perhaps we should not have stayed at The Dolphin. Someone must have recognized me. And you still look like an *agent*, you know."

"What does *that* mean?" asked Cam, visibly perturbed that his partner had put them in such a vulnerable position.

"You gringo federales all look the same," he said casually, as if a scientific study had been conducted on the issue. "Shall we go back for our bags?" he asked with a mischievous grin.

"No. I don't need my toothbrush, and we have tempted fate enough today, don't you think? But now that we've identified our terrorists, and we know they are not at home, let's find a good surveillance spot for their safehouse. Then we can head home. This gringo federale has had enough excitement for the day."

As Cam's adrenaline rush subsided, fatigue set in, and he stole a moment to evaluate what had just happened. Throughout his twenty-six-year career, Cam had always responded to every dangerous situation with calm and calculated professionalism. The incident in the hotel lobby was no different. Five to one had been tough odds. It was unclear what his adversaries' specific intentions were in the lobby, but the element of surprise had caught them off guard, and he had taken full advantage of it. Having a partner helped. The confrontation had lasted only a few seconds, but the incident was a reminder for Cam that when confronted with danger his nature was to react with focused confidence—win, lose, or draw. While he was satisfied to find his basic agent skills still intact as far as the Dolphin incident was concerned, Cam was happy with a draw. Live to fight another day.

As their truck approached the terrorists' safehouse, Oscar slowed and then turned left onto a rutted dirt road that led up into the mountains overlooking the Sea of Cortez. There were no road signs and many forks, but Oscar seemed to know where he was going. About midway up the mountain, Oscar stopped the truck at a sagging metal gate and instructed Cam to open it. Once through the gate, they came to a flat clearing scattered with old broken timbers and twisted scraps of iron. A rusted mining car had been pushed off to the side. Surrounding the area were enough boulders and scrub brush to hide the truck from passing traffic on the highway below. Beyond the highway in the distance was the blue

Cortez, sparkling in the late afternoon sun, and sitting at its edge was the terrorists' safehouse.

"This is a good spot," said Oscar. "The sun is at our backs and in their eyes, and we have good cover among the rocks and the brush. With good binoculars, we should have a clear view of the house."

Cam suddenly remembered that he had left his binoculars in his bag at the hotel. "Dammit," he cursed. Those Nikons were the best pair he had ever owned. The hotel probably has them now … or maybe the terrorists. And his fingerprints would be all over them. "Ugh … sloppy work, Coppenger," Cam mumbled to himself. Surveying the landscape below him, Cam inquired of his partner, "Hey Oscar, how good are the Mexicans at analyzing fingerprints?"

Reading Cam's mind, Oscar said, "If you are talking about your fingerprints, my friend, not very good. They would not have your prints in their database, and it is unlikely they would go to the trouble of sending them to Washington or INTERPOL unless a serious crime has been committed, and you have commited no crime, amigo." Pausing, Oscar added with a smile, "You paid your hotel bill, did you not?"

After a few minutes, a black Ford Explorer passed below them headed north on the highway. "If those are our terrorists, they will have to drive up another mile to the turnoff, then come back down the coastal road to the safehouse. You should see them at the house in about five minutes," Oscar said.

"How do you know these details?"

Oscar grinned. "That house has been used by the Sinaloa Cartel for many years, and I have surveilled it before from this location."

Cam was impressed with Oscar's knowledge of the area and was glad to have him as a partner. Oscar's value as a guide somewhat made up for his disasterous decision to stay at The Dolphin.

Approximately five minutes later, just as Oscar had predicted, the black Ford Explorer came southward down the dusty coastal road and parked in front of the safehouse. Using an old cheap pair of binoculars Oscar provided, Cam saw three men exit the vehicle, the same men he had encountered in the hotel lobby. He noted that one walked with a significant limp as they entered the house.

The sun was beginning to set behind the mountains, and both men were hungry. In spite of the excitement at the Dolphin, their first mission together had been successful. They decided to call it a day and retreated back into the truck. It was still dusk, and Oscar was able to descend the mountain without using the truck's headlights. Shifting the truck into its lowest gear, he used the brake lights judiciously, not wanting to reveal their presence to curious eyes.

By the time they arrived to the San Ysidro Port of Entry (SYPOE) at Tijuana, it was dark. Processing over thirty-three million individual crossings each year, SYPOE was a much busier port than El Centro where they had entered, but Oscar advised Cam he had additional business in Mexico and would not be returning to the US quite yet. At SYPOE, Cam could cross back into the US on foot and take the trolly into San Diego.

"What about my firearm? I'm not supposed to have one in Mexico."

"No worries." Oscar pulled down a narrow alley on the outskirts of Tijuana and into a vacant lot not far from the pedestrian entrance at the border. At the edge of the dimly lit lot, a massive metal border fence separated Mexico from the US. A few dusty vehicles were parked randomly in the lot. Oscar reached behind the seat of his truck and retrieved a used Burger King bag. He opened the bag, popped a couple of stale leftover French fries into his mouth, and instructed Cam to place his 9mm inside the brown paper bag. "Is the safety on?" Oscar smirked.

"Always," replied Cam, somewhat perplexed.

Oscar wrapped the gun inside the bag, stepped out of his truck, and walked to the border fence. Looking both ways, he casually tossed the bag over the fence, as if it were a piece of trash, and then walked back to his truck. "After you have gone through security, come and retrieve your weapon. I will keep an eye on it until you return."

"What the hell, Oscar! What did you just do with my gun?"

"Relax, amigo. The bad guys do it all the time, and they never get caught! I told you I'd keep an eye on it."

Cam spent an hour getting through border-crossing procedures. Once clear, he walked to the spot where Oscar had tossed his gun and retrieved it. In the dim light of the parking lot, he looked through the fence to see Oscar snoozing behind the wheel, hat pulled down over his eyes.

"Adios, amigo!" called Cam, alerting his partner to his presence. Oscar sat up, waved, and started his truck. "Where are you going?" Cam asked.

"Plausible deniability!" said Oscar, grinning as he turned his truck around and headed back into the seedy part of Tijuana.

12

SAFELY BACK IN his motel room in San Diego, Cam showered and ordered pizza from Filippi's in Little Italy. As he feasted on some of the best pizza in town, seeing the historic restaurant's name on the pizza box prompted him to think about the Mexican town of San Felipe and how best to neutralize the threat posed by three active terrorists sheltered just across the border but allied with a powerful and vicious criminal cartel that both protected them and supported their operations. Cam had no legal authority nor did he have any real law enforcement resources at his disposal. He was just one guy with a partner who had access to a little intelligence. Cam thought about notifying Sid, his FBI contact, and letting the JTTF follow official channels to coordinate a joint Mexican/US operation to arrest the terrorists. Then he contemplated the rampant corruption within the Mexican Government that would undoubtedly alert the cartel, and in turn the terrorists, before the plan could get off the ground. No, relying on the government with its agendas, political restrictions, and conflicts of interests was not the answer—not in Cam's mind. Then it hit him like a ton of bricks: a cross-border solution made to order.

Cam awoke early the next morning, dressed, and drove his rental car to Imperial Beach. He found a coffee shop near a beach-front park and ordered a breakfast burrito. Sitting outside on another perfectly gorgeous California day, Cam googled *motorcycle repair shops* on his smart phone, then clicked on *Imperial Beach Choppers*. The business had a professional website indicating its hours of operation and directions to the shop. The owner was listed as Angus *Hoss* Cartwright. Elizabeth's fingerprints were all over the well-designed website. According to Google Maps, the business address was not far away. Cam then googled *Vagos Motorcycle Club* and read an assessment of the criminal biker gang. The report indicated that the Vagos were a diverse group, having both Anglo and Latino members with club chapters located on both sides of the border. Allied with the more well-known Mongols outlaw motorcycle gang, the Vagos were based in San Bernadino, California, and were fierce rivals to the Hell's Angels. The Vagos, known also as the Green Nation, had multiple chapters in Mexico, including Tijuana and Mexicali. *Interesting*, Cam thought to himself as he put away his phone.

Cam thought about calling Angus first, but he suspected that his motorcycle repair shop would be well-known to area law enforcement, and there was a strong likelihood that the business phone was tapped. He decided a cold call was his best option. Cam finished his burrito, downed his coffee, then steeled himself for an

unannounced meeting with an outlaw motorcycle gang member
he had met only once. He easily found the address and pulled
into the converted gas station. Angus' blacked-out chopper was
parked to one side of the building. Cam walked over to the open
garage door. The heavy metal band *Def Leppard* was blaring on
a boombox somewhere in the background. Inside the garage was
dark compared to the bright morning sun outside, but Cam could
see it was filled with an array of old motorcycle frames, various
parts, and used tires. A welding torch flashed blinding light in the
back corner of the garage, ricocheting off the ceiling like staggered
flash-bang explosions.

Cam called out over the music, "Hello!" No response. He called
out again, shouting this time, "HEY!" Then the jagged lightning
of the torch went dark, the hissing acetylene gas went silent, and a
big man stood up. Cam's eyes were still adjusting to the dark, but as
the man lifted the welder's mask from his face, Cam could see his
drooping left eye.

Angus' expression revealed no recognition. "Yeah?"

"Cam Coppenger, Caleb's dad!" Cam called out. "Got a minute?"

Angus emerged from the shadows, pulling thick heavy gloves
from his massive hands, his expression still revealing nothing.
"Yeah?" he asked again, setting the gloves down but not offering to
shake Cam's hand.

"I have some information you might be interested in." Cam said.

"Yeah?" Angus repeated, his mind preoccupied with the fact that
a retired Fed had just invaded his territory without an invite. There
was not a hint of politeness in his tone or mannerisms.

Cam was beginning to wonder if he had made a mistake. Cam

sensed he needed to do something quickly to ease the tension, so he moved forward with his conversation, "The other day you mentioned that you wanted to find the men who hurt your daughter."

Angus said nothing, but his eyes narrowed, and his chin lifted imperceptibly.

Cam continued, "The Vagos have chapters in Mexico, do they not?"

Again, the big man acknowledged nothing, his eyes assessing Cam like a wild predator about to strike. After a moment, Angus responded in a voice that sounded like it had been filtered through gravel. "I'm listening."

Several days passed. South of the border at the Sinaloa safehouse located on the outskirts of San Felipe, Abdullah Khalidi had just gotten out of his morning shower when he heard an unusual noise outside. The barrel-bodied Mexican prostitute he had procured the night before at the hotel was still sound asleep, snoring sloppily. The outside noise grew louder, eventually becoming a chorus of deep grumbling engines revving discordantly as if a race were about to start. *Surely they are not having a Baja race today*, Abdullah thought to himself. There is no race scheduled … a practice run, maybe? From his upstairs bedroom window, he looked west toward the mountains and saw nothing. Then he looked out the opposite window toward the water and saw

Yousef and Ramzi on the boat dock scurrying quickly back toward the house. The earlier gunshot wound to Yousef's leg prevented him from moving very well, and Ramzi was trying to help him, but there was panic in their movements. The young Palestinian then went to the north window and finally saw the cause of the disturbance. In the distance was a massive cloud of dust heading down the access road toward the house. *Motorcycles?* Abdullah thought. *They don't race motorcycles in the Baja, not those kind of motorcycles, anyway! It didn't make sense. Maybe they were lost?* But as the dust cloud grew closer, Abdullah could see the riders were in gang attire. Something was very, very wrong. Throwing on trousers without underwear, Abdullah grabbed his pistol and raced down the stairs just in time to see a massive number of bikers in green colors pull into the drive and begin to surround the house. Ramzi and Yousef were just approaching the veranda when Abdullah glanced at them fearfully, then slammed the patio door shut and locked it. Unarmed, the brothers had not yet comprehended the extent of Abdullah's betrayal. They paused at the door, contemplating their options. Abdullah raced back upstairs in a mindless panic. All he could think about was escaping. At the south end of the house, a low wall and ditch had prevented the bikers from completely surrounding it, but they had gathered on three sides en masse, and began to rev their big Harley engines in a thunderous clamor that rattled glass and made it impossible to communicate. The sound was intimidating and terrifying. The prostitute, now wide awake amid the commotion, screamed in terror, but Abdullah couldn't hear her; the revving engines drowned her out. Terrified, Abdullah threw open the window farthest from the bikers. Barefoot and shirtless, he lowered himself down onto the roof of the porch, breaking several tiles and losing his pistol as he slid his way to the edge and leapt down to the ground. Three of the bikers, seeing Abdullah's attempted escape, dismounted their bikes to pursue him on foot.

Abdullah raced painfully across the hard rocky ground to the shelter covering his dune buggy. He jumped in the seat and pushed the starter button. It whizzed dryly. He pushed it again, and the engine grumbled. Praying to Allah, he pushed it a third time, and the Baja racer finally roared into life. Throwing the vehicle in gear, Abdullah accelerated forward out of the shed, recklessly catching a supporting post with his big rear wheel, pulling the structure down behind him. The collapsed structure and clouds of dust served somewhat as a cover for his escape, but as Abdullah raced south across the rough open terrain, a bullet pinged against the steel roll bar near his head. Abdullah was dazed, scared, and confused as he attempted to put as much distance as he could between him and that gang of bikers. His mind was spinning. What was going on? Who were those men? Had the cartel put out a hit on him? Had his father's alliance with the cartel collapsed? Had he been double-crossed? Was it the CIA? Abdullah had many questions and no answers. As the safehouse faded in the distance behind him, the only thing the young terrorist knew for sure was that he desperately wanted to get the hell out of Mexico.

Later that evening, Cam had just sat down to a dinner of fish tacos with Caleb and Elizabeth at the surfers' beach house when Cam's phone rang. It was his buddy Sid from the FBI. Cam excused himself and stepped outside to take the call.

"Hey Sid, what's up?"

"Cop, we just got word that two Middle-Eastern males have been found dead on the steps of a hotel down in Mexico. They had been dragged through the streets by a gang of bikers. The bodies had very little flesh left on them. They must have been dragged a considerable distance before they were deposited at the hotel. Witnesses say the biker gang was the Vagos. Do you know anything about this?"

"This is the first I've heard of the incident," Cam said somewhat truthfully. "Only two bodies? Where did this happen?"

"Two bodies have been found so far," Sid advised. "The hotel was called The Dolphin, located in a small fishing village named San Felipe on the Sea of Cortez."

"Do you think the Middle Easterners were members of The Liberation Brigade?"

"We don't know for sure at this point. But my guess is yes. We just need to find out who did this and why."

"There are very few secrets in Mexico," Cam advised. "Keep me posted, Sid, will you?" As he made the request, Cam reached into his pocket and touched the small wooden baseball bat he had been carrying with him every day since the train crash.

"Will do," replied Sid. Then he added, "Something big must be going on down in Mexico, Cop. We also received information that a former Tijuana police chief who happened to be in the DOJ witness protection program was somehow involved in a shootout with multiple members of the Sinaloa Cartel earlier today. According to reports, he must have had a death wish. Like something out of the old west, he just walked into a known cartel hangout and started shooting the place up. They eventually killed him, but he took eight bad guys with him. Must have been one tough hombre."

Stunned by this news, Cam was barely able to respond. His voice choked with emotion, Cam whispered in return, "Yeah, sounds like it." The strength in his legs suddenly evaporated, and Cam sat down hard on the steps of the beach house. His friend and partner was dead, and Cam knew why. Tijuana Police Chief Roberto Menendez, one of the few honest cops in Mexico, died following an ancient code of honor that for the most part was lost to the modern world. For just a moment, Cam's heart swelled with respect … and then exploded in mournful sorrow.

13

STILL STUNNED AT the news of his friend's death, Cam walked back inside the beach house and looked at both Caleb and Elizabeth. His voice sinking to a simmering growl, he announced, "I need you kids to send a message to The Liberation Brigade."

Caleb had heard that tone in his father's voice before, and he knew his father was deadly serious.

Glancing over at Elizabeth, Caleb whispered under his breath, "You know what Dad did for a living, right?"

Elizabeth nodded her head.

"Well, it's about to get major radical. Are you up for it?"

Elizabeth nodded again.

Then Cam asked the most important question, "Can you keep a secret?"

Elizabeth looked first at Caleb, then at Cam with a serious expression of her own. She pursed her lips tightly and nodded solemnly. She had been keeping secrets with her outlaw biker dad her whole life. She understood the implications.

"Good," Cam said. "But I need you guys to do exactly as I say, no more, no less ... understood?"

They both nodded.

"What is your message?" asked Caleb.

Cam found a scrap of paper and wrote it out. "*Two down, more to come. Crowbar.*"

Caleb looked at the piece of paper. "What is Crowbar?" he asked, thinking it was some secret operational codename.

"Don't worry about it. Just send those exact words. Can you do it today?"

"Absolutely!" said Elizabeth, motioning for Caleb to retrieve her laptop. "Piece of cake."

———

Early the next morning, half a world away, a member of the Liwa Tahrir intelligence wing knocked on the door of Kalid Khalidi's Beirut hideout. When Ismail answered the door, the messenger handed him a note written in Arabic. The message reported that two members of The Liberation Brigade had been savagely murdered in Mexico.

"Who was killed?" asked the terrorist leader, fearing the worst.

"Our martyred brothers, Ramzi and Yousef," advised the messenger.

"And my son?" Ismail asked, somewhat relieved.

"We believe Abdullah escaped, but we haven't heard from him."

"What happened?" asked Ismail.

"Their safehouse was attacked by an OMG from America," explained the messenger.

"A what?" asked Ismail, not fully understanding what an OMG was.

"A criminal gang of outlaws who ride motorcycles," the messenger explained. "The cartel tells us they are very common in America, and ruthless. They dragged our brothers through the streets with their motorcycles while they were still alive."

"But why?" probed Ismail, trying to make sense of the situation.

"The Mexicans do not know," advised the messenger. "They are as confused as we are. The cartels usually have strong business relationships with the motorcycle gangs, and rely on them for drug distribution and protection in America."

"Yet the cartel could not protect our men?" Ismail asked.

"There were many motorcycles in the attack! An entire army!"

Ismail was confused. He was not familiar with American motorcycle gangs, although he had seen the movie *Easy Rider* some years ago. "Get me more information! Find out what our Hezbollah brethren in Dearborn know, and find out where Abdullah is!"

The messenger acknowledged the order, then hesitated before providing one last bit of information. "There is one other thing, commander."

"What is it?" demanded Ismail, bracing himself for more bad news.

"Our website was invaded with a broadcast message this evening. We were hacked."

"What did the message say?"

"*Two down, more to come. Crowbar.*"

"What is Crowbar?" inquired Ismail, growing increasingly irritated.

"We don't know," admitted Ismail's intelligence man. "In English, crowbar is defined as a curved iron bar used to pry things open. It is also used in American slang as a weapon for self-defense."

"Well, find out who or what Crowbar is … and find Abdullah!" he ordered, slamming the door in the face of the messenger. By slamming the door, Ismail intended to show strength, but once the door was closed, what he really felt was deep concern.

———

Later that day, Cam called his FBI contact in Washington. When Sid Lewis answered, Cam asked him, "Have you heard anything more about the attacks in Mexico?"

"We are still investigating, Cop, but our legal attaché in Mexico City believes the victims were the same guys who hit the Amtrak train. There were supposed to be three terrorist cell members hiding in Mexico, so we believe the third must have escaped." Sid paused and then asked Cam, "Are you sure you don't know anything about this?"

"Just what you've told me, Sid." Cam felt a hint of guilt for not being completely honest with his friend.

"That doesn't really answer my question, Cop." Senior Supervisory Special Agent Sid Lewis was an experienced investigator. He, better than most, understood that how a question was worded was key to getting to the truth. So this time, he asked Cam a direct yes or no question. "Cop, did you have anything to do with the death of those two terrorists?"

By asking the question in such a way, Sid had given his former task force member very little wiggle room. Cam took a moment to formulate his response. He didn't want to break the trust of his friend, but he also didn't want to expose his friend to risk should the details of the San Felipe operation come to light. By keeping him in the dark, he was protecting him. And it was not just Sid who needed cover. Kate, Caleb, Elizabeth, even Angus were all connected to Cam's bizzare counter-terrorist operation in one way or another. There was also the memory of Roberto to take into consideration, the safety of his family, *and* the viability of the DOJ's Witness Protection Program. Still, trust was critical in his line of work, and intelligence sharing was a two-way street. Moreover, Cam was well aware he might require FBI assistance in the future. So he answered Sid's question in a way he hoped would be truthful and informative yet protect the sources and methods of his operation.

"Maybe," Cam replied. Then he assured his friend, "And I am reasonably confident that the cross-border terrorism threat has been neutralized." Cam finished his response with a bureaucratic curve ball, "We are on an unsecured line, you know. I'll need to brief you later." By introducing the need for secure communications, Cam had used government bureaucracy to his own advantage. But he had also provided Sid the critical information he needed, and that satisfied him for the time being.

Cam couldn't see it, but Sid was shaking his head in disbelief on the other end of the phone line. "You are one slick son of a gun, Agent Coppenger. I'll be on the West Coast next week, and I will expect a full *secure* briefing from you at that time. Meanwhile, I'll let the Director know your professional assessment is that the threat has been addressed." Cam heard considerable exasperation in Sid's voice as his friend hung up.

You mean 'retired' Agent Coppenger, Cam thought to himself as he put his phone away. And then his phone rang again. "Uh oh," Cam reacted, looking at Kate's number. *She wants to know what happened to her protected witness.* That was not a discussion he was prepared to have just yet. Cam sent the call to voicemail.

⎯⎯⎯⎯

One week later, Cam agreed to meet with FBI Joint Terrorism Task Force leader Sid Lewis in San Diego. The site Cam chose was a memorial park located right in the middle of Little Italy. The park was named in honor of US Marine Gunnery Sergeant John Basilone, an Italian-American hero of the World War II battle for Guadalcanal and Medal of Honor recipient. After Guadalcanal, Basilone could have spent the rest of the war stateside, out of harm's way, healing from his injuries, participating in bond drives, and training young Marines for combat. He had done his part. But Basilone and others like him lived by a different code. Basilone volunteered to return to combat in the Pacific. Sadly, he was killed by enemy fire soon after landing at Iwo Jima.

As Sid approached the designated meeting place, he could see his friend standing in front of the bronze bust of Basilone. Cam was staring intently into the eyes of the statue, taking full measure of the medals and the metal of the man memorialized before him. "Hello Cop!" Sid called out, interrupting Cam's train of thought. "Good to see you!"

Cam turned, and they shook hands vigorously.

It was another gorgeous winter day in California, so Cam suggested they walk down India Street as they talked. "What brings you to the West Coast?" asked Cam, already knowing the reason for Sid's visit.

"You, primarily," advised Sid. "The Director is all over my ass to find out about your operation, but I will also be meeting with our LEGATT agent at the embassy in Mexico City later this week."

Cam glanced around before responding. "It wasn't really my operation, Sid. My plan maybe, but not my operation. I simply provided some information to an outlaw motorcycle gang, and they conducted the operation."

"But why a biker gang of all things? What's the connection?"

"The terrorists made the mistake of targeting an OMG family member. Everybody knows you don't mess with a biker's family."

"The Amtrak attack?"

Cam paused before responding. He knew the FBI had the resources to thoroughly investigate the background of every victim of the train wreck, and through link analysis they would eventually be able to associate Elizabeth with the Vagos. "Sid, in the interest of protecting sources and methods, I need you to back off on the specifics of the who and the how. Just know that the terrorists picked the wrong group to mess with and paid a severe price for it. Justice has been served."

"Fair enough, but what about the Mexican police officer who was in our Witness Protection program?"

Still grieving over the loss of his friend, Cam paused again and looked around cautiously before continuing. "Sid, I need you to back off of that one, too. He was one of my confidential sources, and I need his identity protected. I was not part of that operation in Mexico. His actions against the cartel were completely unknown to me, but I believe justice was served in that instance as well. To my knowledge, no US laws were broken. He still has family in the WP program, and I want them protected."

"Understood," replied Sid. "I doubt the Mexicans knew anything about the circumstances of his relocation to the US anyway." After walking a block or so in complete silence, Sid slowly put the missing puzzle pieces together. His mind still churning, Sid asked, "So what next?"

"You mentioned one of the terrorists might have escaped?"

"Yes, it appears that one of Ismail's sons was the leader of The Liberation Brigade's cell in Mexico. Our intelligence indicates he survived the OMG attack and has returned to Lebanon."

"Ismail's son? How?" Cam asked.

"Hezbollah has a solid base of operations in the tri-border region of Brazil, Paraguay, and Bolivia, and their tentacles reach throughout South and Central America. We suspect Hezbollah facilitated the son's return to Beirut as a favor to Ismail."

Cam was well aware of Hezbollah's presence in the lawless tri-border region and their involvement in smuggling, money laundering, and espionage there. It was a little-known fact that an estimated 25,000 Arabs had relocated to the tri-border region, many involved in smuggling drugs, guns, cigarettes, even cattle. The FBI believed that one of its *Most Wanted* fugitives, Hezbollah commander Imad Mugniyah, had operated out of Ciudad del Este, Paraguay, for a period of time. In the early nineties, Mugniyah was believed to have been involved in two attacks against Jewish targets in Argentina. In 1992, a car bomb at the Israeli Embassy in Buenos Aires killed twenty-nine people. In 1994, a suicide bomber at the Argentine/Israeli Mutual Association killed eighty-five people. INTERPOL and the FBI both linked Hezbollah and Iran to the 1994 attack as retaliation for Argentina's suspension of nuclear cooperation with Iran. Sid's assessment made sense.

"Whatever happened to Mugniyah, anyway?" Cam asked, well aware that the Hezbollah operative was believed to have been the planner for the 1983 bombings of the US Embassy and Marine Barracks in Beirut.

"He was killed in 2008 in Syria. Israel's Mossad, in possible collusion with our CIA, put a bomb in the spare tire of his vehicle and blew him to pieces."

"You've got to give the Israelis credit. They are cunning, and they are good at what they do."

Sid nodded in agreement.

Moving the conversation back to The Liberation Brigade, Cam asked, "So our job is not finished?"

"Not when it comes to terrorism. Terrorists are like termites, if you don't get the queen, the nest keeps growing."

"Sounds like a return visit to Beirut may be in order."

"That would be a reasonable assumption. Come back to the task force, and we'll see that you are well-positioned within the embassy … with strong White House backing this time, I promise you."

"Not a chance, Sid. I'm done working for the government."

Sid paused, obviously disappointed. Then he probed deeper, "But are you done serving your country?"

"I don't have an answer for that yet. I make no excuses. It's mostly personal for me now. But I may need your help, Sid … off the record, of course. Are you good with that?"

"Absolutely, Cop. You are a patriot and a team member, whether you are on the books or not."

"Standby to standby then." Cam turned to walk away. "I'll keep you posted."

"There's one other thing you should know," Sid called out. "Our cyber guys intercepted an encrypted message sent in English to The Liberation Brigade. We're not sure who sent it, but contained within the message was the term *Crowbar*. We learned from your task force members that you used the code name Crowbar while assigned to Beirut. If we were able to figure that out relatively quickly, there is a good chance Ismail will, too."

"Good," Cam retorted, still walking away. Then he stopped and turned back toward Sid, adding, "I want Ismail to know he is in my crosshairs. I want him looking over his shoulder every day. He has grown too comfortable in his protected little refugee camp. It's time for him to become *uncomfortable*."

14

A WEEK LATER, Cam was back in Beirut. Passing through Lebanese customs at BIA without embassy assistance was slow and tedious. As a common citizen, Cam was unarmed. He rented a car at the airport and drove to the Commodore Hotel where he used a portion of his boat insurance money to pay for a week in advance. With the Syrian civil war raging just across the border, the Commodore was still packed with journalists from all over the world.

Cam ordered room service and ate alone in his hotel room. Jet lagged and unable to sleep, he ventured down to the hotel bar packed with half-lit professional story-tellers exchanging war stories. The ratio of men to women in the bar was at least 12:1. The limited number of attractive female reporters, each striving to be taken seriously, were surrounded by gaggles of male reporters, each competing to win the room key raffle. Among journalists, the best bar scar stories scored bonus points, but the truth was, the producers had the best shot at winning the raffles. They were the ones who controlled the assignments, resources, and airtime. For ambitious, attractive female reporters trying to establish a reputation as a serious journalist, the scales always seemed to be weighted in favor of the producers. Unfortunately, half the successful producers were women ... at least among western news agencies. There were exceptions to the producers-first rule, of course. Heading the short list in every war/disaster zone were a few famous journalists, usually men, whose names and faces were recognized worldwide for their brave demonstrations of *daring and caring*. Throughout his career, Cam had observed these glorified news readers drop into a war zone or disaster scene and be handed a script by the producer, who then rumpled his freshly pressed Royal Robins safari jacket and touseled his hair a bit for authenticity just before airtime. Then acting as if he had just come from the front, the famous reporter would deliver a perfectly worded and heartfelt eulogy on the plight of some victim caught between a rock and a hard place. These dandies were the rock stars of international journalism, and if their reputations preceeded them sufficiently, they were often awarded a reserved table in the corner of the hotel bar where only invited guests were allowed to sit basking at the feet of the master. In reality, during his twenty-six years with the State Department, Cam had saved more superstar reporter butt than he cared to remember. Reporters were always stumbling into dangerous situations: villages overrun by rebels, hijacked airplanes, hostage situations, natural disasters, sexual assaults, or simply finding themselves in the wrong place at the wrong time. It was always something, and they all needed help at some point in their overseas ventures. In Cam's experience, DSS agents were usually the first ones called.

Cam was not accustomed to the amount of cigarette smoking still prevalent overseas. Clouds of smoke hung like tear gas in the air of the bar. He positioned himself at the corner of the bar nearest the entrance and ordered a Blue Moon. Of course, they didn't have that brand. Nor did they have Shock Top. So he ordered a Heineken; they had those. Cam looked around the bar. At one elbow, two Korean male journalists in poorly tailored suits and oversized neckties were having a discussion in Korean. They didn't have a snowball's chance of scoring with one of the cute female journalists in the bar, not even the Chinese one, and they knew it. At his other elbow, a rotund, older female producer for one of the major American networks had hooked up with a skinny little Italian freelancer with greasy hair and bad teeth. Through the shared language of Spanish, they were earnestly engaged in an intense but limited discussion about the future of the EU.

Soaking it all in, Cam realized international hotel bars were no longer his scene, and drunk journalists trying to land their next gigs were not his people. Cam finished his Heineken and paid his tab. As he turned to leave, he spotted none other than Hans Kolb sitting alone at a table. They nodded in polite recognition, and Cam proceeded to his room. Within minutes there was a knock at his door. Cam looked through the peep hole and saw Hans. With the door chain in place, he cracked the door open.

"Hello, Mr. Coppenger. Perhaps you may remember me, Hans Kolb of *The Arabic Eye*." Hans glanced around cautiously. "May I come in?"

"Yeah, sure Hans. Come in!" Cam opened the door and motioned Hans over to two chairs positioned around a small table near the window. Then he flipped the deadbolt and chained the door.

Hans opened the conversation. "You disappeared on us, Mr. Coppenger."

"Yeah, the ambassador and I had a conflict of interest."

"Ah yes, the earnest Wilson Pruett … friend to the Iranians and savior of the Syrians. How is he?"

"I wouldn't know. I'm not here on government business."

"What kind of business are you here for then?"

"*Personal business.*"

"You are self-employed now?"

"Something like that."

"Perhaps like me, a freelancer?" Hans asked with a smirk, seeking more detail.

Cam shrugged in response.

Hans evaluated Cam's responses for a moment and then asked, "Are you open to the possibility of a partnership? I know some clients who may be interested in pooling resources."

"Clients? Who?"

Hans peered over the top of his European-framed eyewear and responded to Cam knowingly, "In Tel Aviv … and other interests in Lebanon."

Cam narrowed his eyes as he contemplated the suggestion. It wasn't a bad idea, actually. The Israelis were the best in the world at what they did. They were smart, savvy, cunning, and ruthless. In his official capacity with the embassy, he had followed the advice of the Chief of Station and initiated contact with them. Now as a civilian, Cam could use all the help he could get. "I might be open to further discussions on the topic."

"Excellent!" responded Hans. "Let's stay in touch. There is a wood carving of a Lebanese cedar tree on my news desk downstairs. It has a Lebanese flag painted on either side. Should you or one of your acquaintances wish to contact me, stop by my desk and turn the tree over on its side. That will be our signal to meet at the marina the next day at ten o'clock. There is a bench that faces the water situated exactly between the Zeitouneh Bay Marina and the St. Georges Hotel. A large Pepsi Cola sign is just behind it. If I cannot meet you at that time, or it is not safe, I will place a rock on the park bench. Next to the rock will be a number written in chalk suggesting an alternative time to meet. Understood?"

Cam confirmed the instructions. "Flip the tree on your desk/ Pepsi Cola bench next day at 10/one rock/alternate time written in chalk … got it."

With a basic communication plan in place, Hans stood, shook Cam's hand, and moved toward the door. He asked Cam to check that the hallway was clear first, and then he exited quickly and quietly. Cam dead-bolted the door behind him.

———

The next morning, Cam placed a call to his old friend Elie who answered with considerable traffic noise in the background.

"Crowbar!" he announced enthusiastically. "It's good to hear from you!"

"How are you, my friend?"

"I am good, considering the circumstances of life in Lebanon," Elie replied in good humor. "And you?"

"I'm good. I thought we might have lunch together?"

"Lunch? You are back in Lebanon?"

"Yep. Got in yesterday."

"Well, of course, my friend. Lunch it is! Where are you staying? I will pick you up!"

"The Commodore. Around 12?"

"See you then!" said Elie.

Standing outside at the entrance to the hotel at the designated time, Cam did not recognize Elie when he pulled up driving a white taxi. Elie honked the horn and waved. Cam climbed in the front seat. "What's with the taxi? Are the Nasty Boys using taxis for counter-surveillance now?"

Elie went awkwardly silent. After a moment, he said, "I am no longer employed as a Nasty Boy, Crowbar. The ambassador fired me."

"What! What do you mean he fired you?"

"Ambassador Pruett concluded that I had been a party to your insubordination, and he dismissed me soon after your team departed."

"But you weren't insubordinate! You were assigned to our team on embassy business!"

"I guess the ambassador thought I should have reported your every movement to him. He knew my loyalties were with you and not him." Smiling faintly, Elie looked over at Cam, "So now I drive a taxi."

"That jealous prick!" Cam slammed his fist against the dash, and steaming with anger, took several deep breaths to regain control of his temper. "Elie, I am so sorry. I had no idea!"

"Not your fault, Crowbar." Elie nudged his friend with a forearm. "Politics in Lebanon takes many turns."

Cam stared blankly out the window of the taxi. He was angry, but what he felt most of all was guilt. His actions had gotten his friend fired. Back in October, Cam could have followed the ambassador's directives to the letter, but he chose not to. He cut corners, crossed boundaries, got caught, and his team was sent home. No big deal. Now, months later, he finds out that his friend Elie paid a severe price for those decisions. Overseas American Embassy jobs are much sought-after. In some countries, like Lebanon, the stability and benefits of working for the Americans were particularly desirable. Elie, over fifty and with a family to support, had protected American interests for twenty-five years as a loyal embassy employee. But without warning he had been callously kicked to the curb by an ambassador with an ego and an agenda, and Cam was responsible. He felt gut-punched.

As they descended the hill from the hotel down toward the sea, the taxi became entangled in a jumble of gnarled traffic. Horns began to blow like a badly tuned orchestra. Cam's attention turned to a parking lot off to the side that was filled with brand-new American-made garbage trucks neatly parked side-by-side. Standing at the entrance to the parking lot was a man in a US Embassy guard uniform. Noting the mountains of garbage piled on the street in front of the dusty lot, Cam asked, "I guess the garbage strike is still going on?"

"It's not really a strike, Crowbar. The government just can't agree on where to dump it."

"Do you mean like Christian east or Muslim west?" asked Cam.

"Something like that. But it's more complicated than that. Politics permeates every aspect of life in Lebanon."

"Whose garbage trucks are those?"

"Ha! They are a gift from the US Government! USAID bought twenty-four garbage trucks for Lebanon to resolve the crisis: twelve trucks for the Christians and twelve trucks for the Muslims. But once the trucks arrived to the port, embassy officials realized they wouldn't fit the narrow congested streets of Beirut, so they parked them there."

"Unbelievable," Cam sighed. "Government at its best, spending massive amounts of money on equipment that doesn't work to address a political problem that has yet to be resolved."

Elie chuckled. He had seen the misapplication of USAID resources many times through the years. To make his friend feel a little better about the waste of his tax dollars, Elie added, "The trucks have not entirely gone to waste. The RSO filled some of them with sand and used them as barriers to protect against truck bombs during the Syrian peace conference hosted by the American ambassador last month."

Cam looked over at Elie. "Tyrone is a smart guy. We could have used a couple of those garbage trucks in '84 when Hezbollah blew up the Baaklini Building, couldn't we?"

"It would have saved many lives," sorrow seeping into Elie's words.

Cam counted the plain white garbage trucks in the lot. They were four short. "There are only twenty trucks in the lot."

"Yes, some have disappeared," Elie said. "It is believed they fell into the hands of Hezbollah and are being used in West Beirut for public relations purposes. American-made garbage trucks have been seen in the most impoverished neighborhoods with the Hezbollah flag emblazoned on the side."

"So Hezbollah is in the garbage collection business now?"

"Garbage collection, schools, healthcare, funeral expenses … you name it! The poor Muslim neighborhoods in Lebanon see Hezbollah as more effective than the government in providing the services they need."

Just past the American University of Beirut, Elie finally broke clear of the traffic congestion along the Corniche Mazraa. He pulled the taxi into a spot in front of a sidewalk café. Their table had a nice view of the Mediterranean. It was still an unusual feeling for Cam to sit outside a café in Beirut in broad daylight. He was accustomed to controlled events, perimeter security, armed bodyguards, and protected motorcade movements. Casual days under blue skies along the waterfront were just not part of his slide show, but on this day everything seemed normal, pleasant even. Elie ordered two espressos from the waiter.

"I feel horribly about what has happened to you, Elie."

Elie shrugged. "Do not worry yourself, my friend. We Lebanese are a very resilient people. We've had to be."

"But I want to make it up to you, Elie … I will make it up to you. I don't know how or when … but I will. You have my word."

Elie smiled at his friend in reply. "So what brings you back to

Lebanon?"

"Personal business."

"Unfinished business?"

"Something like that."

"Have you talked to the RSO? He could be helpful."

"No, I'm not sure I want him to know about my presence here, or my activities." Then looking directly at his friend. "I have already cost one colleague his job."

Elie nodded in vague acknowledgment. "But you are going to need help, correct?"

"Perhaps. May I call on you from time to time?"

Elie chuckled again. "The ambassador may have fired me, but I am still a Nasty Boy ... and I always will be!"

"Excellent!" responded Cam. Pausing, he added, "There is something I could use, but it might be a bit risky."

Elie clicked his tongue. "Anything for you my friend. What do you need?"

"Something for self-defense," Cam said in a low whisper. "The embassy armorer, Sami, is he still around?"

Elie broke into a wide grin, patting the bulge under his shirt. "Sami retired several years ago. His sideline business was becoming too profitable, so he quit embassy work." Pausing, Elie surveyed his surroundings and then continued. "What do you need? AKs, RPGs, Ponzi mines? You should see Sami's basement!"

"Just a handgun for now. Something American-made and high-capacity, a Glock or a Beretta. Let me know how much. I'll get you the cash."

Elie nodded.

On the drive back to the hotel, a thought came to Cam. He asked Elie to stop by the local American Express office. Cam went inside and came out with an envelope containing 7,500,000 Lebanese pounds, the equivalent of five-thousand dollars, and handed the envelope to Elie. "This is a down payment for the debt I owe you."

Elie took one look inside the envelope, and his jaw dropped. He tried to hand the envelope back to Cam.

"Keep it," Cam said.

"Crowbar, I can't take this!"

"It's not a gift, Elie. I'm putting you on salary. You work for me now!"

⸺

After lunch, Elie dropped off Cam at the hotel. Before going to his room, Cam walked down to the journalists' work space and looked around casually. Hans was not at his desk. Cam walked among several rows of news agencies, but when he got to *The Arabic Eye* desk, he allowed his shoulder bag to accidentally knock over a wooden tree on Hans's desk. Without slowing or stopping, Cam meandered among several other desks, acting as if he were looking for someone specifically. Feigning failure in his search, Cam exited the work area and went to his room.

The next morning just before ten o'clock, Cam drove his rental car, a Peugeot, down the hill to the Zeitouneh Bay Marina and parked on the street near the Hariri Memorial. He wandered down

to the waterfront without hurry. To his left was the abandoned
and war-damaged St. Georges Hotel, and to his right was Beirut's
sleekest and most modern shopping district. Cam found Hans
sitting on the designated bench reading a paper. Cam and Hans
greeted each other like old friends in a chance encounter. Hans
suggested they walk. As the men strolled casually among the mega-
yachts and sidewalk cafés, Hans pulled from his pocket a string of
Arabic prayer beads and begin fingering them as was the Muslim
tradition in Lebanon.

Nice prop! Cam thought, as he paused from time to time to
carefully survey his surroundings. A fit young dark-skinned man
seemed to be following their movements at a moderate distance.
For the first couple of blocks, Cam and Hans talked about the
weather, boats, and their favorite restaurants in Beirut. Eventually,
Cam moved the conversation to a more serious topic. "Hans, I have
decided I could use some help during my stay in Lebanon."

"That is good to hear. I suspected you might need help. What is
your plan?"

"I don't have one, yet. I was hoping you might have some ideas."

"Our varmint is very deep in his hole. He will be very difficult to
dig out."

Cam stopped again and looked around. He knew a strategically
placed parabolic microphone could pick up even whispers
from a considerable distance. The sea breeze coming off the
Mediterranean was to his advantage. He lowered his voice. "Do you
have anyone inside the refugee camps?"

"We have sources but not operators. Operators are the key. We
either need to get operators inside the hole, or we have to lure the

varmint out of his hole."

"What about remote operations?" asked Cam, fully aware of Israel's history of targeting its enemies with mail bombs, cell phone bombs … even poisoning.

"If you mean a drone strike, that's out of the question. Tel Aviv doesn't want anything sensational at this point. They have a vested interest in the Syrian peace talks and don't want an incident to sidetrack that effort."

"I was thinking something more subtle. See if your people can come up with some options."

"I shall do that. Let's talk again in a week."

"Sounds like a plan," said Cam in a southern drawl that sounded much less refined than the accent of his counterpart. The men parted ways without shaking hands. After walking several steps in the opposite direction, Cam turned and observed another fit dark man fall in line behind Hans at a moderate distance.

———

Cam left his meeting with Hans and returned to his rented Peugeot. In order to get onto the main road that led back to his hotel, Cam entered St. Georges Square, the site of Prime Minister Hariri's assassination in 2005. As he negotiated the sea of cars rounding the square, Cam's attention was diverted momentarily to the movement of one white car that came too close, even by Lebanese standards. A quick glance to his right revealed the unmistakable forestock and barrel of an AK-47—the terrorists' weapon of choice—and there immediately erupted an explosion of noise and shattered glass. Ambush! Cam's reaction was instantaneous and reflexive: duck, scream something unintelligible, steer into the attacking vehicle, and accelerate! As he jumped the curb and maneuvered the Peugeot around the tangle of traffic, another Kalashnikov, this one with legs, appeared in front of him. Briefly, he peeked above the dashboard just long enough to identify the threat, then instinctively gunned the speeding vehicle straight toward it. He wasn't thinking, just reacting to a plan he had rehearsed in his mind time and time again. Events blurred quickly. Cam felt a heavy bump against his vehicle, but he never hesitated, never slowed down. Bouncing off other vehicles and curbs like a bumper car at a fairground, Cam plowed over piles of garbage along the street. He accelerated erratically as the fractured windshield blocked a clear view ahead. The way forward became completely blocked with traffic, and Cam slammed into the back of two stopped cars. Gunfire behind him continued, shattering his rear window into small fragments of shrapnel. Still hunched over, Cam cracked his door and peered behind him. A shooter had opened his car door and had assumed a firing position on the passenger side. Cam accelerated hard in reverse and struck the open door, slamming it against the shooter, snapping his legs and crushing his torso. Cam had to get off the X. A sloppily executed reverse J-turn got his vehicle pointed in the direction of an open side road, and Cam floored his sputtering vehicle out of the chaos. After a block or so, the automatic weapons fire ceased, but he could still hear car horns and the swelling screams of innocent bystanders behind him. A clear view of his surroundings was impossible through the broken window glass, but Cam continued along his escape route, scraping the sides of cars like some drunk on a bender, causing terrified pedestrians to scramble for cover. He took one last evasive turn to lose any following vehicles before heading in the direction of the hotel.

Cam limped his smoking Peugeot back to the Commodore. He literally had no other place to go. The rental was shot to pieces, its glass completely shattered, two blown tires, and steam pouring from its radiator. Only then did Cam notice the blood-splattered interior of his car. He was bleeding profusely from head wounds. He had multiple lacerations on his face from fragmented glass, and one bullet had found its mark. Miraculously, the 7.62 mm round had not penetrated Cam's skull; his instinctive flinch had been sufficient to deflect the angle of trajectory. The bullet did penetrate his skin, however, just behind his right ear; it had burrowed beneath his scalp like an invasive mole in a well-manicured lawn, plowing a furrow in an arc across the top of his skull and exiting in a bloody mess out the left side of his head. Realizing he had been centimeters from certain death, Cam emerged wobbily from his Peugeot at the hotel entrance. He had an exploding headache. Thick, sticky blood blinded his vision, and shock began to set in. Weak-kneed from the post-adrenaline crash, Cam collapsed in the lobby of the hotel, his blood smearing the white marble floor. Hotel staff reacted hesitantly, stunned at the bloody mess that had just been delivered to their door.

Cam had survived, due primarily to a life lesson he carried in the core of his being. When attacked, take the offensive. By ramming the attacking vehicle and accelerating toward the attacker ahead, he had taken the initiative, disrupted the ambush plan, and saved himself. His reactions had worked. Three automatic rifles, each with 30-round magazines fired at close range, had found their intended target only once. A trail of large-caliber bullet holes beginning at the front grill of the Peugeot and continuing straight up a billboard sign behind the square indicated the blocking assassin had lost his sight picture, and apparently his composure, as Cam accelerated toward him. Police had found the mangled attacker near the site, apparently mashed and dragged for several yards by the speeding Peugeot. A second shooter was found in the middle of the street, his shins snapped like twigs, his chest crushed by the slamming car door. The shooter's driver had abandoned him there in his own panicked escape from an attack plan that had gone horribly wrong. In a classic moving ambush scenario, Cam survived because he had become the aggressor.

15

CAM AWOKE GROGGY in the hospital. His head was pounding, a huge bandage covered his bruised head, and one eye was swollen nearly shut.

"Do you know how lucky you are?" asked a smooth soft female voice in a foreign accent that sounded familiar to him.

Cam took a chance with his response. "Sabrina?" he asked. She laughed that laugh, and he knew it was her. "What are you doing here? How did you know I was here?"

"There are no secrets in Lebanon," responded Sabrina with the same sultry, sophisticated voice he remembered. She spoke impeccably, though English was not her first language.

Cam peeked under the bandage with his one good eye to confirm that she was his friend from long ago. Beautiful Sabrina, wealthy daughter of a prominent Christian Marionite businessman. She was educated, smart, tri-lingual, and politically connected.

Shapely and with stunning dark features, she was significantly younger than Cam, but their stars had collided during the war.

"You made the news, and from all reports, you caused quite a stir in the lobby of the Commodore today," she teased.

"But how did you know it was me?"

"Silly American secret agent. I knew when you were here with your task force, I knew you departed unexpectedly, and I knew when you arrived alone from London just last week."

The information didn't surprise Cam, Sabrina had connections throughout Lebanon.

"Why didn't you contact me?"

"I'm married now, Cop, and it wouldn't have looked right," she explained, giving credence to Lebanon's provincial culture.

"But you are here now," Cam said.

"You are my friend, you are in trouble, and I'm here to help you." Sabrina paused for a moment, touched his cheek, then added in the same velvet exotic voice that had captured his heart so many years ago, "I still care about you, Secret Agent Coppenger."

"That's *Special* Agent, and I'm not an agent anymore."

"Oh yes, you are. Just not officially." She changed the subject. "Do you feel like moving? We need to get you out of here."

"Now?" asked Cam, incredulously.

"Yes, now. The police have already been here once, and I sent them away. They will be back soon."

"Where are we going?"

"Stop asking questions. We need to go," Sabrina ordered, as she began disconnecting the monitors and tubes attached to her patient. "I've sent the nurses on a break. Here are some clean clothes."

Cam looked into the bag she brought and saw a shiny blue Adidas track suit, the kind worn by slimy Russians or Italian mobsters on holiday. "Your husband's stuff?"

"I told you to stop asking questions … we must go!" Sabrina raised him from the bed, spanked his bare bottom as it protruded from the hospital gown, and helped him into the tacky blue track suit. She placed his phone, passport, and wallet in her purse and eased him into a wheelchair. As she wheeled him past the nurses' station, not a soul was in sight. Cam wondered how on earth she had pulled that off. As they moved swiftly down the hallway, Sabrina's Gucci stilettos clicked noisily on the linoleum floor like a slowly spinning wheel of fortune.

The meds were still firmly in control of Cam's lucidity as he faded in and out of consciousness. He remembered Sabrina tumbling him into the back seat of a big white Mercedes and her hiding him under a smelly blanket covered with dog hair. He bumped his head against the armrest and was paralyzed with lightning bolts of pain. As she got behind the wheel, Cam peeked out from the blanket to see a nervous little lap dog peering at him from the front seat.

"Where are we going?"

"We are going to The Chouf. My family has a place in the mountains. You will be safe there."

Cam fell back into a drug-induced sleep, awakening at the metallic clang of an iron gate closing. He wondered how long he'd slept. The white Mercedes turned up a twisting gravel driveway and stopped in front of an ancient stone house that resembled a small fortress. Sabrina beeped the horn, and two servants walked out into the chilly night air to help Cam inside. They carried him up a stone stairway to a room on the top floor and laid him in a huge canopy bed. A wood fire crackled in the fireplace. Fragile tapestries of Christian crusader battles lined the tall stone walls of the room. Before Cam fell into a deep sleep, he looked out the leaded-glass window to see an armed man illuminated by moonlight standing watch under a tall stand of cedar trees. *Safe refuge among the famous Cedars of Lebanon*, Cam thought to himself, and he drifted off.

Cam slept well into the next morning, finally awakened by a knock at his door. His bandaged head throbbed, but through one blurry eye he could see Hans Kolb standing in the doorway. Cam looked at his visitor in disbelief. "Hans? What are you doing here?"

"Have you not learned by now that Lebanese politics are complicated?" Hans grinned like a riverboat gambler.

"Sabrina told you I was here?"

"Sabrina is on our side. I told you I have many clients in Lebanon."

Cam slumped back into his canopy bed. His swollen head pounded as he assessed Sabrina's association with the Israelis. In many ways, it made sense. While most Lebanese despised Israel and were extremely resentful of Israeli invasions into Lebanon, many in the educated class recognized that the only reason Israel invaded was to stop rocket attacks launched from Lebanese territory by Hezbollah, the Palestinians, or any number of other enemies of the Jewish state. Well-positioned Lebanese understood that Israel could be an important ally in the region if only the schizophrenic government would stop Israel's enemies from using South Lebanon as a base of operations.

Hans continued. "It appears our varmit knows you are at his hole."

"Do you think it was Ismail?" asked Cam.

"The two dead attackers were known members of Liwa Tahrir. And eye witnesses to the attack recognized one of the drivers to be Ismail's son."

"Abdullah?"

"Yes, his eldest. Do you know him?"

"I know of him. He orchestrated the recent train attack in America."

"Apparently, Abdullah is very much the coward. He left one of his colleagues to die in the street."

"It wouldn't be the first time," replied Cam, thinking of Abdullah's escape from the Mexican safehouse.

Hans nodded in agreement. "We have now entered the cat and mouse phase of counterterrorism operations."

"So who is the cat, and who is the mouse?" inquired Cam. The bandage on his head made the question a genuine inquiry.

"That is for you to decide. Are you ready to begin the game? It's your move."

Cam touched his bandaged head. "I'll need a few days to recover. My head is killing me. Besides, I can't go out in public looking like Frankenstein!"

"Very well then, Mr. Coppenger. Just don't take too long. One of our key targets will be slithering out of his hole in the coming days."

"What do you mean by that?"

"Abdullah Khalidi fancies himself as a racecar driver, and he and his friends have been known to race cars through the streets of West Beirut from time to time, usually on Thursdays after midnight. But no need to concern yourself with that right now. Take some time to recover. We will talk again." Hans stopped at the door. "You are quite the warrior, Mr. Coppenger. There are not many men who, unarmed and outnumbered, can turn an ambush into a counter-attack and survive. You have our utmost respect."

Cam spent the next week recovering from his injuries. He had a houseful of servants to attend to his every need. Sabrina checked in on him from time to time and arranged for her personal physician to make daily house calls to change his bandages and monitor his progress. The doctor said there would be minimal facial scaring and predicted Cam's full head of graying hair would conceal most of the damage from the bullet.

After several days, the swelling around Cam's headwounds decreased significantly, and he began to move freely about the fortress-like compound. He stopped shaving, thinking a full beard might help hide his identity once he ventured back out into Lebanese society. Gradually, his thoughts turned from recovery to response. It was time to go on the offensive. Using his smartphone and Sabrina's encrypted wifi, Cam sent a brief email to his son in California. *Need a new message sent: Two more down, more to come. Crowbar.*

Within twenty-four hours, Ismail, the Palestinian thug-turned-terrorist, received a knock on his door. Cam's message had been delivered.

By week two, the police had stopped looking for the missing American who had mysteriously disappeared from his hospital bed. Inquiries with the American Embassy came to a complete dead end. The RSO was not even aware that Cameron Coppenger had reentered the country. Police suspected that Sabrina may have had something to do with the American's disappearance, but they did not dare question her. Her family was too powerful. So the investigation died a quiet death. Lebanon had a long history of unsolved assassinations and assassination attempts. From the police perspective, such cases had a way of resolving themselves.

Thursday rolled around and Cam made a call to his friend Elie.

"Crowbar! How are you?"

"I'm okay. I feel like I've been kicked in the head by a mule, but I'll live."

"That is good to know. I suspected you were the one in the news, but I did not know what had become of you. I was afraid to call your number in the event the police had your phone!"

"Good thinking, Elie."

"Do you need anything?"

"Actually, I'd like to get out of the house for a while … I'm going a bit stir-crazy. Can you pick me up?"

"Of course, my friend! Where are you?"

"Do you remember Sabrina from my early days in Beirut?"

"Sabrina Khoury, the most beautiful woman in all of Lebanon? Of course, I remember her! She married very well, as you may know, but with a broken heart it is said."

"Oh, come on, Elie. Sabrina had her pick of any man in Lebanon."

"Maybe so, but she went years without the company of a man after you left. So Sabrina has rescued you?"

"You might say that. I'm at her family's estate in The Chouf. Do you know it?"

"Yes, yes – we come from the same village. Shall I pick you up after work? I have something for you, something you requested."

"This evening works. It's perfect, actually. I look forward to seeing you."

———

Elie drove his taxi to the Khoury estate after work but hardly recognized Cam sporting a full beard. "What is this?" Elie grinned widely. "In two weeks you have become a man of the mountains?"

"I thought it would help hide my American face. Like it?"

Elie clicked his tongue. "You look like Hezbollah!" he said, breaking into his trademark smile.

In the front seat of Elie's taxi was a heavy object in a brown paper bag. "Excellent!" Cam exclaimed, as he opened the bag and found a full-size Glock 17. He extracted the magazine and found it double-stacked with seventeen rounds of 9mm. He pulled the slide back slightly and saw the additional eighteenth round already chambered. He grimaced as he tucked the high capacity firearm under his shirt; the assassination attempt had reinjured his ribs. "This is perfect. How much do I owe you?"

"Nothing," Elie said. "When Sami found out the request came from the one and only Crowbar, he gave it with his blessing! All the retired Nasty Boys send their blessings!"

Still in the mountains, Elie pulled into a restaurant that was not too far from Sabrina's estate. They sat at a table on the outside patio that commanded an excellent view of downtown Beirut, East and

West. The hour was still too early to eat by Lebanese standards, and they were alone on the patio. Elie ordered appetizers of stuffed grape leaves and kebbeh nayyeh.

Then Cam queried his friend hesitantly, "So the Nasty Boys know I'm here?"

By this time Elie had already stuffed his mouth with flatbread and the raw ground lamb meat mixed with spices. He washed it down with a swig of red wine and explained, "Just our old team. They know you are in Lebanon, and they know you survived the attack, but they do not know where in Lebanon you are. I took it upon myself to tell them. We may need their assistance in the future. Do not worry. They can be trusted."

"I know they can be trusted. Does the embassy know I am in Lebanon as well?"

"The police asked the RSO if he knew where you were, and of course he did not. And I doubt he said anything to the ambassador about the police inquiry. He was pretty upset with the way the ambassador handled your dismissal and then mine."

"Was the ambassador curious at all about the news reports that an American had been attacked in Beirut?"

"Are you kidding?" joked Elie. "The ambassador is only concerned about one thing, and that is his role in the next round of the Syrian peace negotiations."

The traditional Lebanese meal of falafel, tabbouleh, and rice was excellent. And as darkness crept slowly over the city, hiding its scars and revealing its beauty, the slums grew quiet, with only the modern highrise buildings capturing the remaining sunlight to reflect its colors at the water's edge. To his right, Cam could see the gleaming Zeitouneh Bay Marina with its rows of extravagant yachts, and next to it St. Georges Square, the scene of the assassination attempt against him just weeks earlier. As so many times before, the city had resumed its life as if nothing had ever happened there. Farther south was the brightly lit Corniche, filled with people enjoying an evening stroll along the waterfront esplanade.

Cam began to formulate his next move. "I hear that one of Ismail's sons thinks he is a race car driver."

Elie chuckled, "Ah yes, Abdullah, the playboy/prince racecar driver! He and a group of his punk friends have formed an auto club, and they terrorize the streets of West Beirut in their fancy race cars late at night. They call it touge racing."

"And the police allow that?"

Elie clicked his tongue again. "The police are powerless in West Beirut. Ismail's thugs are aligned with Hezbollah, and Hezbollah rules West Beirut. Once a gang of terrorists themselves, Hezbollah has emerged as the most powerful of the Muslim political parties in Lebanon. Nothing happens in West Beirut without the approval of Hezbollah. They have even launched public service projects to win the hearts and minds of the people."

"I hear Abdullah likes to race on Thursday nights" Cam said.

"Yes, usually after midnight. We will probably be able to see them from here later tonight. They are impossible to miss. They make a lot of noise."

As the sun sank completely below the Mediterranean, Cam and Elie continued to drink red wine from a traditional goat skin flask well into the night. Below them, the streets in the less affluent western sector of Beirut emptied early. It appeared as if East Beirut would remain vibrant throughout the evening. Then just after midnight, the faint sound of high-revving engines could be heard drifting up the mountainside. "It sounds like our race has begun!" announced Elie.

"I see only one car," Cam said as it topped a hill, raced beneath an overpass, braked hard, and then turned sharply left toward the water. Not long afterward, a second car topped the hill and followed the path of the first.

"They play cat-and-mouse," said Elie. "They do not race against each other but against time. If one catches up to the other, he wins the race!"

"What kind of cars do they drive?"

"Typically the smaller turbo-charged AWD models used in rally races: Subaru, Mitsubishi, or Audi. Our would-be prince drives a lime-green Subaru WRX. Rumor has it he stole it from a shipping container down at the port. It was apparently bound for some exotic dealership in the Gulf States, and it was seized as, you might say … *tribute*."

"Funny how that works. Is Abdullah the only racer in a lime-green Subaru?"

"Oh, yes. The little prince would not allow anyone else to imitate him!"

Pride before fall, Cam recited quietly under his breath. "So Elie, how difficult would it be to borrow one of those USAID garbage trucks for an evening?"

Elie read Cam's thoughts immediately. "Not impossible," he answered with a twinkle in his eye. "As I said before, four have already fallen into Hezbollah's hands."

"And how in the world did that happen?"

"Hezbollah has eyes everywhere. They simply waited until the guard called in sick. The keys are already in the vehicles."

"What kind of car salesman leaves the keys to all his inventory inside the vehicles?" Cam asked incredulously.

"Uncle Sam, of course!" replied Elie with a smile. "Personally, I think USAID is secretly hoping all the trucks are stolen to cover up their incompetence!"

Cam shook his head. He wasn't surprised, just disgusted as a taxpayer. That said, in his role as a counterterrorism operative, he hoped to use the government's incompetence to his advantage. Looking directly at Elie, Cam made a cryptic request. "See if you can get the embassy guard to call in sick next Thursday evening."

Elie acknowledged his request with a nod.

16

THE FOLLOWING THURSDAY evening, Elie dropped Cam off along the Corniche at eight o'clock. Armed with his Glock and sporting a full beard befitting the finest middle-aged Muslim male in Lebanon, Cam pretended to pay Elie a taxi fare and proceeded to walk along the esplanade for a couple of blocks. Cam's Chocktaw lineage had given him a dark complexion that aided his disguise. After checking and double checking for possible surveillance, Cam turned up the road that led to the parked garbage trucks. Once there, he found a small sidewalk café nearby and ordered a Nescafé. Cam watched the parking lot. As had been requested, the embassy guard was nowhere in sight. It was a dark part of town, and only a single dim lightbulb illuminated the guard shack. After several minutes, Cam walked to the parking lot, found the rusty gate unlocked, and walked in. He wandered among the neatly parked trucks until he got to one surrounded by what appeared to be small piles of beach sand. *Must be one of the sand-filled trucks the RSO used for perimeter security during the last Syrian peace talks*, he thought to himself. He knocked on the metal side of the truck and found it to be solid and full of sand. Cam pulled on a pair of heavy work gloves and climbed up into the cab. He studied the cab interior with the light from his phone. *Four forward gears … looks simple enough*, he surmised. Just as Elie had said, Cam found a key in the ignition and started the diesel engine. It grumbled, then rumbled to life. He checked his watch and saw the time was 2200 hours. Ten minutes later, Cam put the heavy garbage truck in gear, pulled out of the lot, and headed deeper into West Beirut.

Cam followed the route along the waterfront where he had seen the racecars the previous week. He found the underpass the cars had passed through before turning toward the sea. Just beyond the underpass was a small auxiliary road that descended from the mountains and intersected with the main racing route. Cam backed the big truck along a dirt patch next to the road, applied the parking brakes, and waited. Hoping the engine would restart without a problem, he turned it off and checked his watch. Almost midnight. From his position, Cam had a clear view of the small hill the cars would clear before plunging down into the underpass. The surrounding community was quiet with only an occasional passing car, none of which took notice of the garbage truck. The garbage feud had been lagging on for months. Out-of-place garbage trucks roaming the city at odd hours was nothing new to the citizens of Beirut. The barking of stray dogs echoed along the dark narrow streets.

Just past midnight, Cam heard in the distance the faint whines of high-revving engines. He sat up and started the truck engine. It vibrated and rattled noisily. Peering through the darkness toward the hill, Cam could see headlights bouncing off the sides of buildings. He buckled his seatbelt, put the truck in gear, and waited. The first racecar to top the hill was a white Mitsubishi Lancer covered in racing stickers. The Lancer crested the hill, then descended quickly down the other side, disappearing behind buildings until it entered the underpass. Accelerating loudly through the tunnel, the Mitsubishi had to downshift and brake hard before immediately making a sharp left toward the sea. That sharp turn was the target zone. Cam timed it. All in all, he would have about twelve seconds to identify his target at the top of the hill, get the garbage truck rolling, and make contact. His timing had to be perfect; there would be no second chance.

Exactly one minute later, Cam heard the roaring turbine of a Mazda RX-7 cresting the hill. The car was dark gray or blue and covered in stickers. Like the Mitsubishi, the RX-7 accelerated loudly down through the underpass, then braked hard before entering the sharp turn. *Not bad driving*, Cam thought to himself as the Mazda accelerated cleanly out of the turn and disappeared into the darkness.

Instinctively, Cam prepared himself for the next car. Something told him the Palestinian playboy/prince would be next, and he was right. Exactly one minute after the Mazda crested the hilltop, a lime-green Subaru WRX Sti popped up. Like the others, after topping the hill, the Subaru disappeared momentarily behind some buildings but could still be heard screaming its way toward the underpass. Cam released the clutch and floored the massive diesel down the short but steep incline. The diesel rattled and strained, but momentum built quickly; it simply became a matter of timing. From the corner of his eye, Cam spotted the green car emerge from the underpass. Whether Abdullah saw the speeding garbage truck or not, it didn't matter. He was already beginning to brake for the turn and had no place else to go. For just a split second, Abdullah glanced to his right and saw a bearded man in a garbage truck headed straight at him. Almost instantaneously, the small Subaru disappeared beneath the hood of the thirty-ton Mack truck moving at 50 mph. Like a locomotive under hard braking, the speed wasn't deadly, but the weight and momentum behind the massive t-bone impact were. Under normal circumstances with normal vehicles, the Subaru should have been knocked down the street like a tin can kicked to the curb, but the height of the truck's bumper trapped the Subaru beneath it, and the garbage truck rolled over the racecar's sheetmetal with bone-crushing weight, mashing it flat with all of its contents. By the time the big truck stopped, the Subaru looked like a crushed soda can.

Stepping down from the cab of the truck, Cam didn't even bother to check for signs of life. There was nothing left to check, really. Except for a faint hissing coming from the Subaru's radiator, the crash site was silent. Debris was scattered everywhere. A scuffed and dented racing helmet rocked awkwardly on the sidewalk, the young terrorist's head still strapped firmly inside. Cam looked around numbly. Lights were beginning to turn on in the surrounding residences. Discarding his gloves, he paused, reached into his pocket, and touched a small wooden bat. Then he began walking calmly back toward the center of town where Elie was waiting in his taxi.

Ismail received the news of his son's death stoically. He had no way of knowing for sure who had targeted Abdullah. That was the way such events happened in Lebanon. There would eventually be whispered rumors, but at present all Ismail could do was speculate. It could have been any number of his enemies—America's CIA, Israel's Mossad, Lebanese intelligence, the illusive Crowbar—or any combination of the aforementioned. Given the unexpected turn of events in Mexico, Ismail even wondered if one of the cartels had ordered the attack. He had to be careful about jumping to conclusions, though. Some of his adversaries were particularly adept at making their actions appear to be those of another. Unlike his own organization, which celebrated its deeds publically and thrived on the emotional impact its terrorist operations had on the intended victims, the assassination of his eldest son had been implemented quietly and professionally, and for no clear reason. If there were an intended message, Ismail didn't get it.

This time around, Cam did not have Caleb send a personal note to Ismail. By design, he had the FBI's most wanted terrorist just where he wanted him: stunned, confused, and scared.

Seven months had passed since Ismail's reign of terror had come to America. First the attack at the San Diego airport, followed by the 4th of July bombing at the nation's capital, and then the train wreck in the Arizona desert. All the attacks had originated with the same terrorist organization, headed by a man who seemed untouchable. Although the immediate threat from across the border in Mexico had been neutralized, America was still in a state of unease regarding the security of its homeland. That was in America.

In Lebanon, an American citizen had been ambushed in the streets of Beirut, but the only issue that had the attention of Ambassador Wilson J. Pruett was the Syrian peace process. Pruett's diplomatic skillset suited him perfectly for his role as America's chief negotiator to bring the Syrian conflict to an end. When properly motivated, the ambassador could indeed be a very good negotiator – maybe too good. Hezbollah, along with its ally Iran, were key supporters of the Assad régime in Syria, and they had taken notice of the ambassador's role in the negotiations. From the Iranian's broader perspective, the Americans were playing too big of a role in the Syrian negotiations. In Hezbollah's more myopic view, the American ambassador had become too sympathetic with the Syrian rebels. From both viewpoints, something needed to be done to regain and hold momentum for the Assad régime. So with another round of negotiations coming up, Hezbollah, at the behest of the Iranians, turned to Ismail to bring things back into balance.

Just as before, Beirut was to be the venue for the upcoming peace conference, and as expected, Ambassador Wilson Pruett had positioned himself for a seat at the head of the table. The Phoenician Hotel was the preferred site for the negotiations due to its proximity to a Lebanese army camp located next door on the grounds of the now-abandoned Holiday Inn. The hotel also served as an important symbol of the renewal and rejuvenation of downtown Beirut. The embassy's RSO, Tyrone Bell, had a significant role as a security consultant for the event, and despite the highly suspicious use of a reportedly *stolen* USAID garbage truck in the recent attack against a Liwa Tahrir member, the embassy's sand-filled trucks were once again used as security barriers on the roads leading up to the hotel. Lebanese security precautions for the event were extensive, but the host country made one particular security decision that was of serious concern to the RSO. Lebanese authorities decided that all conference participants would have to stage their vehicles at any one of several security checkpoints located a full block from the hotel and then walk to the event on foot, accompanied by only one bodyguard. That meant Ambassador Pruett and his small entourage would have to leave the safety of their armored limousines, as well as a security contingent of Nasty Boys, and walk unprotected one block to the entrance of the hotel. Given Lebanon's history of assassinations, the arrangement was reckless. Who within the government made the decision was unclear, but it seemed to have been made under a cloud of secrecy.

The RSO recognized the vulnerability immediately, but the decision was beyond his control. In reality, any location in downtown Beirut would have had the same vulnerability. The abundance of high-rise buildings surrounding the site were perfect platforms for a sniper attack. RSO Bell was extremely dissatisfied with that aspect of the Lebanese security plan and argued his case vehemently. He proposed that authorities erect an enclosed walkway for the dignitaries that would shield them from any observation from above, but the Lebanese were more concerned with Improvised Explosive devices (IEDs). Ultimately, the RSO's warnings, while heard, were ignored. Separate appeals to Ambassador Pruett himself went unheeded.

A few days later at the main entrance to the Phoenician Hotel, a single sniper's bullet exploded Ambassador Pruett's head like a ripened melon before a live TV audience, and the incident sent shock waves throughout the entire western world. Wilson Pruett's assassination had been the first of an American ambassador since 1979. The RSO was devastated—it happened on his watch afterall—as was every member of the embassy's bodyguard force. The Nasty Boys had never lost an ambassador before. The last American ambassador assassinated in Beirut was Francis Meloy in 1976, and that assassination led to the formation of their elite protection unit in the first place.

Of course, the American press went crazy. The international press corps at The Commodore buzzed with rumors, conspiracies, and lies. Sid Lewis of the FBI placed a call to Cam's cell phone, but his friend and contact had long since gone to ground and could not be reached. In response to the assassination, the Syrian peace negotiations were postponed indefinitely. Embassy operations were reduced to essential-personnel only, the State Department imposed a ban on travel to Lebanon, and it also ordered the Beirut International Airport off-limits to Americans. Even American air carriers were prevented from flying into or out of BIA. The end result was that Hezbollah's objectives had been achieved; America's presence in that region of the world had been significantly reduced.

Understandably, Liwa Tahrir claimed no responsibility for the act. The implications were just too great.

In the wake of Ambassador Pruett's assassination, the embassy's Deputy Chief of Mission, Bill Romano, was promoted to Chief of Mission (COM). His first challenge as the new COM was to get the ambassador's body back to the US for burial. As an experienced veteran of several conflict zones, and with the airport closed to American carriers, the COM turned to the military. The US Navy's Sixth Fleet, headquartered in Naples, Italy, was the closest military asset. Working through the embassy's Defense Attaché (DATT), the White House ordered the US Sixth Fleet to recover the ambassador's body and bring it home. There was just one problem. In retaliation for the US Government decision to close BIA to American air carriers, the Lebanese Government had denied US military access to Lebanese airspace. As happens so often in diplomatic stand-offs, the US Navy decided to proceed with its mission through alternate channels. The decision was made to ignore Lebanese restrictions and retrieve the body by helicopter on embassy grounds. Emergency evacuations from embassy grounds by helicopter had been common during the war, but they were risky. In preparation for the undertaking, the DATT, an experienced veteran himself, advised the COM that a commercially manufactured casket would be too large and too heavy for a standard helicopter. The ambassador's remains would have to be transported in a lightweight wooden box. After learning this, Romano instructed the embassy's maintenance shop to build one. The embassy carpenter had been around a long time, going back to the early days of the civil war. He knew exactly what to build.

The day after Ambassador Pruett's assassination, Hans Kolb visited Cam at Sabrina's estate in The Chouf. Cam greeted his guest on the ivy-covered veranda that overlooked the city. The beautiful Mediterranean could be seen shimmering in the distance. After a few minutes of chit chat over espressos, Hans transitioned the conversation to official business. "Congratulations on the garbage truck accident by the way – very clever use of government resources. But it appears you lost an ambassador in retaliation."

"Do you really think Pruett's assassination was related to the hit?" asked Cam.

"We can never know these things for sure. Our evaluation is that Ismail did not know for certain who had targeted his son. It is more likely that Pruett's assassination was part of a greater geo-political move related to the Syrians. We believe the Iranians ordered the assassination. In any event, if Ismail had even the slightest suspicion that the American government was behind the death of his son, killing your ambassador was an efficient way of addressing both scenarios."

"Are we sure Ismail did it?"

"A reliable source has identified the ambassador's assassin as Asem Zaydani, Ismail's driver and most trusted bodyguard. He was a long-range specialist during the war."

"Will Washington be provided that information?" Cam knew that his friend Sid would eventually be among the recipients in the dissemination chain.

"That would be normal procedure under such circumstances."

"Yes. I know people in Washington who need that information."

Moving the conversation back to the purpose of his visit, Hans asked, "Have you given more thought about how to lure Ismail out of his hole? He is not as foolish nor as reckless as his son."

"Not really," admitted Cam. "I'm a little short on ideas right now. What are you thinking?"

Hans looked out toward the sea and contemplated his response. "I have some information that could be of use. But it may present somewhat of a moral dilemma for you, depending on how you make use of it."

"Oh? What do you mean?"

Hans paused and looked down into his coffee cup. "Ismail has another son, Jamal. He is twelve and currently away at boarding school."

"Twelve years old? Where is he?"

"Switzerland. Reportedly, Ismail sent Jamal away when he was ten after the boy began questioning his father's involvement in Liwa Tahrir."

"So the boy has the conscience his father lacks?"

"Something like that. The fact is, there may be hope for the boy to have a different life than that of his father. That's why I was reluctant to even mention him."

"I understand. Let me think about it."

Hans's phone buzzed, and he looked at the screen. "I have another appointment in town. Shall we continue this conversation later? I'd like you to meet someone."

"Yes, of course," Cam replied, as he walked Hans down to his vehicle. "We'll be in touch."

Hans turned before getting into his car. "So are you glad Pruett is dead?"

Cam took a moment before responding; he had asked himself that same question. Cam recalled his frustration at being dismissed by the ambassador, purely for political reasons. He thought about Elie and the heartless disruption Pruett had brought to his life and family. Then he thought about Ismail. How ironic that Ismail had just killed the one American who, in his own twisted way, had helped shield the terrorist from justice. The truth was Pruett had been the absolute embodiment of the confusing contradiction of priorities that existed in the world of international diplomacy, so Cam's response to Hans's question was sincere. "I'm not sure."

Later that week, Sabrina stopped by her family's estate to check on Cam. She found him in the garden under the shade of a cedar tree where he was reading a history of the Israeli/Palestinian conflict. Dressed in a white tailored pantsuit and stilettos with her raven-black hair pulled tightly back in a ponytail, Sabrina looked like she had just walked off the front page of a fashion magazine. "How is my *secret* agent doing today?" she asked in a voice that reminded Cam of one particularly warm night on the French Riviera.

Almost fully recovered now, Cam replied enthusiastically,

"Better than I deserve! I want to thank you for everything you have done for me these past few weeks, Sabrina. I don't think I will ever be able to repay you."

Sabrina clicked her tongue, "You don't have to thank me. You would have done the same for me. Would you not?"

Cam smiled. "I don't think I would ever find you with your head nearly blown off, but you know I would swim an ocean full of sharks for you, right?"

"Of course you would, and I for you." She reached down and touched his shoulder. When she did, he noticed her 3-carat diamond wedding ring turned inward toward her palm. Cam felt its weight press sharply into his shoulder. He didn't know enough about Lebanese culture to know what that subtle gesture meant, so he didn't stand to face her. He thought it best not to. He simply reached up and placed his hand on top of hers and held it there. Momentarily, one of Sabrina's servants came outside with a tray of iced lemon water, unaware of the disruption her thoughtfulness had caused. Pulling her hand away, Sabrina announced to both in a formal tone, "Victor and I will be leaving for Cannes in the morning. I'm not sure how long we will be gone."

"That sounds like a great trip," Cam replied. Then he asked, "Do I need to find other accommodations?"

"Absolutely not!" snapped Sabrina. "You will be my guest for as long as you want!" Turning to Trina, her servant, Sabrina instructed, "Mr. Coppenger will be a guest of this estate indefinitely. Please see that his every need is met. Should anyone inquire about his presence here, the police or anyone else, say nothing and contact me immediately. Is that clear?"

Looking over at Cam, Trina replied with a smile, "Yes, of course, Ms. Khoury. We like having Mr. Coppenger here very much!"

By this time Cam was standing.

Having delivered her instructions, Sabrina turned and gave him the customary cheek-to-cheek, double-air kiss, bidding him goodbye. When she reached the garden gate, she spun and blew another kiss, shouting, "Ciao!"

"Ciao!" Cam called back and offered a weak wave that somehow seemed empty to him. He owed her much more than a thank you and a simple wave goodbye.

———

A few days after Sabrina's departure, Hans returned to the Khoury estate. He brought with him a very serious man with close-cropped hair and a thick athletic build. The man was about the same age as Cam, and he looked vaguely familiar. On the veranda, well out of hearing range, Hans made the introduction. "Mr. Coppenger, allow me to introduce to you one of my colleagues from Tel Aviv, Mr. Avi Levine, of Israel's Shin Bet."

"Ah yes, Shin Bet – Israel's *Unseen Shield*!" Cam shook Avi Levine's hand. "You look familiar!"

Avi seemed to carry very little emotion with him.

Cam continued the one-way conversation, trying to find some connection. "I wonder if we have ever worked dignitary protection together?"

"Possibly," Avi replied stiffly. "I worked on the Prime Minister's protective detail for several years."

"Oh yes, I remember now," recalled Cam. "You were with Sharon in New York at the UN General Assembly. Your team handed out baby blue bonnets to all the American security personnel and told us that if anything went down we were to place the bonnets on our heads! You said anybody not wearing a bonnet would be shot!"

"Yes, that is right," Avi replied curtly. "In those days, our instructions were to shoot anyone not wearing a bonnet."

Cam smiled. "That's pretty intense."

"We live in an intense world." There was no hint of humor in Avi's voice.

Hans sensed the friction immediately and suggested the men sit down. A servant brought out a tray of fruit juices, and the three sat in silence. The chirping birds made the silence all the more obvious. To break the tension, Hans began laying out his plan to lure Ismail into the open.

"History has shown that every protected target has at least one vulnerability," Hans stated. He looked at Cam and continued. "It is our evaluation that Ismail's son Jamal is his greatest vulnerability."

Cam raised his eyebrows and tightened his lips. He was not sure he liked the direction the conversation was headed.

"Jamal could serve as an important bargaining chip for us," Hans said.

Avi said nothing and showed no expression.

Cam knew that Avi was prepared to do whatever was necessary to protect Israel. Like any good soldier, Avi was simply at the meeting to receive his marching orders.

"What are you suggesting?" Cam asked.

"I am suggesting that we seize Jamal and use him as bait to bring Ismail into the open so he can be dealt with," replied Hans.

"*Dealt with … do you mean killed?*" asked Cam.

"Not necessarily," replied Hans. "Tel Aviv doesn't want any fireworks at this point in the Syrian negotiations. *Captured and imprisoned* would be a satisfactory alternative. Of course, politically speaking, holding Ismail in an Israeli prison would not be an option. His imprisonment would simply serve as a lightning rod for more terror attacks. We were hoping you Americans might want him."

"That could probably be arranged … preferred even," Cam replied. "But my concern is the kid. I'm not so sure I want him involved."

"Do you have a better idea for getting our target out of his hole?" Hans asked.

The truth was Cam didn't have a better idea. Frankly, he was out of ideas. Since the death of his son Abdullah, Ismail had become extremely wary, and that made Cam's mission more difficult. "I wouldn't want the kid harmed in any way."

"Harming the boy would not be our intent," replied Hans.

"Intentions and outcomes are two different things," Cam retorted.

Hans said nothing in response.

Disturbed, Cam stood and walked to the edge of the patio. Below him was the beautiful ancient city of Beirut with its storied history of hate, violence, death, and resilience. Beyond Beirut was the tranquil blue Mediterranean, and beyond the Mediterranean was America. Cam thought about the countless American deaths caused by Ismail and his terrorist organization. Innocent men, women, *and* children had died in San Diego, Washington, and Yuma, and there was no guarantee that the slaughter would end until Ismail was stopped. Then Cam thought about Joshua, the Amish boy who had died in his arms in the cold Arizona desert. He reached in his pocket and retrieved the small wooden bat Joshua had given him the day before he died. The hand-carved wood had turned to a dark amber from all the handling it had received over the past several months. Using an innocent kid as bait did not sit well with Cam. It seemed unethical and immoral. It *was* unethical and immoral. Yet, Ismail had to be stopped. When Cam emerged from his thoughts, he did so with the realization that a solid combination of sound planning, precise execution, and expert skills might allow him to step across a moral boundary and achieve a greater good without putting Ismail's son at too much risk. Those were his instincts anyway, and through the years he had learned to trust his instincts. Cam turned and walked back to the table where Hans and Avi were sitting. Taking a seat between the two, Cam leaned forward and asked, "What is your plan?"

17

ONE OF THE most beautiful locations on earth, the small mountain village of Leysin, Switzerland, overlooks Lake Geneva in the Swiss Alps. Cars are not needed. A cog-driven tramway traverses up and down the steep mountain, taking passengers to and from larger towns in the valley below. Above Leysin, the tramway climbs to the internationally renowned Foret School for Boys (FSB). Built on the grounds of a former tuberculosis sanitarium, the international boarding school has educated the children of Europe's wealthy elite for more than one hundred years.

Jamal Khalidi, known to his teachers and classmates as Jamil Said, had just stepped off the tram in town with a group of his friends when a serious man with a thick athletic build approached the boys. Speaking in Arabic, the man said he had a message from Jamal's father. None of the other boys understood Arabic, but Jamal was accustomed to serious, tough men delivering messages from his father, so he left his friends and followed the man to a waiting car. And just like that, he was gone.

The reputable school had never lost a student before, and the boys who had been with Jamal were confused and clueless in their descriptions of what had happened. The police were slow to respond, suspecting the boy to be a spoiled runaway seeking attention from absentee parents. Switzerland's strict secrecy laws only complicated matters. Even after school authorities realized Jamal had been enrolled under an assumed identity, it would take police several days in court to learn his true nationality. The boy's father, once notified, proved to be uncooperative at best. Jamal Khalidi simply vanished into thin air, and Leysin's tranquil facade was shattered.

When Ismail received the news of his son's disappearance, the terrorist leader was visibly shaken. In a matter of months, Ismail's world had suddenly come crashing down around him. He had already lost his eldest son, and now his youngest was missing. Liwa Tahrir's alliance with the Mexican Sinaloa Cartel had come apart, and the Brigade had been decimated by a wave of unanticipated casualties. Seemingly out of nowhere, Ismail had encountered a formidable unseen enemy, an enemy who had turned the tables of fortune against him.

An unmarked package was delivered to his door several days after his son's disappearance. Ismail already knew what it contained. Inside the package was a non-traceable cell phone with a note attached, handwritten in English: *If you want to purchase your son's life for a modest fee, pack two large metal zero cases with 1,000 gold Krugerrands each, and await further instructions. The enclosed phone has been modified to receive only my call, do not lose it. You have one week to procure the ransom. Crowbar.*

Through the years, Ismail had learned to be wary of unmarked mail and cell phones. In 1996, one of his Palestinian brethren, Yahya Ayyash, Hamas' most well-known bomb-maker, was killed when Israel's Shin Bet detonated explosives they had placed in the cell phone he was using. Phones were much larger then and had room for enough RDX explosive to blow off a man's head. Modern phones were much smaller, and the likelihood of a repeated event was minute. Still, Ismail turned the phone over to his chief technician and asked him to check it out.

Ismail had no one to whom he could turn for help. He wasn't a citizen of Lebanon, and Hamas was nothing more than a collection of corrupt politicians with no real functioning government. Hezbollah was useless in any kind of diplomatic capacity; the only respect they received was what they extorted through threat of force. There was Liwa Tahrir's benefactor, Iran, but Ismail was so many steps removed from Tehran that he didn't even have a point-of-contact within the government. So Ismail was alone with a problem of his own making. Moreover, he found himself in unfamiliar territory. Ismail was accustomed to being the antagonist, not the target. He had made many enemies in his lifetime, certainly, but none had ever gone after his family before – not until now. A mysterious, illusive American had apparently declared a one-man war on Ismail and his terrorist organization. Ismail didn't know who this man was or where he came from, but one thing was certain: with all the losses Ismail had suffered in recent months, he did not want to lose the only son he had left. So Ismail procured the gold as instructed, and he waited. Ismail desperately wanted to meet the man who had brought so much misery to his life; therefore, he agreed to deliver the ransom in person. And perhaps most importantly, Ismail wanted the violence to end. Not surprisingly, that was what Cam wanted, too.

Over a period of several days, arrangements were made for Ismail to purchase the life of his son for two-thousand pieces of gold. The exchange would be strictly controlled. Cam, with the help of his friend Elie, picked his security team carefully. All five members were retired Nasty Boys. They were men with whom Cam had entrusted his life many times before. Though all had aged somewhat, now with thinning hair and hints of paunches, the Nasty Boys were still a solid team of professionals. Elie was to be Cam's bodyguard and driver. A backup security vehicle would be driven by Navi, nicknamed *Bullitt* for his superior driving skills. Next to Navi in the front seat was Sami, the weapons expert who had provided Cam the Glock. In the back were Henri and Souk, reliable men with clear eyes and sound hearts.

Early in the discussions, Ismail had demanded that his son Jamal be delivered at the time of the exchange, but that was not going to happen. Ismail had no leverage. Cam held all the cards. Jamal would be released the day after the exchange. One concession Cam pretended to make to Ismail was the meeting location. Cam and his team agreed that the location for the exchange would be a small abandoned farmhouse situated in a desolate area called Gemelt, just outside the ancient Lebanese city of Sidon about twenty-five miles south of Beirut. Gemelt was an area populated primarily by displaced Palestinians and considered to be Hezbollah territory. Elie had served there for a time in the army and knew the area well. Gemelt was also where Sami had grown up before the Palestinian refugees flooded the area prior to the war. The designated house sat in a dry shallow valley surrounded by barren rocky hills. The dusty landscape offered no shelter from the sun. A good location for both parties, any uninvited vehicles could be seen approaching from miles in any direction.

A few days before launching the operation, Cam sent two interesting text messages. The first text was to his friend Sid Lewis of the FBI. *Strongly advise you get aboard Sixth Fleet in the Med ASAP. Have your Director pull any strings necessary for authorization. National security implications. Notify USMS Dep Kate Allison as well. Do not delay.* The second message, even more interesting, was to RSO Tyrone Bell. *Request embassy maintenance shop build second casket matching AMB specs. No questions please. Crowbar.*

On a Tuesday morning at exactly ten o'clock, Cam's party of two vehicles crested the hill overlooking the meeting location and parked. Across the shallow valley, a dust cloud could be seen on the road approaching the far hill to the south. Emerging from the dust, two older-model Mercedes arrived at the top of the hill and stopped. The vehicles exchanged flashes of headlights, and after a moment, one vehicle from each hill descended slowly toward the house. The two backup vehicles remained parked at the top of their respective hills. The two lead vehicles met in front of the house and stopped, facing each other about ten yards apart. From his place in the back seat, Cam could see two men in the opposite vehicle: a driver and in the backseat a balding heavyset man wearing dark glasses. Cam could tell by the distorted windows of the old Mercedes that it was armored with ballistic glass. Elie's taxi was not.

After several long seconds, the driver of the opposite vehicle opened his door and walked around to the back of his vehicle and waited. "That is Asem Zaydani," whispered Elie. "He is Ismail's most trusted bodyguard and is believed to be the assassin who killed Ambassador Pruett."

Cam processed that bit of information silently.

After several more tense seconds, Elie asked, "What do you want me to do?"

"Get out and do the same thing Ismail's driver did. Just be careful."

Once Elie did as he was told, each driver moved cautiously around to the sides of the vehicles and opened the doors for their respective passengers; then all four men moved warily in front of their cars. Like opposing team captains awaiting a coin toss, the four men faced each other. The tension was palpable.

Standing only feet apart, Cam made a quick assessment of his opponents. Ismail was unimpressive physically. They were about the same age, but Ismail had grown fat over the years. He was balding, and his clothes were rumpled. He looked like he hadn't slept in days. He had the look of defeat in his eyes. Cam felt a hint of satisfaction in seeing Ismail's deteriorated condition. Asem, the bodyguard, was the youngest and most fit of the group. He had the cold eyes of a killer. Cam noted that Asem was wearing a ballistic vest that partially covered a sidearm. Elie wasn't wearing a vest, but he, too, was armed. Cam was not overly concerned about any tricks at this point. He still held all the cards. Jamal was still under his control, half a continent away, and the wanted terrorist would be stupid to cause an incident before Jamal was released.

As had been agreed, the two bodyguards moved forward and frisked the opposing adversaries for weapons or electronic devices. Both men were clean.

"Where is the gold?" asked Cam, giving his pretense lip service.

"It is in the trunk," replied Ismail flatly. "But we must talk first."

Cam nodded and motioned toward the door of the house. The bodyguards went in first and conducted a security sweep of the room. With the exception of a small table and two chairs, the room was bare. Ismail flicked his head, and both bodyguards retreated back to their cars where they remained standing twenty feet apart.

Alone inside the house, the two men faced each other. The morning sun had risen above the mountain and was beginning to heat the walls of the old stone building, already hot inside. Perspiration had accumulated in drops on Ismail's balding forehead. They sat down at the table across from each other and paused in a self-imposed silence. Ismail's breathing revealed him to be a mass of controlled rage.

In perfect English, Ismail opened the conversation. "Well, I finally meet the illusive Crowbar," he said, sarcastically.

"We have met before," replied Cam calmly.

"Oh?" Ismail was intrigued. "How so?"

"During the war. More of an encounter than a meeting."

Ismail shifted his eyes up and to the right, signaling to Cam that he was genuinely trying to remember the encounter by triggering the memory portion of his brain. "What do you mean? You fought in the war? When?"

"I didn't say I fought in the war. I said we had an encounter. It would have been 1984 or 85, and I had a warrant for your arrest."

"Arrest? You are police?"

"I was at the time." Cam didn't have the time or inclination to explain the subtle differences between police and federal agents, so he let the statement stand unchallenged. "We had you surrounded in an abandoned mosque near the Green Line during a ceasefire, but my ambassador would not let me execute the warrant for your arrest."

Ismail remembered the mosque and the ceasefire, but he had no idea an American policeman had been waiting outside with an arrest warrant. Nor did he know an American ambassador had saved him from capture. Ismail responded indignantly. "So what was this warrant for?"

"The hijacking of that Pan Am flight and the murder of two Americans."

Ismail dismissed the event's relevance. "That was a long time ago."

"Yes, and you have lived a long life that you've denied many others."

Ismail shrugged, indifferently. "Warriors sometimes have to take lives of other warriors."

"You are a terrorist, not a warrior. Many of the lives you took were innocent women and children."

Cam had just insulted him, and Ismail's nerves grew on edge, his pulse quickening. "And what about you, Mr. Crowbar. You are the man who cowardly took the life of my eldest son!"

"You go after my family, I go after yours," Cam said.

"What do you mean, your family?"

"My son was on the train you ordered destroyed in Arizona."

Ismail's eyes narrowed as he contemplated the information he had just received. A glimmer of comprehension flickered across his face. All the schemes and plots and paranoia he had envisioned fell away. The circumstances became more clear. Crowbar's presence in Lebanon was not part of a government operation or a CIA plot. It was personal.

"You are not CIA, then? Because that is the reason I ordered your assassination. We assumed you were CIA." Ismail was trying to provide some degree of justification for the attack.

"Never have been, never will be."

Possibly showing a hint of humanity, Ismail asked, "Your son died on that train?"

"No, he didn't die ... but he could have."

Ismail leaned back in his chair. "Yet you killed my son anyway?"

as if Cam should have ignored Abdullah's *intent* that night in the Arizona desert. Ismail leaned forward, "I should kill you now with my bare hands," he said, revealing his deeply ingrained sense of *eye for an eye* justice.

Cam ignored Ismail's threat, but prepared himself for a fight. "Your son killed many innocent people," Cam stated firmly. He could see that his strategy was working. He continued to push Ismail's emotional buttons.

"He was just a boy," Ismail replied, his grief welling up inside him.

Ismail needed one more push. Gripping both edges of the table, Cam leaned forward and hissed, "Abdullah was a terrorist, and he deserved to die!"

Ismail was a violent man with a short fuse. He exploded across the table at his tormentor. Cam was prepared for the explosion, but he was not prepared for the buckle blade Ismail pulled from his belt. As he lunged at Cam with a sweeping slash, Cam was able to raise his hand just enough to deflect the jab. Still, the razor-sharp blade slid across the front of Cam's arm, cutting small muscles and slicing his arm open like a banana peel. Adrenaline masked the pain, and Cam caught Ismail's knife hand at the wrist. Bringing both hands to bear, he twisted the wrist sharply backward against the thumb, and Ismail's radial bone audibly snapped. Ismail screamed like a wild animal as his stronghand became useless and his weapon clanged noisily to the floor. Falling backward together, Cam twisted his body just before impact, causing Ismail to hit the floor first with his face. The blow stunned Ismail, and Cam reacted immediately. From behind, Cam hooked Ismail under the chin with his elbow, then rolled onto his back, locked his long legs around Ismail's torso, and squeezed his forearm and bicep tightly against his victim's carotid arteries. Desperate, Ismail groped for Cam's face, then slid his one good hand across the floor until he found the knife. Cam saw the blade flash, and defenseless with both hands engaged, all Cam could do was lower his head, protect his neck and face, and absorb the blows. The blade slashed wildly across his scalp and the side of his head, reopening old wounds, and slicing his ear in random but painful jabs. Ismail had a thick neck that impeded Cam's ability to cut the blood flow. Cam held on tightly despite his own devastating wounds and counted the seconds. Ten seconds passed, then fifteen, and finally the struggle was over as Ismail's body went limp and his eyes lost focus. He had passed out from lack of oxygen to his brain.

The moment Elie heard the disruption inside the house, he launched into action. Drawing his weapon, he turned to face his counterpart. Asem had noticed the noise as well, but as he reached for his pistol, the thick vest he was wearing interfered with his draw. That gave Elie the advantage needed, and he used it to deadly effect. A brief flash of panic froze Asem's face with the reality of his predicament. Elie's quick and skillful double-tap to Asem's throat and head dropped him like putty. Now time became critical. Elie quickly reholstered his weapon, popped the trunk of his taxi, and rushed into the house. Cam, weak from the adrenaline-induced struggle and blood loss from his wounds, was slow getting to his feet. Ismail was still out on the floor, but he would regain consciousness soon. He was a big man, and Elie had to get him to the car quickly. Rolling Ismail awkwardly into the trunk of his taxi,

Elie fastened plastic zip ties to his hands and feet as Cam moved in a daze toward the car. Ismail moaned as he slowly revived, and Elie, a big man himself, slugged Ismail solidly on the temple, knocking him out cold. If he had wanted, he could have easily killed the terrorist with a couple more well-placed blows, but he didn't; that wasn't the plan. Elie slammed the trunk shut and moved quickly to help Cam into the back seat.

On the opposite hill above the house, Ismail's bodyguards had heard Elie's shots. Confused at the commotion, they sprang into action. The Nasty Boys were *not* confused. As scripted, they pulled their AKs from the brackets of the Suburban and unleashed a torrent of covering fire downrange. By this time, Ismail's security team was speeding down the hillside toward Elie's taxi. One straggler who had fallen from the moving vehicle was running to the site on foot, a cellphone in one hand and a useless machine pistol in the other. An AK round hit him in the ankle, taking his foot clean off, and he went down holding his shattered leg in horror and agony. Then Sami went into action. Pulling a can-fed M-60 machine gun from the back of the Chevy, he laid the tripod-mounted man-eater across the hood of the truck and unleashed 7.62 millimeters of holy hell into the terrorists' vehicle. Smashing rounds tore into the Mercedes' radiator and engine block, shredded tire rubber and ripped sheet metal, then showered the ballistic windshield with broad splotches of glass and plastic until its integrity gave way and its passengers were exposed. Sami continued to pour his leaded death and destruction into the car's interior. Crimson-and-pink matter instantly exploded inside the vehicle as if someone had detonated a grenade. The plastic runflat inserts that had been installed on the car's wheels allowed the stricken vehicle to continue its descent down the hill, but the loose desert sand held its momentum in check. Elie, with his friend slumped in a bloody heap in the back of his taxi, peeled his tires aggressively in the loose dirt as he spun away from the site of the snatch, their precious cargo strapped securely in the trunk. The driverless Mercedes, still with a remnant of momentum, slowly crept its way to the scene of the disaster until it bumped meekly against the corner of an old stone wall and stopped. Elie accelerated his taxi hard and turned it northward toward Beirut. The Nasty Boys, their gun barrels still too hot to touch, inserted fresh magazines, piled into the Suburban, and followed the taxi in close pursuit.

18

AT THE EMBASSY, the Chief of Mission had just concluded the memorial service for Ambassador Pruett. The service was a solemn affair, held outside in the chancery garden, with sobering words and ample opportunities for those in attendance to contemplate the rewards and the risks of serving one's country abroad. The ceremony was depressing, made more so by the diminished numbers in attendance. Non-essential personnel had been evacuated after the incident, and all who remained at post were a handful of Americans. The ambassador's casket, a plain wood box made of Lebanese cedar, contributed to the mood of the event. Beautifully made and draped with a colorful American flag, the casket seemed inadequate for the circumstances it represented. Such sacrifice, so little recognition.

The Sixth Fleet helicopter was already en route to retrieve the ambassador's remains when Elie excitedly pulled his taxi up to the embassy gate. The guards knew Elie, but he was no longer an employee, and they had been instructed by the ambassador months ago to restrict his entry. Then they looked in the back and saw a blood-soaked man slumped over in the seat. They called the RSO. Tyrone Bell was just leaving the memorial service and noticed the commotion at the front gate. He raced over and found his former Nasty Boy sitting in a taxi with an anxious look on his face.

Elie shouted as the RSO approached. "I have Crowbar in the back, and he is hurt pretty badly!"

The RSO glanced in the back seat and saw Cam covered in blood, looking as if he'd been attacked with a chainsaw.

More lucid now, Cam managed to sit up in his seat and motioned for the RSO to come to his window.

"We have the FBI's *most wanted* terrorist in the trunk, and we need to get him on the ambassador's chopper," Cam explained with slurring words, sounding like a hungover delivery man late with his shipment.

The RSO, a combat veteran who had experienced plenty of blood amidst the fog of war, was knocked off balance by this startling turn of events.

"Tyrone, I need you to *let us in … please!*" implored the former agent, barely able to maintain consciousness.

Had it had been anybody else but Cam Coppenger, the RSO would have hesitated. But he knew the man, had heard the stories, and knew that Coppenger was involved in something big. He waved the taxi through. The distinctive thumping of a helicopter could be faintly heard in the distance.

Elie sped onto the compound past the tennis courts and down

into the basement of the old Baaklini building. There in the corner of the maintenance shop was a second cedar box identical to the one that held the ambassador. As Cam stumbled out of the car, Elie opened the trunk and lifted the incoherent terrorist out and onto the ground. He motioned for the shop workers to help him load the human cargo into the box. Hesitantly, they followed Elie's command. Slowly regaining his senses, the terrorist began to resist as they attempted to place him in the box, but Elie raised his big ham of a fist and slammed it into the terrorist's temple again, knocking him out cold. The carpenters, hoping desperately for someone to explain what was going on, followed Elie's command and screwed the lid solidly onto the box.

Weak and in extreme pain, Cam slowly worked his way up and out of the basement to the tennis courts just as the Sikorsky SH-60 Seahawk was landing. Touching down, the pilot kept the turbines running at half power, blades flat; it couldn't stay there long. Without proper clearances, the military aircraft risked a serious diplomatic incident if discovered to be in Lebanese airspace without authorization. The tennis courts had not been used in a while, and the downdraft of the chopper blades had stirred all kinds of debris into the air. The scene was loud and chaotic. Off to the side were six current Nasty Boys standing as an honor guard with the ambassador's casket at their feet. The rotor blast was threatening to blow the American flag off the casket, and several of the Nasty Boys were attempting to hold the flag in place. Next to them stood the COM and the RSO. The RSO, dressed in a suit, had been designated as the embassy representative to escort the ambassador's body back to the US. His wind-blown necktie slapped him in the face as he gestured emphatically to the COM, his words drowned out by the turbine engines.

As the Nasty Boys bent forward and moved the casket to the wide side door of the helicopter, Cam approached the pilot. Barely audible, Cam shouted, "I need to get some TS cargo back to the fleet!"

The pilot, who had seen plenty of bloody men in his career, was not affected by the sight of Cam at his window. He just shook his head. "What?" he asked. "Say again!"

"Top Secret cargo!" Cam shouted. "I need to load it on your chopper!"

"Can't do that!" shouted the pilot. "The manifest calls for one casket and one embassy escort! Somebody higher than my pay grade will have to approve it!"

By that time, the RSO had hustled over to the pilot's window, hoping to gain some perspective on the situation. On the other side of the helicopter, Elie and the carpenters had moved the second cedar box next to the open door and sat it on the ground. The pilot looked at his watch. Time was running short. Then he looked at the RSO and shouted, "This guy wants to load a second box onboard. It's not on the manifest. I need the COM to approve it!"

Bell looked at Cam skeptically and shrugged his shoulders. "Romero wants to know what you are doing here."

"Tell him we have the ambassador's killer boxed up, and we need to get him back to the US for trial!" advised Cam, trying to make the COM's decision as simple as possible. "He's America's most wanted terrorist!"

"I'll try," Bell said. Bending at the waist to avoid being

decapitated, he jogged back over to where the COM was standing. Cam could see the RSO pleading his case. He saw Romero look over at Cam and shake his head. Procedures had been violated. Laws had been broken. Boundaries had been crossed. Careers were at stake. Cam understood all that. The pilot looked at his watch again. Finally, after what seemed like an eternity, Romero bowed his head, kicked the dirt, and nodded his approval. The RSO turned, smiled, and gave Cam a thumbs up.

Both boxes were loaded, and the pilot was pumping his fist; there was no time to properly secure them. The crew chief helped Cam, still wobbly, into the back seat of the helicopter and strapped him in behind the pilot. The chief then took a position on the other side, sitting in the door next to the hoist. Over water, the side doors of Navy helicopters stay open to facilitate emergency evacuation, and while the policy made sense, Cam felt nervous to be sitting next to the open door, but it was time to go.

The Seahawk pilot steadily increased the RPM of the rotors, and the military bird lifted reluctantly above the embassy tennis court, pivoted slowly 180 degrees just feet above the ground, and then climbed deliberately toward the sea. Looking out his side door, Cam spotted a shiny white Mercedes parked on an overpass below the embassy. Standing next to the Mercedes was a beautiful Lebanese woman, immaculately dressed, watching the chopper leave Lebanon. Holding a little lap dog in one arm and shielding her eyes from the sun with the other, the wind was blowing her long, dark hair across her nearly perfect face. It would have been impossible for Cam to have seen the tears streaming down her cheeks.

Within minutes of entering international airspace, Seahawk pilot Lieutenant Rusty Baird received an unusual radio message on the international emergency frequency. "US rotary wing aircraft departing Lebanon, this is Islamic Republic of Iran Air Force Commander Farhad Farzan. You have departed Lebanese airspace without authorization and are instructed to return to Beirut International Airport immediately!"

Co-pilot Chuck Easley, hearing the message, looked over at Lieutenant Baird. "Iranians enforcing Lebanese airspace?" he asked.

"This is not about airspace; it's about our TS cargo," replied Baird. Before responding to the radio transmission, Baird reported the communication to Fleet Command. "Fleet Command, this is Egg-Beater Six, we have departed location and are returning to base. Be advised, however, we have been instructed by the Iranian Air Force to return to Lebanon."

The Iranian Air Force? Fleet Command was perplexed, completely unaware of the special cargo that had been loaded at the embassy. Why are the Iranians involved? Are they simply looking for another opportunity to taunt the Great Satan? Or flexing their newly acquired military muscle? As a precaution, the XO ordered a squadron of F/A-18 Super Hornets aboard the carrier USS John F. Kennedy to Alert-5 status. Fleet Command responded, "Negative, Egg-Beater Six, you are instructed to return to base in due haste, understood?"

"Understood, returning to base."

Moments later, the Iranians radioed a second message, "US rotary wing aircraft departing Lebanon, you are warned to return to Lebanon immediately. Fighter aircraft have been deployed to intercept."

The American pilot gave a skeptical glance to his co-pilot. "That's a negative, Commander," replied Baird in a slow, calm southern accent. "This United States Navy aircraft is in international airspace. You have no authority, and we have no authority to utilize BIA."

The Iranian Commander responded, "I repeat, Iranian fighter aircraft are en route your location; you are instructed to return to Lebanon immediately!"

Lieutenant Baird reported the exchange to his fleet flagship. "Fleet Command, be advised the Iranians have deployed fighter aircraft."

With this unexpected escalation and potential for hostilities, US Navy Sixth Fleet Admiral George Cockren ordered full battlestations. A squadron of four FA-18 Hornets were scrambled and ordered launched. Destroyer escorts deployed sounding bouys and activated their Phalanx systems fore and aft. An airborne EA-6B initiated radar jamming procedures. A Los Angeles class fast attack sub locked torpedo guidance on the Russian sub that had been shadowing the fleet since Newport News. The most formidable projection of nautical forces the world has ever known was on high alert. The aircraft carrier USS John F. Kennedy was positioned in the middle of the Mediterranean, just south of the Italian boot. It would take the Hornets several minutes to launch, organize, and reach the threatened whirlybird.

Two Iranian MiG-29's were already enroute to the slow-moving helicopter, and within seconds, the Seahawk's co-pilot detected on radar two bandits approaching from behind at closing speed. "What do you want to do, Rusty?" he asked. "We can't outrun them."

"They're probably bluffing," advised Baird. "We shall proceed at speed and hold course."

With their maximum low-altitude speed of 930 mph, it didn't take the Russian-made Fulcrums long to catch up to the 168 mph Sikorsky. Approaching their target, the MiGs slowed and leveled off on either side of the Seahawk. Wearing a headset the crew chief had given him, Cam was aware of the crew conversations that had taken place. He peered out the open door at one of the aging Iranian fighters, it's tri-colored green, white, and red circle insignia clearly visible on the fuselage. Four air-to-air missiles were slung underneath each wing. The twin-engine MiGs looked remarkably similar to the older American F-14 Tomcats of *Top Gun* fame, but this was no movie.

Emerging from his fog of pain and weariness, Cam chuckled to himself, *Hezbollah must really want their boy Ismail back.* The helicopter was particularly noisy with its doors open, but Cam could hear a vague bumping coming from inside one of the boxes and thought to himself, *Sounds like somebody is finally waking up, and I'm pretty sure it's not the ambassador!*

The Iranian commander gave one final warning to the American helicopter.

Baird replied calmly to his adversaries, "No can do, Frito Bandito, we are in international airspace over which you have no authority. Sorry, Charlie." Baird was hoping his use of slang would perplex his adversaries long enough to buy him more time.

The two MiGs peeled off and disappeared from view. In a matter of seconds, however, the MiGs returned in a sweeping arc toward the chopper. In staggered formation they closed in fast and hard toward the starboard side and, with afterburners fully lit, they screeched loudly as they crossed in front of the chopper. As the Seahawk entered their jet wash, its rotor lift was drastically reduced, causing the chopper to plunge sharply. Cam could see the pilot in front of him struggling at his controls with both hands and feet.

"Dammit," Baird cursed. After regaining level flight, he radioed Fleet Command. "Fleet Command, be advised we have just been aggressively buzzed by two Iranian bandits."

"Copy that," replied Fleet Command. "We have Hornet interceptors launched and en route to your location."

Cam could see the Iranian MiGs taking another broad sweeping turn back toward the Seahawk, and within seconds they were speeding into a second run directly at the defenseless helicopter, this time from the port side. The sound they made was deafening as their jet blast sucked all the air beneath the chopper, causing it to dip sharply and spin askew 90 degrees.

The ambassador's casket was nearest Cam, and the twisting action of the helicopter slammed it into his knee, causing him to cringe in pain. Cam closed his eyes and held tightly to the web strap with his one good hand. He was about to lose his cookies. He clenched his stomach tightly to hold his spew. All he could think about was getting off that damned helicopter.

Radio communication within the helicopter became chaotic jabber as the chopper pilots fought valiantly to maintain control of their aircraft.

Looking out the opposite door, Cam saw the Iranian fighters turn tightly for another pass. He braced himself as the fighter jets split high and low, creating a tornado of turbulence that threw the chopper into a sideways tilted spiral. The two boxes slid toward the open door on Cam's side. Grasping desperately but helplessly, his seatbelt was the only thing that held him inside the aircraft. The boxes shifted again dramatically. Cam stuck his foot out just enough to stop the box nearest him from sliding all the way out the door; it was the ambassador's casket. But Cam was in no position to block Ismail's box, which launched from the spinning chopper like a clown shot from a circus cannon.

Like a glob of spit spat from a windy bridge, the box containing the FBI's most-wanted terrorist arced poetically in midair, hesitated, and—dropping gently—drifted sideways, shrank from view, and tumbled a bit before splashing silently into the sea. The box was well made, and it held together nicely. Still, water quickly began to seep in. Baird had miraculously regained control of his aircraft, and from his position at the door, Cam had a good view of Ismail's box. The cedar wood box, now a coffin, rocked briefly on the surface of the water, and then like an enemy ship torpedoed at sea, it rose deliberately at one end, hesitated, and slipped stern-first below the waves, bubbling as it sank. The Navy crew chief, peering in astonishment from his open door, glanced at Cam in panic. Cam shrugged in reply, closed his eyes, and laid his swooning head back against the bulkhead in an effort to calm his queasy stomach. The MiGs didn't return for a fourth pass. Cam wondered if the Iranian pilots even knew what they had done. He planted both feet firmly against Wilson Pruett's box. Justice had been served. Mission accomplished.

As if on cue, two American F-18 Super Hornets whooshed

past the helicopter in pursuit of the MiGs, but there would be no dogfight that day. The Iranians were long gone, having no desire to play a part in US Navy target practice. Disappearing on the distant horizon, the Hornets eventually turned back, slowed, and leveled off on either side of the beleaguered helicopter as they escorted her home.

Once the Seahawk landed safely on the deck of the command frigate, and after the bluster of the rotors had subsided, six sailors in parade dress solemnly off-loaded Ambassador Pruett's casket, draped it with an American flag, and snapped a sharp salute before taking it below deck.

FBI Agent Sid Lewis was standing next to the admiral and the XO. Deputy US Marshal Kate Allison was there as well, handcuffs ready, waiting to place the notorious terrorist under arrest. Behind them, a squad of US Navy SEAL team members in full combat gear served as backup. Cam, a bloody mess, stepped gingerly out of the empty helicopter, and the reception committee moved forward.

"Are you the RSO?" asked the admiral suspiciously, stunned at the amount of blood that saturated Cam's clothing.

"No sir, I'm not," replied Cam, respectfully.

"Who the hell are you, then?" demanded the admiral.

Admiral Cockren wasn't in Cam's chain of command, but out of respect for the rank, he extended his bloody hand and offered his US passport as identification. "My name is Cameron Coppenger, sir. I am simply an American citizen." The admiral looked over at Sid, confused by the idea of an uncleared civilian boarding one of *his* helicopters and landing on the deck of *his* flagship without authorization.

Sid intervened, "He's part of our team, admiral." Then turning to Cam he asked, "Where's Ismail?"

Cam looked back at the crew chief who was busy securing the chopper to the deck, "Buried at sea."

"*Buried at sea?* What do you mean buried at sea? Is he dead?"

"He is now."

The admiral looked past Cam and called out sternly to the crew chief, "Front and center, Chief!" he ordered.

The crew chief hustled past Cam, faced the admiral squarely, and snapped a salute. Returning the salute, the admiral demanded, "What happened out there, Chief?"

The Chief stammered for a split second, then stiffened. "We loaded two boxes in Beirut, sir, but we got buzzed by Iranian MiGs over the Med, and their jet wash dumped one of the boxes overboard, sir!"

By this time, the Seahawk pilot had ambled calmly over to the conversation. Baird offered a professional salute to the admiral, which the admiral then returned.

"Is this true, Lieutenant?" asked the admiral.

Lieutenant Baird responded confidently, "I didn't see exactly what happened, sir. I was pretty much occupied with the hostiles. But I did authorize taking on a second box of cargo, and I can report we took some pretty severe dips in the MiG jet washes. I almost lost control of the aircraft."

Sid's forehead was furrowed as he shook his head in disbelief. He was already thinking about the mounds of paperwork and Congressional testimony to come. "Is that the way it went down, Cop? Ismail was in the box that went overboard?"

"That's the way it went down, Sid,"

"Why are you so bloody? What happened to you?"

"I made the mistake of bringing fists to a knife fight," Cam said, struggling to keep his balance on the deck of the rolling ship.

Kate, eyes wide with concern, almost stepped forward to steady Cam, but stopped.

Staring up at a beautiful Mediterranean sky, the admiral let out a heavy sigh and replied, "Very well, then, let's go below and get you patched up. Then I'll expect a full briefing. There are going to be a lot of questions on this one."

As the team exited through the companionway one by one, Kate positioned herself beside her old friend, still woozy from the harrowing flight. While waiting their turn, Kate threw a quick nudge into Cam's re-injured ribs.

"Ouch!" he cried out. "Be careful!"

Cam shoved her back with a blood-caked forearm. Their eyes locked for a brief moment.

Moving deeper into the bowels of the ship, Cam made a discreet inquiry to his former boss. "Does the State Department's *Rewards for Justice* program still have a bounty out on Ismail?"

"Yes, a five-million-dollar reward, dead or alive ... but it's not available to government employees," advised Sid. "Why do you ask? Were you thinking about putting in for it?"

"Not for me," replied Cam. "But I do have someone in mind. His name is Elie Najjar. He is the one who should get the reward. I'll write it up for submission. Think you can make that happen?"

"Absolutely!" Sid replied, "We'll get right on it."

"Good," Cam smiled, "It's the right thing to do."

Epilogue

IT WAS HURRICANE season, and another Cat 4 was headed for Mobile Bay. The heavy wooden tiller felt good in his hand. Of solid ash and well-varnished, the wood grain glistened a deep amber. Cam had spent a week refurbishing the tiller, seven days, seven coats of varnish. As thick as the business end of a baseball bat, the tiller was as substantial as his new boat. Steel-hulled for strength, full-keeled for stability, with a cutter-rig for power, his sailboat was strong and solid. Compared to the sharp narrow lines of *Fadeaway*, the design of the smaller twenty-eight-foot cutter was short and stocky. Tapered at both stem and stern, the wide girth of the double-ender gave the sailboat a compact shape like a thick slice of cantaloupe. The single oak mast was heavy and short, encased in aluminum sheathing for strength and supported by six heavy-gauge stainless-steel cables through-bolted to welded chain-plates. Two small, round portholes on each side of the low, square cabin were designed to keep seawater out rather than letting in light. The hatches were aircraft-grade aluminum with over-sized brass wing-nut fasteners. Inside the cockpit were four bolted eyelet rings designed for securely lashing items to the deck in heavy weather, including the boat's pilot. The heavy steel deck was slathered with a thick coat of non-skid paint. The boat had no name; it was simply a shelter for survival.

Mobile Bay was metallic gray and restless as Cam left his Dog River berthing and approached the eastern end of Dauphin Island. He plotted a reaching course east/southeast for Fort Morgan, located three miles across the mouth of the bay. Cam was sailing alone, and he was comfortable with that. Looking down, he noticed he was wearing the same scuffed and stained boots that had carried him across the globe. They were probably inappropriate for use aboard a sailboat, but they had a history. They were the same boots that had climbed the debris of a fallen embassy in Beirut, waded through the slick bloody aftermath of a suicide bomber in Islamabad, and stepped over mounds of butchered bodies in Haiti. The boots had carried Cameron Coppenger through a lifetime of horrors. They had been tested, tried, and proven, and they belonged with him now.

It was early evening on Mobile Bay, daylight fading. The bay had become abusive, the air stiff. As he rounded the eastern end of Dauphin Island, Cam noticed a modern contradiction, a Confederate flag, flying defiantly from the ramparts of old Fort Gaines. Fort Gaines, and its counterpart, Fort Morgan, had been the lone defenders of the Confederacy's last major port in 1864. Here Admiral Farragut, in the midst of battle and having just lost a ship to an underwater mine, is alleged to have exclaimed to his Union fleet, "Damn the torpedoes, full speed ahead!" It made a good story, and Cam thought of those words as he left the shelter of Dauphin Island and headed south into the open Gulf, toward the threat of the approaching storm.

Cam liked his boat's cutter rig. With two forward stays, he could preset a storm jib on the half stay and hoist his working jib ahead of that. That was the sail plan he wanted to use when foul weather was expected. A system of blocks/tackle allowed him to drop the working jib from the cockpit without having to go forward on a pitching deck. With his mainsail already reefed down to heavy-wind proportions, Cam headed to open water.

Clear of sheltering islands, the wind began to pick up in the Gulf. Cam sensed anger in the wind's voice as it bundled the waves into heavy swells, six to eight feet from crest to trough, rolling but not yet breaking. Cam liked the way his boat handled swells. He could tell by the steady angle of heel and firm, even pull of the tiller that the boat's designer had experienced rough weather and built the boat accordingly. That gave him confidence. Darkness approached, and as he tacked diligently southwest toward Sand Island Lighthouse, the strength of the approaching storm grew, and the foamy seas began to exert themselves against the steel hull of the cutter. Cam shackled himself into the deck of the cockpit, his tethered safety harness fixed fast to the bolted eye-rings. Behind him, the faintly glowing lights of Mobile could be seen reflecting off the low-hung, fast-moving sky. The rumbling thunder and lightning flashes reminded him of Beirut at war with itself so many years before.

The seas were much heavier now, and the winds began to whistle through the boat's rigging and whip the foamy tops from the huge, house-size waves. With the winds came spume and blinding rain. The outer edge of the storm was approaching. Cam knew its rhythm. There would be chaos, then the eye, then chaos reversed. Daylight was at least ten hours away, and with it would come the worst of the weather. Cam planned to be thirty miles out to sea by daybreak. From there, he would heave-to, deploy the sea anchor, screw down the reinforced hatches, lash himself below deck, ride the storm like a corked bottle … and survive. That was the challenge, to survive, boat and man intact. Into the darkness he plunged with a sound plan, wearing the boots that had overcome challenges before. Retired Special Agent Cam Coppenger was not afraid, but he was keenly aware of the dangers. Hurricane *Lana* was going to be a formidable challenge. The VHF crackled with a monotonous chant of hurricane warnings and small craft advisories. Cam turned the radio off. Unexpectedly, a rogue wave slammed over the boat's starboard side, knocking Cam off balance, soaking him to the bone and briefly filling the self-bailing cockpit with seawater. "*Damn the torpedoes,*" he cursed to himself. "*Damn the torpedoes.*"

Acknowledgments

A BOOK IS not written in a vacuum. It's a team effort, and I had a good team. First, thank you to my writing group leader and mentor, Cheryl Elliot Lewis, who inspired me to start the project, encouraged me along the way, and served as the voice of experience I needed; to Lesley Cole who introduced me to important elements of the writing community; and to graphic artist and long-lost-friend Sarah Turner who helped me capture my story in the single image I found myself reviewing for inspiration throughout the course of writing the book.

Every good work of fiction must be accurate in its details. To that end, I consulted a host of experts in their given fields. Thanks to LTC Mark Pierson (USA/Ret), Amtrak Conductor Jeff Omspaugh, fellow DSS Agent and USMC helicopter pilot Don Gonneville, Captain Fred Carter Smith (USN/Ret), CDR Patricia Galeki (USNR/Ret), and LCDR Leon Galeki (USN/Ret). RT, thank you for your insight into the culture and politics of the very diverse country of Lebanon. FH, thank you for reminding me just what a special group of guys the Nasty Boys still are. DW, thank you for assistance with the country of Mexico, its culture, and its language.

Finally, thanks to Mindbridge Press for knowing *Boundary Hunter* is a story worth telling.

About the Author

A.R. MOORE SERVED AS a Special Agent with the State Department's Diplomatic Security Service (DSS) for twenty-four years and spent much of his career overseas, including missions to Australia, Lebanon, Sri Lanka, and Haiti. Domestically, Mr. Moore worked in a broad range of Washington-based assignments, including stints with the DSS Anti-terrorism Assistance Program (ATA), the Office of Intelligence and Threat Analysis (ITA), Passport Fraud Investigations (DS/PF), and the Office of International Programs. Prior to 9/11, he served as a Pearson Fellow for the State Department with the Congressional House Government Reform Subcommittee on National Security and finished his DSS career as chief of the San Diego Office. During his career, Moore received numerous awards for meritorious service. Originally from Mobile, Alabama, Moore was awarded a B.A. in Criminal Justice and a M.S. in Political Science from Auburn University. An avowed cabinologist, the author spends as much time as possible writing, traveling, and playing outdoors.